# IN
# SEARCH
# OF
# ETHEL
# CARTWRIGHT

*Also by Tom Winter*
31 Days of Wonder
Arms Wide Open
Lost & Found

# TOM WINTER

# IN SEARCH OF ETHEL CARTWRIGHT

corsair

CORSAIR

First published in the United Kingdom in 2024 by Corsair

1 3 5 7 9 10 8 6 4 2

Copyright © Tom Winter 2024

The moral right of the author has been asserted.

A CIP catalogue record for this book
is available from the British Library.

ISBN 978-1-4721-5830-7

Typeset in Garamond by M Rules
Printed and bound in Great Britain by Clays Ltd, Elcograf S.p.A.

Papers used by Corsair are from well-managed forests
and other responsible sources.

Corsair
An imprint of
Little, Brown Book Group
Carmelite House
50 Victoria Embankment
London EC4Y 0DZ

An Hachette UK Company
www.hachette.co.uk

www.littlebrown.co.uk

"We are like islands in the sea,
separate on the surface but connected in the deep."

# The story of Norman, Ethel and Flo

# NORMAN

# 1.

They weren't funerals, they were leaving dos, that's how Norman liked to think of them. Though, like any social occasion, some gatherings were better than others. A lovely person might have a dreary send-off, while someone at the other end of the spectrum – a bit of a knob, if you will – could leave this world on a high simply because there was chorizo in the potato salad.

Today's dearly departed had been a sweet old thing, though you'd never know it from the state of the finger food. Much like the people in the room, the sandwiches were visibly stale; bread dry to the touch, surrendering to gravity as if resistance was futile.

Norman had just started another egg sandwich when he spotted Sally, an elderly neighbour from across the street, her frizzed mass of curls bouncing in his direction.

'Gertie deserved better,' she said, shaking her head at Norman's sandwich. 'The least her family could have done was get some decent cakes. Gertie was very partial to a Victoria sponge.'

Another acquaintance, Ernie, approached on his mobility scooter, a four-wheeled Moses, people parting for him as he slowly advanced across the room with a sausage roll in hand.

'I give this funeral a six out of ten,' he shouted, still some way off. He didn't notice how some of the other guests looked aghast, but that had always been the thing about Ernie, he never noticed anything. When it came to the art of conversation, you could say he was a sort of human blowhole, everything just blasting out at once, salty and a shock to the senses.

Sally glanced at her watch, her manner prim and proper as always. 'I should get a move on,' she said. 'But I trust I'll be seeing both of you tomorrow. My place, three sharp.'

Ernie spoke through a mouthful of sausage roll. 'So we're still having the meeting as usual?'

'Of course,' she replied, looking affronted by the question. 'Gertie would want us to. Not to mention, it'll be a chance to give her a proper send-off.'

Norman watched her leave, striding away with the certainty of someone who considered herself to be a pillar of the community. He was about to take another bite of his sandwich when he realised Ernie was staring at him, flakes of pastry scattered down his shirtfront.

'Can I be honest with you?' said Ernie. Given that his honesty was often a concussive experience, Norman braced himself for what might follow. 'I worry about you.'

'I'm fine,' replied Norman, his voice nevertheless rising an octave.

Ernie shook his head, as if he alone could see the truth of the situation. 'Now that Betty's been gone a while, may she rest in peace, you're looking, how should I say? *Old*. Like fruit withered on the vine.'

'I'm eighty-six,' he replied, the uneaten remains of his sandwich beginning to droop between his fingers.

'Same as that bloke a while back,' said Ernie. 'The one that got hacked to pieces.'

Norman gasped. 'I didn't hear about that.'

'A bunch of kids it was. They gutted him like a fish.' Lest there be any doubt, he demonstrated the movement in a stabbing, twisting motion. 'And it wasn't even to rob the bloke, that's the worst thing. It was just for sport.'

'But I couldn't have missed news like that,' said Norman. 'People would have been talking about it.'

'It's probably sub-conscious,' replied Ernie, nodding at his own wisdom. 'You blocked it out because you know it could happen to you. I mean, if it wasn't for Sally keeping an eye on you, the police might not find your body for weeks, even months. You could be half eaten by flies before anyone realised.'


In retrospect, Florence regretted wearing a hoodie. Clacton was much colder than she'd expected, far chillier than a September day had the right to be. She wasn't sitting on Norman's door-step so much as huddled there, her face hidden from view as he pulled up in his car. The thought that this might be alarming to an elderly person – to find a hooded stranger camped in front of their door – only occurred to her after she realised Norman hadn't got out. That, instead, he was sat staring at her, the engine still running.

Granted, they'd both changed in the twelve years since they'd last seen each other. In the same way that he wasn't the grandfather she remembered – a ten-foot giant who used to scoop her up like a rag doll – it probably went without saying that there wasn't much left of that young girl either, but still Florence had assumed there'd be *some* recognition.

The look on Norman's face said otherwise.

Deciding there was no point in waiting this out – that, from an environmental perspective alone, it would be better to talk to him so that he'd at least turn his engine off – Florence got up and approached the car.

Norman inched down his window as she got closer, not enough to get a hand through, but sufficient for some other form of attack, as though the possibility of being sprayed with acid was just the price he had to pay for being polite.

'Hey, Granddad.'

Norman's mouth fell open and for a few seconds it seemed that he'd lost the power of speech.

'Florence?' he said, his attention focused on her pierced eyebrow and grey-dyed hair. He opened his door, his movements slower and stiffer than Florence had expected. 'For the life of me, I didn't recognise you.'

'Yeah, I got that feeling. I hope I didn't, like, freak you out.'

'Don't be silly,' he said, nothing in his tone to suggest that he'd just been cowering in a locked vehicle.

'I was thinking we could, you know, hang out together.' She saw him glance at her bags, so full they were straining at the seams. 'Maybe for a while.'

He smiled, trying to make it seem like it was the most natural thing in the world that a granddaughter he hadn't seen in twelve years had just turned up out of the blue.

'That sounds lovely,' he said. 'How about we get you inside and make a nice cup of tea?'

# 2.

Even once she was indoors, Florence remained bundled up, hunched at the kitchen table while Norman busied himself making tea.

'So how are you?' he said. 'Were you outside long?'

'Not really. But then I started thinking maybe you'd gone away or something. I don't have your number on my phone.'

'But your mother has it.'

'Yeah,' she replied, making the word sound like teenage code for all the things she wasn't ready or willing to say. 'The whole trip was kind of, you know, spontaneous. Mum thinks I'm at uni.'

'Then surely she'll worry?'

Florence frowned. 'If there's a problem, she'll call. And I'm wherever my phone is. The geography doesn't matter.'

'But you're not at university.'

She looked at him differently, as though worried about his mental faculties. 'No,' she said, more slowly. 'I'm here.'

As she stopped speaking, Norman found his eyes drawn back to her hair, a grey so reminiscent of battleships, the overriding impression was of war and conquest.

Trying not to stare, he got on with making tea while Florence peered at a crossword on the table, not unfinished so much as un-started.

'Is it a difficult one today?' she said.

'Oh, it's always difficult. I'd like to say it's my age, but you could have put it in front of me sixty years ago and I still would have struggled. I'm sure your Uncle Gerry could do it with his eyes closed; he got all the smarts in the family. You're welcome to have a go at it.'

'Crosswords aren't really my thing.'

'No?' he replied. 'So, what is?'

'I guess you could call me a nerd. Maths, science, stuff like that.'

'Your grandmother would have approved. She was always dipping into the encyclopedia, wanting to learn something new.' He handed Florence a steaming mug of tea. She took it in hands still covered by the stretched arms of her black hoodie, holding the drink close, absorbing its warmth. 'I wish Betty was still here. She would have loved to see how you've grown.'

Florence looked away. 'I'm sorry we couldn't make it to the funeral,' she said.

'Well, your mother was sick. There was nothing to be done about it, was there? I'm just glad she had you to look after her. Are things all right now?'

'Yeah . . .' she replied, the word sounding even more vague than before. 'She's fine.'

Norman waited for her to say more, but the silence hung heavy. Unsure what to say – but certain that this wasn't the right moment to comment on the weather or the latest episode of *The Archers* – Norman sipped his tea while waiting for it to pass.

Sure enough, Florence eventually began to relax, swapping her frozen huddle for a more comfortable position. As her hands came into view, the first thing Norman noticed was her rings: chunky silver skulls, piled up across both knuckles like a metallic deformity. Then the entire hoodie came off, yanked away as tomboyishly as the garment itself, to reveal yet more layers of black beneath – so much black, anyone would think *she* was the one who'd just been to a funeral.

'That's interesting jewellery,' said Norman, trying to make conversation.

'Thanks,' she replied.

'Do they not get in the way?'

She glanced down at her fingers. 'In the way of what?'

'I don't know,' he said. 'Life.' Her puzzled expression suggested not. 'I still remember the last time you were here. You had this lovely pink dress.' He smiled at the memory, hopeful that it might prompt something in Florence, but she remained impossible to read. 'It's funny how much we change over the years, isn't it? Though I daresay I've changed a bit as well.'

And, as their eyes met, he realised that Ernie was right: he *had* withered on the vine.


Florence wouldn't have *said* it, of course – 'Yeah, you're looking old. Really, really old' – but there were limits to how much control she had over the rest of her physiology. Which was unfortunate, because Norman now sat there with a dejected air. It was the same thing she'd seen in her mother in recent years, like there was some point in midlife when your age went from something you *are* to something you *have* – an aggressive python, say, or an especially venomous spider – and your remaining decades were spent either struggling to put it back in its cage or living on the run.

'I should go unpack,' she said, thinking that some alone time might be a useful reset for both of them.

'I'll sort out the bedding for you. And let me give you a hand with your bags.'

'No,' she replied, a little too quickly. 'I'm fine, really.'

'But they look heavy,' said Norman.

*Exactly* was the correct response, but this, too, felt like a trap. The Norman of her childhood memories could have tossed both bags up the stairs with one hand behind his back, but it seemed probable that *this* Norman would die in the attempt.

'Let's just say I like a challenge,' she said. 'You know, girl power, that sort of thing.'

'Well, if you're sure.'

Leaving him in the kitchen, Florence dragged her bags upstairs, rising *thud, thud, thud*, one rung at a time, each step taking her further from the secrets she'd left behind.

It was an odd sensation to be back in this house after so many years. Like Norman, it was smaller than she remembered, yet other details were just the same as twelve years earlier; such a profound sense of time having stood still, it was easy to believe the pig-tailed seven-year-old she'd once been was about to jump out from some hiding place. Even Betty felt present, the scent of her cigarettes so ingrained into the fabric of the building it was plausible that she'd be joining them at any second, cooing over Florence, her face unexpectedly stubbly, every kiss an exfoliation.

As she dragged her bags into the bedroom, the first thing she noticed was the lace doilies, one on almost every surface, akin to a heavy frost – a fitting reflection of the temperature in the room. She wouldn't have chosen the doilies for herself, but the more she considered them, the more they felt appropriate. She'd always thought it likely, after all, that she'd been born a middle-aged woman trapped in the body of a baby. This at least would account for her teenage years, which had had a distinctly menopausal quality: not a sense that she was growing into something, but rather withering away; on the outside a young woman, but on the inside a joyless old crone.

She went out to the landing and shouted downstairs. 'Granddad.' Then, unaccustomed to the response time of the average eighty-six-year-old, called again. 'Granddad.'

'Is everything all right?' he said, shuffling into view at the bottom of the stairs.

'It's pretty cold up here. Can I turn the heating on?'

'I'll bring you some blankets in a jiffy.'

'It's not the bed,' she replied, 'it's the room.'

'Would another cup of tea help?'

'I was thinking we could just turn the heating on.'

Norman looked confused. 'It's much healthier to sleep in a cold room.'

'Yeah, it's not sleeping I'm worried about. It's staying alive between now and then.'

This teenage desire for comfort seemed to be new territory for Norman. 'I daresay the radiator works just fine,' he said, sounding more speculative than Florence would have liked. 'If you just turn the knob a bit, I'm sure it will come on sooner or later.'

Returning to the room, Florence did as instructed, but like Norman the mechanism had calcified and stiffened with age. Spurred on by mental images of sleeping in a woolly hat and gloves, she persisted, tugging first this way and then that. Yet when it finally came loose, the pleasure she found in turning it gave way to the disappointment that nothing was happening: no reassuring hum or satisfying hiss, just a cold silence.

Since Norman's likely response would be a blanket, or a cup of tea, or a cup of tea under a blanket, Florence got on with unpacking, deciding that warmth, like so much else in her life, would have to remain a work in progress. Far more pressing was trying to understand why she was there at all, something she couldn't explain to Norman because she still couldn't explain it to herself; still couldn't decide if she'd come in search of comfort – to a distant memory of a man, a vague notion of belonging – or whether the whole trip was more of a post-mortem, literally going back to the family's source in an effort to understand where everything had gone wrong.

# Six years earlier

## 2016

Faced with the prospect of turning eighty in a few weeks' time, Norman couldn't decide which was more surprising: that there was no one he wanted to invite to his birthday party, or that he didn't care. Undeterred, Betty tried to sell the idea to him with enthusiastic talk of balloons and finger food and a gathering of acquaintances from across the decades. And yet the more Norman pictured the scene, the less excited he felt.

'There must be *some* people you've liked over the years,' she said, the two of them discussing it over a breakfast of tea and toast.

'Of course,' he replied. 'But that's the thing about turning eighty, isn't it? Lots of them are dead already.'

Betty sighed. 'I suppose we could just have Sally and some of the other neighbours over.'

'But that wouldn't feel very special,' said Norman. 'We see those people all the time.'

There was something about the reply that seemed to irritate Betty. She lit a cigarette, a grey cloud forming around her as she glared at him across the table. 'Just how *special* would you like your party to be?'

'I don't know,' he said, unnerved by her change of tone. 'All I really want is a cheese and pineapple hedgehog.'

Betty continued staring at him. 'I mean the *people*, Norman. What kind of "special" people would you like to invite?'

He looked away, tried to busy himself with his breakfast: another smear of jam, another sip of tea.

'There's no point inviting the kids, is there?' he said, as he took a bite of toast, still avoiding her gaze. 'They won't want to come.'

'They might if you actually have a party.'

'No,' he replied, dismissively. 'They're busy with their own lives, aren't they? A birthday card is more than enough for me.' He glanced out the window, eager to be away. 'I should probably get started in the garden before it starts to rain.'

He was still thinking of his birthday as he stepped out into the cool fresh air of the garden. Turning eighty felt important somehow, rather like turning forty all those years before but with one key difference: when he'd turned forty, he'd felt that he was lurching into old age – ludicrous to think now – whereas in turning eighty there was a clear sense that he was running out of time.

He started tending to one of the rose bushes, doting over it with more than the usual care. When he'd bought the plant years earlier, he hadn't dared tell Betty that the variety was called Ethel – the name that may never be mentioned between them. Over the years, its pale pink flowers and heady fragrance had defined many of their summer days together and yet whenever Betty had asked what it was called, he'd always claimed he couldn't remember.

He smiled to himself as he trimmed away some withered leaves. If he was lucky, there'd be a flower or two he could pop in a vase for his birthday. In that sense, at least, Ethel would be present for the occasion, which was more than enough for him.

He noticed Betty in the kitchen window, watching him as she washed up their breakfast things. For an instant he felt guilty, but of course Betty suspected nothing. A person need only look at the splendour of Norman's vegetable patch to understand that the garden was his happy place; why wouldn't he be smiling to himself while he was out there?

15

# 3.

By the time Norman and Florence had finished breakfast the next morning, Norman was certain of only one thing: Florence had dropped out of university. Although the way she presented herself should have made that obvious from the start – her clothes, her jewellery, her hair – Norman still felt a pang of disappointment to think that she was giving up on her education just like her mother before her. He was still none the wiser as to why she'd come to him, but it was so lovely to see her again after all those years, it surely didn't matter.

After they'd cleared away the last of the breakfast things, Norman led her out into the back garden, unable to hide his excitement.

'You could say I've saved for the best for last,' he said, raising his voice over the sound of the wind as they progressed away from the house. 'I would have shown you yesterday, but I didn't want you getting cold again.' He came to a stop beside a dense profusion of greenery, gesturing at it with parental pride. 'This is my vegetable patch.' Florence stared at it blankly. 'Look at those leeks,' he added. 'They're absolute beauties.'

Florence merely nodded.

'There are cabbages, too,' he said, hopeful that he might still spark some interest. 'And some marrows.'

Florence nodded again, more awkwardly this time, and then looked away.

They clearly needed a Plan B.

He glanced up at the sky, dark clouds threatening rain. 'How about I show you around town? I doubt you remember much from your last visit.'

They left the house soon after, the weather growing greyer by the minute. As they went out to the car, Norman noticed Sally in her living room window, watching them leave, doubtless wondering what he was doing with a teenager who looked like that.

'Who's she?' said Florence, as Norman waved to her.

'Sally. She's been living here almost as long as I have. We're both on the local Neighbourhood Watch committee.'

Florence laughed. 'She's definitely watching.'

'We're supposed to be looking out for criminals, of course, but Sally's never been one to limit herself.' Feeling self-conscious, he waved to her again as they pulled away. 'We have a meeting at her place this afternoon, just to update everyone on what's been happening.'

'And what has been happening?' said Florence.

Norman hesitated. 'Well, the meetings are a chance for tea and cake as much as anything.' The first drops of rain spattered across the windscreen. 'Oops, there we go. It does tend to rain a lot here. That's the downside of living by the sea, I'm afraid.'

'So what's the upside?' she replied.

Norman was taken by surprise, never having known anyone to ask a question like that. 'Well, it's the seaside, isn't it? Everyone loves the seaside.'

Florence said nothing, perhaps feeling that their surroundings were response enough: some of the houses were well past their prime; all peeling paint and rust.

She remained like that while Norman tried to think of what to talk about next. They were nearing the town centre when he spoke again. 'Back in the war, we were on the flight path for

17

German bombers heading into London. There was a fair bit of damage.'

'And you were like, what, a teenager back then?'

'I'm not that old! I only remember bits and bobs. There was a plane loaded with mines that crashed into the town. That wiped out lots of houses. And there was the occasional doodlebug, of course.'

'A doodle*what*?' she replied.

'Doodlebugs. Flying bombs from Germany. I can still picture the rubble. It took a fair while to get the place back on its feet.'

Driving at a measured, sedate pace, they passed a boarded-up shop.

'Is that what it is now?' she said. 'On its feet?'

Norman sighed. 'It used to be such a buzzing place back in the sixties, a real holiday resort. Had you told people back then it would end up like this, they would have thought you mad. It's a bit like old age, I suppose; it just creeps up on you. You notice the odd thing here and there – a new wrinkle, say, or a few grey hairs – but it doesn't seem that important, until one day you look in the mirror and realise your whole body is falling apart.'

Florence giggled. 'I don't think the local tourist board would be thrilled with your tour.'

'But there's no point sugar-coating it, is there? The sparkle's gone. It's still a lovely place, but it's a shadow of what it once was.' He pointed at a block of flats as they drove past. 'There used to be a cinema there. Art Deco it was, quite striking.'

'Was that hit by a doodlething, too?'

'No, no,' he replied, sadly. 'We destroyed that one ourselves.'


The more Florence considered it, the more it felt possible that Norman wasn't showing her around at all, but rather trying to scare her away: *See, this place is awful. Whatever you're running from, it can't be worse than this.*

On that basis, at least the progression of the morning made sense. After driving at a ceremonial pace past discount stores and tattoo parlours, Norman suggested they have an ice cream on the seafront. It was during a temporary break in the rain, but still the day was cold and grey, a chill wind blowing in from the North Sea.

'It's not so bad when you find a bit of shelter,' he said. 'And when you think about it, it's much more practical to eat ice cream on a day like this; there's no danger of it melting.' After finding them an appropriate spot, he set about the task at hand, enthusiastically licking his cone of vanilla ice cream. 'Do you remember any of this from your last visit?'

'Not really,' she replied. 'Mum sometimes talks about the place. I've spotted a few of the things she's mentioned.'

'I dread to think what she says. She got away as soon as she could.'

'Yeah, I get that impression.'

The wind tugging at her hair, her clothes, Florence took in the surrounding scene. Further up the beach was a big wheel, stark white against the grey sky. The town's pier stretched out to sea in front of it, the sound of screams drifting on the wind from its amusement rides.

Norman followed her gaze. 'I've always thought it strange that people pay good money to be scared witless. As if life isn't frightening enough already.'

Florence pointed to a group of wind turbines far out to sea, their massive blades turning on the horizon. 'They look great in this light. Very Zen.'

'But birds don't like them, apparently.'

'I'm guessing birds dislike climate change even more,' she replied.

'They fly into them, that's what the papers say. Imagine, flying along, not a care in the world, and then *thwack*.'

Florence dismissed it with a shrug. 'Is that really any different to being human?'

'Well, true,' he said. 'I hadn't really thought of it that way.' He broke into a smile, and before he knew it she was smiling back. 'Ah, that's more like the Florence I remember!'

She blushed even more. 'Sorry, I have a terminal case of resting bitch face.'

'Well, *that* wasn't the word I had in mind,' he replied, with a chuckle. 'As long as you're okay, that's all that matters.'

'I've had a lot on my mind, that's all.' She watched his reaction to that titbit of information; how he leaned a little closer, expectant for what she might be about to reveal. 'I was dating someone for a while.'

'Oh, yes?' he replied, trying to sound offhand. 'Who was the lucky man?'

Florence frowned. 'What makes you think it was a man?'

Norman froze mid-lick, looking much like the ground had just given way. 'Well, of course, I, er, well, yes ...'

'I mean, it *was* a guy,' she added. 'I just don't see how it's helpful to make those assumptions.'

'Well, that's a fair point, I hadn't really thought of it that way. So things didn't work out with the young man you were seeing?'

'God, no,' she scoffed. 'But it was pretty full-on for a while. I mean, he wanted me to meet his family, and he was constantly going on about wanting to meet mine. And it just made me think, *what family?* Dad doesn't even try to get in touch on my birthdays any more. And I hadn't seen you in years and years.'

Norman looked concerned. 'The relationship didn't end because of that, did it?'

'No, of course not. I dumped him because he was a bell-end. But it's going to happen again one day, isn't it? Or at least I hope so. And I want to feel good about it when it does.' She licked her ice cream, distracted by the thought. 'As a family, I think we need to acknowledge that we're not very good at relationships.'

'Just because your parents' marriage didn't work out, it doesn't mean *you* can't be happy with someone.'

'But it's not just them, is it?' she replied. 'Uncle Gerry and his wife crashed and burned. And then there's you and Gran.'

Norman stopped eating. 'What on earth are you talking about?'

'Hey, don't shoot the messenger. I'm just repeating what Mum's said.'

A look of genuine shock set in, Norman shaking his head in such disbelief; even the remains of his ice cream offered no solace. 'Your mother really said that? I can't imagine why. Betty and I were very happy together.'

'Look, maybe I misunderstood her,' said Florence, the lie having an instant calming effect. 'Things can get lost in translation, you know how it is.'

Temporarily soothed, Norman returned to his ice cream, but Florence saw him glance at her every now and then, until finally –

'Has your mum said anything else about me and Betty?'

She took a deep breath, deciding now was not the time for more honesty. 'I wouldn't stress over it. It's probably all a misunderstanding.'

# 4.

Even under the best of circumstances, Norman wouldn't have been in the mood for one of Sally's committee meetings, but all the more so having just had his marriage called into question. It didn't help that everything he'd shown Florence so far had elicited the same underwhelmed response – a gnawing sense that it wasn't just his marriage that she thought had problems, it was also his hometown and all his life choices.

'I don't get why you need a crime committee,' she said, as they crossed the street to Sally's house. 'It doesn't look that bad round here. Or, at least, it doesn't look *dangerous*.'

'But it's going downhill,' he replied. 'One look at people's flowerbeds should tell you that. I even find beer cans in my front garden sometimes. Empty ones, obviously.'

'And these people we're meeting, they're all old friends?'

Norman hesitated, trying to find the right words. 'I wouldn't say we're *friends*, exactly. We're really just the last ones standing. Everyone else from the early days has either moved away or died.'

'So, the biggest thing you all have in common is being alive?'

'Well, yes,' he replied. 'You could put it like that. There used to be five of us, but Gertie died last week. It was her funeral yesterday.'

They'd barely started up the garden path when Sally opened the front door, watching them approach.

'I noticed you had company,' she said, as they got closer. 'I was going to come over and ask, but then I thought we'd see each other this afternoon.'

Norman beamed. 'My granddaughter, Florence. She's visiting for a while.'

'Little Florence?' said Sally, sounding genuinely shocked. She ushered them indoors, her gaze lingering on Florence's clothes, her hair, her pierced eyebrow. 'You're not *at all* the little girl I remember.' Before Florence could reply, Sally turned back to Norman. 'And how come you never mentioned this yesterday?'

Norman struggled to think of an appropriate response. 'Well, it's a nice surprise, isn't it?'

Sally picked up on his hesitation, but said nothing. Instead, she hovered in the hallway while they removed their shoes, Norman kicking himself as usual for not checking his socks before putting them on that morning. Sally glanced down at his feet, a yellow toenail poking out from a nest of bobbled wool – something she saw almost every time he visited, and yet each time she managed to look shocked afresh.

'Horace and Ernie are already here,' she said, as she ushered them through to the lounge.

'What's this I hear about a granddaughter?' yelled Ernie, as they entered the room.

'This is Florence,' replied Norman. 'She's my youngest.'

Florence seemed unfazed by the attention, standing there while elderly strangers scrutinised her.

'And here was me thinking you'd got yourself one of those mail-order brides,' said Ernie. 'I was about to ask you how they got her through the letterbox.' He turned to Florence. 'I'm just kidding with you. I see the family resemblance. Though that's not to say you look like a balding geriatric man, of course.'

'That's Ernie,' said Norman to Florence, the words sounding like an apology. 'He lives around the corner. We used to work together, too, back when I was a lorry driver.' He gestured at another, much older man in the corner of the room. 'And that's Horace.' Horace offered a subtle nod and a faint grunt as Norman leant closer to Florence, lowering his voice. 'Horace had a stroke a few years back . . .'

From behind them, Sally breezed into the room carrying a Victoria sponge on a porcelain cake stand. 'In honour of Gertie,' she announced, as she set it down.

'Thank God she had decent taste in cakes,' said Ernie, watching excitedly as Sally started plating up. 'Imagine if her favourite food had been, I don't know, tripe and sauerkraut flan. We'd all be like "Gertie who?"'

Sally served him first, presumably in the hope that a full mouth would stop him talking. She then handed a plate to Horace, beaming with pleasure as he used his one functioning hand to scoop up a forkful of cake; lifting it, trembling, to his gaping crooked mouth.

'How is it?' she said to him, speaking louder and slower than normal.

Horace grunted a response.

'I'm so pleased,' she replied. 'There's plenty more if you want it.'

Norman still couldn't decide if Sally really understood Horace's monosyllabic pronouncements or whether it was just wishful thinking. Judging by the way she spoke to him since his stroke, anyone would think Horace's communications had taken on the complex tonal quality of Chinese, every sound conveying a wealth of information, but all of it lost on Norman because he wasn't clever enough to learn the language.

'Last but not least,' said Sally, handing a plate to Norman and finally to Florence, her eyes this time settling on Florence's chunky jewellery, her disapproval plain to see. 'Are you at university now?' she asked as Florence started to eat.

Norman jumped in. 'She's with me now, that's all that

matters. I've been showing her around. Showing her what a lovely town we have.'

Sally responded with a thoughtful nod, as though this, too, had been a revealing response. Retreating to her usual armchair, she put on her glasses – propping them on the bridge of her nose – and began reading from a list. 'On today's agendum, we need to discuss how we can take on Gertie's responsibilities.'

Ernie spoke through a full mouth. 'She never really did anything.'

'She was still another pair of eyes,' replied Sally, in a chiding tone. 'I was actually thinking you could pass by her street on your scooter from time to time, just to keep us informed.'

'I suppose I could,' he said, reluctantly. 'Though I'm not going any further than her place. People say there's a bloke a couple of streets over, he's murdered at least three people. With a chainsaw.'

Sally shook her head. 'Ernie, I'm sure that's not true.'

'That's easy to say, isn't it?' he replied, becoming animated. 'Easy to say when you're sitting here in broad daylight with a plate of cake in your hand. But tell me how true it is when you hear that *vroom, vroom* in the middle of the night and realise he's cutting through your front door.' He turned to Horace. 'Tell me, Horace, would you go poking around that bloke's place?

Horace grunted.

'Exactly,' replied Ernie. 'I rest my case.'

There was a strained silence in the room, Norman thinking how unfortunate it was he would forevermore associate Victoria sponge with death by chainsaw.

Sally took a deep breath and returned to her list. 'I had a run-in the other day with the same offender I mentioned at our last meeting. On this occasion, I witnessed him toss something from his car window before driving off. On closer inspection, it was the wrapper of a chocolate wafer bar – generic, not branded. Needless to say, I disposed of it in the proper manner. I also passed details of the car – make and model, et cetera – to the police.' Seeming to realise that she was still playing second fiddle to Ernie, she spoke in a more dramatic tone. 'Undoubtedly, the most important task we all have ahead of us in the coming weeks is to be vigilant for slashers.'

Florence gasped. 'There's knife crime here?'

'Absolutely,' replied Sally, peering over the top of her glasses. 'It's a constant and very real threat. If someone were to slash Norman's leeks now, we'd stand no chance at the annual competition.'


Despite Norman's garden being a veritable jungle of vegetables, they never appeared to make it into the house. For the second night in a row, their dinner revolved around tinned food: a mechanical process of emptying one metal object into another and then introducing heat.

Since cheese on toast was the pinnacle of her culinary repertoire, there was no point Florence offering to cook, but still she couldn't shake a sense of complicity. It was one thing to know of someone whose entire dietary intake was canned, who seemingly lived life like a never-ending Arctic expedition circa 1829, but quite another to sit and eat it with them. To participate in the process, as she had tonight, by opening the can of beef stew for Norman, while he spoke about its contents as if it was an old family recipe.

When they were finally sitting down to eat, he watched as she took her first bite.

'What do you think?' he said, eyes sparkling with anticipation.

'It's nice,' she replied, impressed not so much by the food itself as by the fact that Norman had been able to survive on it for so long. The label claimed it was a beef *and vegetable* stew, but it seemed they weren't actual vegetables so much as early prototypes – before someone had the bright idea of adding taste and texture – only the colour indicating that this lump was a carrot, that lump a potato.

'It's my favourite,' said Norman with a slight blush. 'I make sure there are always a few tins of it in the cupboard.' They remained like that, eating in silence, until Norman spoke again. 'So, have you thought about what you're going to do with your life?'

'Wow,' she replied. 'It sounds so profound when you say it like that. My *life*.'

'But you need to think about it, don't you? That's the thing about the years, they slip by whether you're ready or not. You said you like science. How about being a hairdresser? It's quite technical, what with all the potions they use. And let's not forget, it's a growth business, no pun intended. The whole world could go to pot – icebergs melting, and all those other things you young people worry about – and the thing is, people will still need their hair cut. You don't even need to be very good at it. I've had lots of bad haircuts in my time.'

Florence laughed. 'I think you're supposed to tell me I should pursue my education.'

'Not necessarily,' he said, placing unnatural emphasis on the words. 'It's not the end of the world if you don't have an education. Look at Bill Gates and Richard Branson. They didn't worry about bits of paper. They just rolled up their sleeves and got on with it.'

'They're not hairdressers.'

'But I'm sure they could have been if they wanted to,' he replied. 'And I dare say they would've made a real success of it. Bigger than that Gore Vidal bloke, the one with all the fancy shampoos.' Florence opened her mouth to correct him, but then let it go. 'Or you could follow in my footsteps. The world will always need lorry drivers.'

'It does sound kind of cool,' she said politely, deciding this wasn't the right moment to explain self-driving technology. 'The variety, I mean. Being on the move all the time.'

'Do you know how to drive?' he replied.

'I took some lessons a couple of years ago, but I couldn't really afford to keep them up. I mean, my instructor was also a total sleazeball, so it wasn't a hard decision.'

'Getting my licence was probably the best thing I ever did. Everything came from that: the house, the lot of it. My job took me everywhere, the length and breadth of the country.'

*So many opportunities to cheat on Betty*, thought Florence.

'You must have met a lot of people along the way,' she said, her tone betraying nothing.

Norman looked down at his food. 'If anything, it was the opposite,' he said, avoiding eye contact. 'It was just me and the open road. But I loved it, I really did.' He paused, a hint of regret in his expression. 'Though maybe I shouldn't have loved it as much as that.'

'Why not?' replied Florence, fascinated by the change in tone.

Norman seemed to choose his words more carefully than usual. 'Because it took me away from home so often. I was hardly ever there, it was just Betty and the kids. I was away for days and days at a time.'

'Was it lonely, living on the road?'

'Of course,' he replied, the words sounding well practised rather than sincere. 'I hated being away.'

And in that instant, it was obvious. He was lying.

# Twenty-one years earlier
## 2001

It was the end of an era, that's what everyone kept telling Norman.

'Retirement,' people would say, unable to hide their envy, as though it was a good thing that he was now deemed too old to be useful any more. 'You'll be as free as a lark. Imagine all the things you can do.'

As long as it doesn't require youthful vitality, Norman would think to himself. Or more money than his modest pension would allow.

If Norman's greatest wish in life was to spend endless time at home drinking tea and listening to the wireless, then yes, his impending retirement really was a dream come true. But what he couldn't admit was that in saying goodbye to a life on the road, he was also bidding farewell to Ethel and any chance of spending time with her again.

It really was the end of an era.

On his last day of work, Norman arrived back at the depot to find the inevitable 'surprise' party in the forecourt. As he parked his lorry for the final time, he looked out at the assembled faces: colleagues he'd never liked that much; acquaintances who knew almost nothing of his life. And in the middle of them all stood Betty, looking as uncomfortable as Norman already felt.

He took the keys from the ignition, at that moment wanting nothing more than to have it all back; another forty-odd years of driving his lorry across the country; perhaps even a rewinding of the years, so that at the end of it he might be twenty again, his whole life ahead of him.

With a deep sigh, he opened the door and climbed out. His feet hadn't even touched the ground when Ernie rushed up and fired a party streamer over him: a loud bang of gunpowder followed by multi-coloured paper rain. 'Norm, you old fart. Happy retirement!'

This prompted applause from everyone else, Norman feeling more and more awkward while he stood there picking confetti from his thinning hair. As the clapping died down, he realised they were waiting for him to say something. After trying to think of the right response, he simply gestured at the crowd, at the balloons dangling from the depot girders, and the large silver and gold banner saying "GOODBYE NORMAN" in glittering capital letters.

'You shouldn't have,' he said, certain this was the only possible statement of truth.

And with that, Ernie fired another party streamer, creating yet more chaos while everyone else descended on the drinks table, determined to down as much as possible before the free booze ran dry.

Norman crossed to Betty and gave her a peck on the cheek. 'Hello, love.'

'How does it feel?' she replied, brushing some streamers from his jumper.

'It doesn't seem real, if I'm honest with you. I *know* it's my last day, but it doesn't *feel* like it.'

A colleague barged between them, raising his plastic cup in a toast even though Norman still didn't have a drink. 'Cheers, mate,' he said, his breath tangy with beer. 'I bet you're glad to get it all over with, aren't you?'

Norman forced a smile. 'It's going to be a big change, that's for sure.'

Already unsteady on his feet, the man bumped against Betty. 'Upsidaisy,' he said, trying not to spill his drink. 'Though you better get used to it. Norman's going to be under your feet every day from now on.'

As the man moved on and the party began to pulse around them, Betty's face reflected Norman's fear that life was about to change in unexpected ways.

He'd just suggested they get a drink, as an anaesthetic if not for actual pleasure, when Ernie's voice boomed through the depot, amplified threefold thanks to a microphone he'd plugged into a portable stereo. 'Ladies and gentlemen,' he shouted, the tinny little speakers straining under the volume, simultaneously rendering his voice too loud and yet utterly without substance. 'Don't worry, I'm not going to start yammering on. I just want to thank you all for coming. Norm's actually been my best mate for as long as I can remember ...' As Ernie's voice cracked with emotion, Norman reminded himself that it was the cheap wine talking, not genuine sentiment. 'Mate, I want you to know you'll be missed, but we're all wishing you well in your golden years. And though, let's face it, sixty-five is bloody old, I reckon we're all as young as we feel.' He shouted to the crowd: 'Let's show 'em how Clacton does it. Come on, everyone, get down and dance!' This was followed by an awkward silence as he unplugged his microphone and fumbled with a CD player until, at length, S Club 7 began blasting at full volume.

Despite being not far from retirement himself, Ernie leapt into the crowd, gyrating his body in ways that matched neither the music nor the occasion.

Norman gave Betty an apologetic look. 'It's the divorce,' he said. 'It's still so fresh. I think it's hit him quite hard.'

'It's not his divorce that surprises me,' she replied. 'It's that anyone wanted to marry him in the first place.' She laughed. 'Gracious, listen to me, I sound like a monster. I'm obviously overdue a cup of tea.'

'Ooh, yes,' replied Norman, 'a cup of tea would hit the spot right now. Come on, we can go and make one in the pantry.'

'But what about your party?' she said.

Norman looked at the throng on the makeshift dancefloor, no one seeming to notice that he wasn't in there with them. 'It's not really *my* party, is it? I'm just a convenient excuse for a knees-up.

And anyway, we're only going to the pantry. We'll be back before they even notice.'

Together, they slipped into the office, the noise growing more muted as Norman wondered if this was how the coming decades were going to be: conversation stumbling into silence as they made cups of tea; life reduced to the distant sound of something happening to other people in some other place.

He gave her a brave smile. 'At least I'll have more time to spend with the kids now, eh?'

They stayed like that, smiling at one another, neither ready to admit that family life didn't quite have the rosy glow that they were implying. One child, trying for a baby of her own, was increasingly unknowable. And then there was Gerry: his marriage had only hit the rocks metaphorically, but he now seemed to spend most of his time like an actual castaway, alone and impossible to reach.

'I was thinking I might take up gardening,' said Norman, needing the refuge of a safe subject. 'Now that I'll be around every day, I can make a proper go of it; a big vegetable patch and everything.'

Betty was about to say something when they heard the sound of people chanting Norman's name.

'Oh, I know what's coming next,' he said, wearily. 'They're about to give me my clock. Everyone gets one when they retire. I swear they probably bought them in bulk years back.'

As the chants grew louder – *Norman! Norman! Norman!* – he braced himself to look happy and grateful. He'd shake hands, he'd smile, he'd hold the clock for people to admire, as though they hadn't already seen one just like it on many occasions before.

'I suppose we ought to go out there,' he said.

'Think of it this way,' replied Betty. 'It'll be a memento of your time on the road.'

And even though she sounded like that was the last thing she wanted, she managed to smile anyway.

# 5.

Florence lay in bed the next morning trying to piece together the facts so far; how all the evidence pointed to Norman being an egregious cheat and liar, and yet her entire experience of him for the past two days had been so different.

She could hear him moving about downstairs, already getting on with the day. Although staying in bed was infinitely more appealing, she hauled herself up and joined him; found him hovering over a slice of toast on the kitchen floor.

'Good morning,' he said, with a cheery smile. 'Would you be a love and pick that up for me? My knees aren't up to it today.'

'Sure,' she replied, swooping upon it like a bird of prey, so swift and effortless she was halfway to the bin when he called to her.

'No, no, give it here. I want to eat it.'

'It's been on the floor,' she replied, giving it to him anyway.

'Not for long. I know some say five seconds is the rule, but I'm sure the real number is much more than that. It's like the expiry dates on things you get at the supermarket: they want you to throw everything away after a week, because that's how they make money. In my experience, once you scrape the mould off, most things are fine.' He blew on the piece of toast before spreading it with margarine. 'Waste not, want not, that's always been my attitude.'

Florence watched in disbelief. 'I don't think you're supposed to say that about bacteria as well.'

'It's not like it had anything on it when it fell on the floor.

Dry toast seems quite antisocial in that respect, don't you think? I can't imagine it does much in the way of making friends with germs.'

While he took a bite of it, chomping away happily, Florence made some fresh for herself; was staring into the toaster, willing the bread to brown faster, when he spoke again.

'I've been thinking, how about I teach you to drive?'

She turned to look at him. 'You what?'

'You already know the basics, we'll probably make very quick progress.' Remembering that this was the man who'd just eaten his breakfast off the kitchen floor, Florence replied with a vague murmur – an acknowledgement of the statement rather than an agreement – and turned her attention back to the toaster. 'If we pop out and get some learner plates after breakfast, we can start by ten.'

Shocked, she span back around to face him. 'You want to do it *today*?'

'Why not?' he said, as he finished his cold toast, unable to hide his satisfaction at wasting nothing. 'You're jobless and I'm retired. I'd say it's the perfect thing to do.'


It was akin to being kidnapped, a reverse carjacking: one moment Florence was a carefree pedestrian, the next she was being forced behind the wheel of a car she didn't want to drive.

Norman had chosen an old industrial estate for their first lesson; a place of dilapidated roadways and weed-strewn car parks. No one else in sight. No one to hear her scream.

'I know it's not much to look at,' he said, stooping on arthritic joints as he attached the plates. 'But it's the perfect spot for a learner. You can't go wrong, really.'

'There are still walls and lampposts to crash into,' she replied.

'But that's the beauty of the place, you don't need to go near them. You can drive in the middle of the road if you want.' He looked at her, sitting forlorn behind the wheel. 'Come on, it's not that bad.'

'Are you even allowed to do this at your age?'

Norman bristled. 'I have to renew my licence every three years. That probably makes me a better driver than most of the other people on the road. Not to mention, I learnt to drive in the army. You can't get better training than that.' He lowered himself into the passenger seat. 'Well, this is a first. Somehow the car feels very different on this side.'

'Trust me,' replied Florence. 'I can totally relate.'

'How much do you remember about clutch control?'

'Enough to still be traumatised by it.'

He hesitated, perhaps deciding that this wasn't the right time to explain the transfer of torque. 'I'm sure it'll come back to you.'

'The knowledge or the trauma?'

'You'll be fine,' he replied. 'Just turn the ignition and we'll get started.' His face lit up as the engine sputtered into life, as though Florence had already nailed the most difficult part. 'Now, just press down the clutch and put her in first gear, and—' The car stalled. 'Never mind, that happens to everyone. If you don't get it wrong, you'll never get it right.'

On that basis, it soon became apparent that Florence would one day most certainly get it right, such was the scale of her failures. If only it was called clutch uncontrol, she could already lay claim to a natural talent, but instead they spent the first few minutes jerking angrily across that weed-strewn expanse.

Eventually, however, she graduated from stalling the car to moving it around the empty lot, climbing up and down through the gears with only the occasional loud crunch. 'Okay,' she said. 'It's coming back to me now.'

'See, it just takes time and practice. And I can guarantee you, it's a useful skill. Even for me, it would be handy if you know how to drive.'

'What are you talking about?' she said. 'You can already drive.'

'But I don't like driving in the dark any more. Imagine what would happen if . . .' He flailed for some compelling argument. 'Imagine if all the lightbulbs at home just blew out one evening, the whole house plunged into darkness. If you can't drive us to the shops, we'll be sitting like that all night.'

'Then buy some candles!' she said, creasing her face in disbelief. 'Why make this about me?'

Ignoring her, Norman pointed at a small incline. 'Tell you what, let's go over there and try some hill starts.'


The hill starts turned out to be a reminder that driving, much like life itself, is easier on a flat, level surface. Although it had been Norman's suggestion, the experience was just as stressful for him, each of Florence's failures now coming with the possibility of rollback, the length of which was determined by her exasperation at that precise moment – at times, almost nothing at all, and at others a sense that it wasn't even in her power to stop the car.

She was restarting the engine yet again when he twisted in his seat to face her. 'I want you to imagine you can do anything. Imagine you're Wonder Woman.'

'Granddad, if I was a superhero, I wouldn't need a driving licence.'

'You just need to believe you can do it, that's what I mean. You can do anything, you're Wonder Woman.'

With a sigh, Florence turned the ignition again, easing the engine into first gear but this time holding the car steady on the hill.

'See,' said Norman, 'that's what I'm talking about.'

Florence rolled her eyes. 'Just to be clear, I wasn't pretending to be Wonder Woman.'

'Well, whatever you're doing, just keep doing it.'

This advice proved more valuable because, over the minutes that followed, Florence became increasingly adept at her clutch control. Making such rapid progress, in fact, Norman's attention began to stray.

'Have you had a chance to talk to your mum?' he said, as Florence climbed the hill yet again and held the car steady.

'Not yet,' she replied, her entire focus on the dashboard, as though the car needed to be kept under close supervision.

'I still can't believe what she said about me and Betty,' he said. 'It's ridiculous, really.' He laughed nervously, desperate not to make it sound like a big deal, even though it had haunted his thoughts for the last twenty-four hours.

Florence shrugged, a teenage dismissal of all his concerns. 'I don't know, maybe she just misunderstood how you felt about your job.'

'What do you mean by that?' he replied, instantly sounding more defensive than he'd expected.

The change in tone wasn't lost on Florence. She glanced at him, her clutch control momentarily faltering. 'You said it yourself, you enjoyed being on the road. You liked being alone.'

'But it wasn't that simple.'

Florence gave him a look of genuine pity. 'If you know Mum's wrong, why do you care so much about the things she's said?'

'So she *has* said other things?' he replied, his tone becoming more fraught.

For a few moments, Florence said nothing, her thoughts seeming to mirror her clutch control: a careful balancing act; the delicate maintenance of order.

'Look,' she said. 'No more shooting the messenger, okay? I only know what I've been told.'

'Of course,' he replied, the words spilling out as a knee-jerk reaction rather than a considered response.

Florence opened her mouth to speak, her expression suggestive of someone about to jump from a great height. She remained like that for a few moments, her unspoken words seeming to take on a life of their own, nothing but the purr of the engine to fill the tense silence. 'Mum said there was another woman in your marriage.'

'She what?' shrieked Norman, much louder than he'd intended. 'Why would she say something like that?'

Florence struggled to hold the car steady. 'Apparently, Uncle Gerry told her.'

Norman gasped. 'Dear God, Gerry thinks I cheated, too?' There was a pained moment of speechlessness, Florence's clutch control in its death throes. 'Right, you're driving us to Gerry's, this instant.'

The engine stalled, Florence looking so anxious at the change in Norman, she didn't seem to notice that they were rolling backwards, the mood in the car – much like the car itself – now in freefall.

'Press the brake,' said Norman, trying to sound calm, but Florence just looked at him. 'Brake,' he said. And then louder. 'Brake! Brake!'

Panicked, Florence stamped on the accelerator instead, appearing confused that the engine was now screaming as they all rolled backwards faster and faster.

Norman was reaching for the handbrake when the car mounted a kerb, jerking to a stop just as a lamppost lopped off the left-hand wing mirror.

After the sound of breaking glass: a long silence.

Florence sat there trembling, her breathing fast and shallow, her skull-encrusted fingers still gripped tight around the steering wheel.

Norman attempted a reassuring tone. 'It doesn't matter. I never used that mirror anyway.'

'I could have killed us!'

'Not really,' he said. 'Somebody else, maybe, but not us.'

'That's even worse!' she replied.

'Well, that would really depend on who they were.' He gave her a smile. 'I think it's time for a cup of tea, don't you?'


After rummaging in the boot, Norman returned with a thermos, two plastic mugs and an entire packet of chocolate biscuits.

'I've already added milk and sugar,' he said, pouring her a steaming mug of camel-coloured liquid. 'I daresay you could use both right now.'

Florence took a sip. Despite its stewed quality – somehow managing to be both too bitter and too sweet – Norman was right, there was comfort in it. And still the car remained exactly where it had come to a stop, the whole vehicle leaning at an odd angle, not enough to make their tea break uncomfortable, but a constant reminder that their world was more skewed and troubled than it had previously been.

'Don't feel bad about the car,' said Norman. 'It's nothing that can't be patched up.'

'Thanks,' she replied, still shaken. 'But it's not just the car I feel bad about. It's my stupidity.'

'You're still learning; mistakes come with the territory. You can't beat yourself up about things like that.' There was a long pause, the two of them drinking their tea in silence. 'It's not true, by the way, what your mother and Gerry said.'

'Just something else lost in translation, right?'

'Well, I can only presume ...' he replied, gazing out the window; the words fading into a sad silence. He didn't speak again until Florence had finished her tea. 'So, are you ready to drive us to Gerry's?'

Her heart sank. 'You really still want to do that?'

'Of course.'

'Shouldn't we at least call him first? Maybe he's not there today.'

'Oh, he'll just say he's busy,' replied Norman. 'That's what he always does with me. Though at least he answers his phone, which is more than I can say for your mother. It's a wonder anyone can reach her.'

Florence considered explaining caller ID – *She's not out, she's ignoring you* – but then more pressing thoughts came to mind. 'Do you honestly want to go on a sixty-mile roundtrip with someone who can't tell the difference between the brake and the accelerator?'

Norman smiled at her – unexpectedly warm considering that a small part of his car was now in fragments on the ground outside. 'I'm not bothered in the least. You're Wonder Woman, remember?'

# 6.

Even with her limited experience, Florence could tell that Uncle Gerry's neighbourhood was the location of choice for two key demographics: first-time buyers and divorcees. Half the residents hopeful for a lifetime of happy memories, the other half now picking their way through the wreckage of those same dreams; the kind of place where a middle-aged man's most valuable possession is visitation rights.

On street after street, there was nothing but identical blocks, so that the overall impression wasn't a community but rather a machine that stamped out the same thing again and again. The same hopes, the same disappointments, repeated over and over.

'He used to have a lovely house over in St Albans,' said Norman. 'It was a step up from where we raised him, that's for sure, but they sold it after the divorce. Maureen got the bulk of it when she and the girls moved to Australia.'

'Do you hear from them sometimes?' replied Florence.

'Not really. They send a card every Christmas, but it never feels very personal. It pains me to think it, but I don't suppose the girls remember anything about me, they were still too young when they moved away.' He pointed to a building at the end of the street. 'It's that one. You can park in front.'

Despite Florence's relief at turning off the engine, other emotions quickly rushed in to fill the vacuum. 'You're not going to tell Gerry what I said, are you?'

'Don't worry, I'll be very discreet. This chat has been a long time coming. Long before you.'

'Then maybe I should just stay down here,' she said.

'Don't be ridiculous. He's your uncle, he'll want to see you.'

'Yeah, but probably not under these circumstances. "Look, Florence is here. By the way, I never cheated on your mother, despite what everyone seems to think ..."' She noticed him flinch. 'Sorry, that came out wrong. This is none of my business.'

'No, no,' he replied, sounding sadder than before. 'It's everybody's business, I can see that now. That's why we're here.'


Someone was coming out of Gerry's building just as they reached the main door, so Norman went straight in, insisting that there was no need to press the intercom first.

After riding up to the fourth floor, the lift doors opened to a long, ill-lit corridor, both sides lined with identical front doors. From somewhere down the hallway, the sound of a daytime chat show drifted through the walls unhindered.

Norman led the way to Gerry's flat, pausing as they reached his door, not a sound coming from inside.

'Do you think he's out?' said Florence.

'No, he always was a quiet boy. The bookish kind.' If that was true of Gerry, it wasn't of his doorbell, which was so loud, so jarring, it felt to Florence that they'd literally broken the silence: smashed it into jagged shards that Gerry would now have to walk across to open the door.

If they'd buzzed from downstairs, he would have at least had time to prepare for their arrival – if not to actually get changed, then a few minutes to steel himself. As it was, he opened the door in a bathrobe that he'd probably considered throwing out on a number of occasions; the kind of thing someone keeps only because they believe no one will ever see them in it. Though

42

Norman was at least right about one thing: there *was* something bookish and educated about Gerry – a hint of Colin Firth, but without the success; Colin Firth after years of setbacks and disappointments.

Expressionless, Gerry stared at them.

'We were just passing,' said Norman, telling the lie with surprising ease. 'I thought it might be nice if we popped in and said hello. You remember Florence.'

Gerry gave her a polite smile. 'All grown up, I see.'

'She's staying with me for a while,' added Norman, unable to hide his pleasure at the statement.

'Well, how lovely for you both,' replied Gerry, looking like all he wanted was for them to leave. The three of them stood there in a sea of invisible tumbleweed until finally he stepped to one side. 'Why don't you come in? I'll put the kettle on.'


Gerry's flat was the opposite of what Florence had seen in glossy magazines. Instead of a décor that transported her elsewhere, Gerry's home managed to reverse the sensation: bringing some other home into this one; cramming in over-sized furniture from a bigger, nicer house, so that the overall effect was of a life derailed – a mockery of everything that had been lost.

'Have you heard from the girls recently?' said Norman, calling through the living room wall while Gerry made tea in the kitchen.

Gerry's voice echoed back. 'Yes, they're doing well. Chloe will finish her masters this year, and Annabel's just got another promotion.'

Norman slumped; each mention a reminder that he was no part of their lives. Still, he called through the wall again. 'You've made it look lovely in here.'

'Have you not seen it like this?' replied Gerry.

'It was almost empty when I was here last. You'd only just got the keys.'

'Crikey,' he said, 'that was years ago.'

The last of Norman's confidence seemed to drain away; a dawning realisation, perhaps, that he wasn't a guest, he was a gate crasher. It was at that moment that he noticed a glass of sherry on one of the bookshelves, within easy reach of Gerry's armchair. He was frowning at the sight of it when Gerry returned with two mugs of tea, handing one to Norman and the other to Florence.

'Are you not having one?' said Norman, making it sound like Gerry was denying them something important; that by not participating in the ritual, the whole process had been rendered meaningless.

Ignoring him, Gerry turned to Florence, who was already blowing on her tea, wishing it to cool down as fast as possible so she could finish it and leave. 'Where else have you been today?'

She stopped blowing. 'Excuse me?'

'Father said you were passing by. I was wondering where else you'd been?'

'Oh,' she said, steam rising inches from her nose. 'Yeah.' She glanced at Norman, hopeful that he might swoop in and save her, but he was just sitting there, looking too sad and distracted to follow their conversation. 'The bigger question is, where *haven't* we been?'

In her mind, the words had such a hint of adventure and mystery about them, the right response was simply to be impressed; the right response was to abandon further questioning because their lives were so rich and full, it would take far too long to explain it all in detail.

'I wouldn't think there's much round here to interest a visitor,' said Gerry.

'Hey, don't knock it,' she replied, gesturing at the window like the view alone was Instagram gold. As she followed his gaze, she realised they were looking out at the blocks of flats on the opposite side of the road, nothing to see between them except scrubland and a distant motorway. 'I mean, it's not, you know, Shakespearean England, but it's all new to me.'

Gerry turned back to Norman. 'I suppose there's something you want to discuss?'

'Actually,' said Florence, putting down her mug, 'if you don't mind, I'd like to use the loo.'

With difficulty, she heaved herself from the armchair, her youth counting for nothing against its worn-out springs.

She didn't want to use the bathroom, of course, but she'd seen enough documentaries about tornadoes to know that this was the time to seek urgent shelter. In the microcosm of Gerry's apartment, the air pressure was plunging, a Category Five twister about to tear through the place at any second. So she sat there in the bathroom, listening through paper-thin walls, both grateful for the refuge and yet frightened of what might come next.

'I came because I wanted to talk,' said Norman. The icy silence that followed suggested that Gerry had less interest, but still Norman persevered. 'It's the past, you see. I need to tell you something important.'

'Father, I don't see how the past is of any use to either of us.'

'The thing is,' said Norman, sounding more diffident, 'I think your mother might have given you the impression that I cheated on her.'

Gerry snapped back. 'We're not going to discuss any of that.'

'But there are things you need to know. Things I need to tell you.'

'No,' he said, louder. 'This is my home, not a confessional.'

'I'm not trying to confess, I'm—'

Gerry cut him off, speaking in the kind of loud whisper that only a man would imagine discreet. 'If Mother knew about this other woman, that's enough for me. The rest is between you and your conscience.'

'But you don't—'

'I don't *want* to know,' said Gerry, even more harshly.

By that point, Florence could imagine that the whole building was coming apart: that beyond the bathroom door, the apartment was being stripped of windows and carpets, Norman and Gerry facing one another in a spinning maelstrom of second-hand furniture and threadbare clothes.

'It's just not what you think,' said Norman, sounding so small by that point, it seemed possible that he'd literally shrunk; reduced in size while the world disintegrated around him.

'Speak honestly,' said Gerry, his voice low and insistent. 'As God is your witness, was there another woman in your marriage?'

Norman hesitated.

Gerry sighed in disgust. 'That's all I needed to know.'

Even from behind a wall, Florence could picture the scene: the two of them sat in that cramped living room, trying to avoid one another's gaze.

But then Norman spoke. 'Do you make a habit of drinking during the day?'

Gerry exploded. 'For fuck's sake, Father, it's one glass of sherry at three o'clock in the afternoon. I would have thought that *pales* in comparison to a lifetime of marital infidelity.'

This was followed by footsteps, too fast to be Norman's. They sounded aimless at first, Gerry presumably only wanting to be in some other part of the flat, anywhere away from Norman, but then the footsteps gained a new sense of purpose: they thundered right past the bathroom and into the bedroom next door. For a brief interlude, there was the sound of clothes being hurriedly pulled on and zipped up, until finally the footsteps resumed, pounding past the bathroom once again and back out to the living room.

'I need to get some fresh air,' said Gerry, still trying and failing to speak discreetly. 'You can let yourself out, just pull the door closed behind you.'

'No, no, you stay,' replied Norman. 'We'll leave.'

'But Florence is ...' His words drifted off at that point, not wanting to say aloud what might be taking her so long on the toilet. 'I'm sorry for your wasted trip.'

He walked away, the front door slamming behind him.

After flushing for authenticity, Florence returned to the lounge, where Norman sat looking dazed, still clutching his mug of tea.

'Gerry had to pop out,' he said, not a hint of irony.

'Okay,' replied Florence, thinking she should play along for his sake. 'Are we waiting for him?'

'Ah, well, he might be a while.' He drank down the rest of his tea, not willing to waste anything even at a moment like that. 'We may as well get going, eh? It's a long drive home.'

# 7.

Given that Florence still drove with the panicked air of some-one who saw every light, every junction, every other vehicle, as a cause for concern, Norman wasn't surprised that she went straight to bed after dinner, not tired by their trip so much as extinguished by it.

Under different circumstances Norman might have listened to the wireless for a while, but the day had been exhausting for him, too. It still stung to think of their time at Gerry's. To realise that he'd lacked the courage to say any of the things on his mind. At the very least he could have told Gerry that it wasn't a wasted trip, but he didn't even do that; didn't tell his own son that seeing him could never be a waste of time. After a lifetime of choosing the things he did and didn't reveal, it was as though the words he wanted to say had become trapped deep down with all the other things he wanted to keep buried.

For a few hours he lay in bed, trying to silence his racing thoughts. As on so many other sleepless nights, though, he even-tually abandoned the pretence that he might drift off to sleep. Moving as quietly as possible, he pulled on his dressing gown and made his way downstairs. It was only when he got to the kitchen that he turned on a light, its harsh glare accentuating the lateness of the hour. He was boiling the kettle when Florence joined him, moving as silently as always.

'I hope I didn't wake you up?' he said.

'No, it's fine,' she replied, looking at him with a concerned expression. 'Are you still thinking of Gerry?'

Norman sighed. 'Gerry, Betty, your mother . . . so many things.'

He turned back to the boiling kettle, waiting for it to turn off. Although he had his back to Florence, he could feel her eyes on him.

'It's okay,' she said. 'If there was another woman in your marriage. I'm not Gerry or Mum, I won't judge you.'

'But it wasn't like that,' he replied, as he poured his drink.

'Then why does everyone think it was?'

'Because you don't understand. You don't know the whole story.'

Florence looked confused; that same slight frown Norman had seen on his own children as they'd grown older, drifting further and further away from him because he'd never given them something truthful to cling to.

He took a seat opposite her, the two of them facing one another across the table, steam rising from his tea like a volcano threatening an eruption. And all the while, she said nothing. Just sat there, waiting, the silence growing louder and louder.

He opened his mouth to speak, but it took a few moments for words to start flowing. 'It's just . . . When people talk about me cheating, it's . . . They've missed the point, they . . . It's all about perspective. Do you understand?'

Florence reached across the table and took his hand in hers. 'Granddad, this is me you're talking to. You can say anything. Anything at all.'

'Yes, yes, I . . . I know you're right,' he stammered – his voice, his body, the whole room feeling more and more foreign and unfamiliar. And yet there was Florence squeezing his hand tighter, her eyes imploring him, until finally the long-hidden words began to bubble free. 'The other woman. It was me.'

# ETHEL

# Twenty-five years earlier

## 1997

It wasn't a lorry cabin, it was a chrysalis. Albeit a chrysalis with cheap velour curtains that did a bad job of keeping the light out at night. And a bed so narrow, there was barely room to breathe let alone move around. Yet despite its discomforts, it was still a place of magical transformations.

Although Norman had parked for the night deep in the Shropshire countryside, he was careful to ensure the curtains in his cab were tightly drawn shut. He knew from experience that it wasn't a spot prone to passers-by, but on the off chance that there were some, it was important not to arouse suspicion. He was just a haulier getting some well-earned rest; there must be nothing else to see.

*Well-earned rest.* In recent years, when he thought of all the miles he clocked up every week, it had begun to seem as though he experienced them in much the same way as his lorry: an extended process of wear and tear; a slow grinding down of bits and bobs that had once worked perfectly.

Sitting there in the cramped, anonymous bubble of his curtained cabin, Norman took his makeup from the glove compartment and started painting his lips a bright red, the colour instantly lifting his spirits. He leant closer to the mirror, his hands moving with a delicacy that belied his thick fingers and calloused skin. There used to be infinitely more pleasure in this process, but as he neared retirement, the reflection peering back at him had grown increasingly unfamiliar. He still *felt* young, but clearly no one had told his face, which now appeared to be separating from his skull in a doomed bid for freedom; a slow-motion process of sagging and collapsing that not only complicated the act of applying makeup, but often made it disheartening to look in the mirror at all.

Pressing his hands on either side of his face, he pulled his skin back, trying to imagine how he might look if he had one of those Hollywood facelifts he'd read about in the newspaper, but the result was somewhere between stretched leather and a startled cat, not a hint of Hollywood glamour about it.

'Better to just grow old gracefully, eh?' he said to himself as he dabbed some lipstick on a finger and rubbed it into his cheeks – an instant blush of vitality, if not youth. He turned his head to better admire the effect, just as his mother used to do so many years before. Back in those days, as a young child, Norman would watch in wonder as she got ready in the mornings, handling her lipstick as though it was a priceless family heirloom. The country had still been at war back then, but one way or another she'd always kept a lipstick on her dressing table. Hitler hated cosmetics, that's what people used to say; women the length and breadth of the country wearing makeup as an act of patriotism as much as beautification.

That's what he told himself when, at the age of seven, he first tried her makeup: that he was just doing his bit for the war effort. As a latchkey child, he had plenty of time alone, but of course there was no knowing if his mother might suddenly have a change of plans. That would certainly account for his trepidation that day. While the adults of Clacton worried about what might fall from the sky, Norman's heart raced at the prospect of who might walk through the front door. And yet he *had* to try the lipstick, never mind the danger or the mystery of what he was doing. Touching that strange waxy substance to his lips was a necessary thing.

Since it seemed unlikely that his mother would share his enthusiasm for this discovery, he spent the rest of her absence scrubbing and re-scrubbing his face, until his skin was so clean it surely sparkled. And that was it. The first act of transformation. And with it the first act of subterfuge. Not a lie so much as a selective withholding of the truth.

When Norman thought back to those days, it seemed odd that swathes of the country had been in ruins, bombs still raining down on London, but his only clear memory was of his mother putting on lipstick. His father was away in the army, he could recall that much, but in every other sense life hadn't seemed unusual. Or maybe it was just that life hadn't changed so very much since: those early wartime years morphing into an embattled existence of a different kind. And yet just like his mother used to say, life must go on.

Content with his red lips and blushing cheeks, Norman gave the mirror a wry smile. 'Up yours, Hitler.'

If his cab was ill suited to putting on makeup, it was even less convenient for getting changed, but still he persisted, lying down on his small cot and wriggling first this way and then that as he squeezed into a second-hand dress, tugging it up his body much like a pork sausage stuffing itself.

When finally he was done, he lay there panting – not quite the Venus de Milo moment he dreamt of, but a step closer nevertheless. Heaving himself upright, he reached into a cubbyhole and took out his brunette wig, moving closer to the mirror one last time as he pulled it into place.

And *voilà*, there she was. Ethel Cartwright staring back at him. She was a lifetime away from the person he'd met in the mirror as a seven-year-old boy, but even after all those years it felt no less right.

They smiled at one another in the weak yellow glow of the ceiling light.

'No one's going to call you an English rose, are they?' he said to his reflection. 'More potpourri, if anything; all withered petals and dried bark. But there's still a place for that, isn't there? People go mad for that stuff these days.' He adjusted his pose, all the better to admire his handiwork. 'Some jewellery would brighten things up a bit, but we can't have it all, eh?'

Most often, that would have been the highlight of the evening, the rest of it spent enjoying Ethel's company in the cramped confines of the cab, but it was getting late and the world outside was dark and silent.

After turning off the ceiling light, he stealthily pulled back a curtain and peered out into the night, nothing to see but moonlit hedgerows and empty fields. Emboldened, he opened the door and – after checking for the sound of distant traffic – climbed down onto the cold, damp earth. A faint smell of cow hung in the air, but Norman was too excited to care. Wandering further from his lorry, he made his way to a three-bar gate, the distant outline of the Shropshire Hills visible across the farmland. It was such a pretty sight, for an instant he wished Betty was there to see it, too – though under the circumstances, it was just as well she wasn't. It was hard to imagine her cooing over the view while he was stood there in a brunette wig and red pleather dress.

No, like so many other moments, this memory would have to be carefully edited before he shared it with Betty. The trouble was that he'd spent so many years doing that – stripping away layers of his existence, erasing the things that other people found unpalatable – it often seemed that he'd reduced himself to something spectral. Not living in the world so much as moving through it as a ghostly presence; privy to an entire lifetime of people and experiences that would forever remain untold.

# 8.

Florence finally understood the true meaning of stunned silence. As she sat there at the kitchen table, still holding Norman's hand, she couldn't be sure how long she'd been staring at him – minutes, hours, weeks, it all felt plausible.

Norman was the first to speak. 'I'm not actually a woman. A transsexual, I mean.'

'Transgender,' said Florence. 'Most transgender people prefer that word now.'

'I'm a cross-dresser. Ethel has always been my alter ego, for as long as I can remember.' Florence only realised that she was still staring at him, still trying to process the news, when he spoke again. 'Are you disgusted with me?'

'Of course not,' she replied, leaning even closer and giving his hand another squeeze. 'I'm ... I'm surprised, that's all.'

'That's a very tactful way to put it.'

'I'll be honest, it's not what I was expecting. But it's a good thing, don't you see? Once Mum and Gerry know the truth, they'll understand.'

Norman stared back at her, his eyes so wide, anyone would think *she* was the one who'd just revealed a shocking secret. 'I can't tell them that!'

'But you have to,' she replied. 'This whole misunderstanding, the longer you leave it, the worse it will get.'

'No, no,' he replied. 'I'm sure there's another way.'

Florence's silence should have been a sufficient answer, but it occurred to her that he'd spent so many years denying his own feelings, it was only natural that he did the same with other people's.

'It's not too late to start patching things up between you,' she said. 'I think they'll be more understanding than you imagine.' Norman still looked unconvinced. 'How much did Gran know?'

'Well, I told her after we got engaged, I felt I owed her the opportunity to back out while she still could. She wasn't thrilled, let's put it that way. More than anything, I think she didn't take it seriously. Most people don't. When a full-grown man tells you he dresses as a woman called Ethel, I suppose it's easy to be dismissive; to think of it as something I *like* to do rather than an important part of who I am. Betty just made me promise to never mention it again.'

'But she never asked you to *stop*?' said Florence.

'Well, that's probably what she meant, but no, she never used the word "stop".' He toyed with his tea, staring into its milky brown depths. 'She didn't want me to mention it, so I never did. All those years the kids were growing up, I never stopped being Ethel, I just made sure she only came out while I was on the road.'

He drank his tea in a ponderous silence while Florence tried to connect the dots between what she thought she knew and where she now found herself.

'So, Ethel is, like, your drag name?' she said.

'I'm not a drag queen,' he replied. 'That's something totally different. Drag is a performance. Ethel is ... just another part of me, I suppose. I chose the name in honour of Ethel Merman; something else that Betty wasn't thrilled about. I don't think she was ever able to enjoy an Ethel Merman song again.'

'Do you still have any clothes of Ethel's?' said Florence.

Norman froze, unaccustomed to being so open. 'I've got one dress,' he said, hesitantly. 'And an old wig.'

'Then go and put them on. I'd like to meet that part of you.'

Norman scoffed. 'I can't, it's not right. Not with my own granddaughter.'

'That's my point. All these years, you've been thinking you can't be yourself with your family. And I'm saying, why not? We should be the first people to see you as you are, not the last.'

'But it's the middle of the night!'

'So?' she replied. 'Neither of us have anywhere else to be.'

Although he still looked burdened by years of shame, his tone began to soften. 'Well, true. I suppose I could. If you really insist.'

She squeezed his hand again. 'I really do.'

'Though it won't be anything special. I don't want you getting your hopes up.'

'Granddad, I'm not expecting anything. I just want to get to know all of you. Now, go ...'

She watched as he went out to the hallway.

'I'll be back down in a jiffy,' he said, already swallowed by the darkness.

It could have been broad daylight and still Norman's curtains would have been drawn shut, the habit of a lifetime. It had always been that way, transforming in shadows of one kind or another.

As on so many other occasions, he pulled on his dress, feeling freer by the second as its soft fabric encircled him. Going to the mirror, he finished the look with his old brunette wig, its long curls making sense of his face in ways that a lifetime of short back and sides had never been able.

Florence called from the hallway. 'Is everything all right up there?'

'Sorry, I've been longer than I thought. You're welcome to come up.'

Seconds later she was in the open doorway. 'Knock, knock,'

she said, stepping into the soft glow of the lamplight, the room a patchwork of shadows.

Norman remained by the mirror, lingering in the half-light. 'Sorry, I'm being slow.'

'Don't worry about that. Let me get a better look.'

She beckoned him forward. Head hanging, he did as commanded; every movement feeling stiff and awkward.

'Was this one of Betty's dresses?' said Florence.

'No, it would have been much too gaudy for her.'

'It's black,' she replied.

'But it has these sequins ...' He touched them with a religious reverence. 'Your grandmother liked many things, but sequins weren't one of them. I found it in a charity shop a while back. It's lovely, isn't it?' Without prompting, he gently twirled, the fabric dancing around him. 'I was too embarrassed to try it on, so I claimed it was for Betty. I was holding it up in front of me, going on and on, pretending to ask the girl's advice, and all the while I was just trying to work out if it would fit me.' He checked his reflection again, performing another subtle twirl for his own pleasure. 'It's the only dress I have. I used to try on some of Betty's clothes when she wasn't around, but the fit was pretty dire, as you can imagine. Not to mention we had very different taste.' He took a small bag from a drawer and began laying out cosmetics on the dressing table, a High Priestess arranging sacred artefacts. 'It's the makeup I struggle with, if you have any tips.'

Florence laughed. 'Do I look like I have makeup tips worth sharing? I'd say, if in doubt, go natural.'

'Easy to say at your age,' he said. 'All my nature is dead. Not to mix my metaphors, but if I don't plaster it on, all you can see is the brickwork.' He took another look at his reflection. 'Maybe we'll just leave it like this for tonight.'

Florence gently motioned him back into the light, taking in

the full view of him: an eighty-six-year-old man standing before her as bashful and self-conscious as a young wallflower.

'You look great,' she said.

He blushed. 'We work with what we've got, eh?'

'And we can go shopping together. We can find you more clothes, more makeup, whatever you want.'

'No, no,' he replied, sighing. 'It's a bit late for that, isn't it? I'm eighty-six, after all.'

'Granddad, it's never too late.'

'Said the teenager.' He turned back to the mirror. 'I'm just grateful to share a moment like this with you. It's more than I would have ever dreamt possible.'

# 9.

The next morning, Florence was still in bed when Norman called to her through the door. 'We should get a move on. There's rain forecast.'

'You can come in,' she shouted.

Norman poked his head into the room, his manner uncharacteristically brittle. 'You can't spend all day in bed.'

'It's only eight-thirty,' she replied.

'And it'll probably be raining soon. We should get going before the worst of it hits.'

Florence propped herself up on her elbows to get a better look at him: his flannel trousers, his old cotton shirt, his remaining wisps of hair slicked back with Brylcreem. 'Why aren't you dressed as Ethel?'

He looked uncomfortable at the mention of that name. 'I think it's best we leave all that in the past, don't you?'

'No,' she said, indignant for Ethel's sake as much as her own.

'Well, *I* think it's best we leave it all in the past. I shouldn't have told you any of it.'

He backed out of the room, his manner so stiff and self-conscious, he was barely able to look her in the eye. 'I'll go and get your breakfast ready.'

Florence called to him as he ducked out of sight. 'If there's no Ethel, there's no driving, that's the deal from now on.'

He slowly came back into view, eyes wide. 'I can't do that.'

'Then I can't drive,' she replied, burrowing under her duvet.

'But you can. You know you can.'

'Right back at you, Granddad,' she said, her head still covered. 'It's all a matter of confidence. Just pretend you're Wonder Woman.'


He shouldn't have told her, that's all Norman could think as he went back downstairs. The proverbial genie had been set free and now it was anyone's guess as to whether he'd get it back in its bottle.

It was hard not to think of Betty at a time like this. She was often in his thoughts, but now more than ever: quietly following him around the house, shaking her head in dismay that their darling little granddaughter had turned up after so many years – something they'd both dreamt of for so long – and what had Norman done? He'd paraded in front of her as a shameless old trollop!

And the worst of it was that he was no closer to understanding why Florence had dropped out of university. There he was, her own grandfather – the most senior member of the family – and so far their only shared confidence had been him in black sequins and a manky old wig. Even at rest in her grave, Betty was probably chain smoking an entire pack of cigarettes.

He tried to keep himself busy with a crossword, but that, too, was only a reminder of his shortcomings, the page taunting him with all its unfillable blank spaces; physical proof that there were so many things in life he didn't understand.

Quiet frustration had turned to irritated muttering by the time Florence entered the kitchen, moving as silently as always. Norman looked up from his newspaper, still feeling too guilty for a warm greeting. This emotional distance clearly wasn't wasted on Florence, her manner instantly cooling.

Unsure what else to do, Norman read from his crossword. 'Maybe you can help with this. "Quiver." Nine letters. It's probably got an L in it.'

Florence shrugged. 'Is that today's?'

'No,' he replied, sighing, 'it's still the same one from a couple of days ago. It seems wrong to start a new one until I've finished.'

'Do you finish?' she said, the words sounding more like an accusation than a question.

'Well, I suppose *give up* is a better expression.' He noticed how Florence looked even more disappointed by that. 'Can I make you some tea?' he added, attempting a more cheerful tone.

'No, I need to do some shopping. I can grab something while I'm out.'

'We can go together,' he replied. 'If we take the car, you could practise some parking in town.'

'No, thanks. I'd like the walk.'

After kissing his forehead, she left the room.

'At least take an umbrella,' he called to her, his heart sinking.

'Yeah, will do,' she replied from the hallway.

Norman waited at the kitchen table, listening as she pulled on her shoes and coat, preparing to leave him. When finally he heard the front door open, he rose from his seat and made his way through to the front room, going straight to the window and watching as she walked away under darkening skies.

It was an aimless wandering at first; through the town centre, past the garish lights of the amusement arcades. It was only as Florence neared the pier that she knew what she wanted to do: the big wheel rising in front of her, offering a ready escape from the cares of life at ground level.

She sat alone in her gondola, slowly rising above the pier, the wind whipping around her as the whole town came into view. Despite her frustrations, she was smiling as she crested the topmost point, overcome by an unexpected sensation of being on holiday. And still the wheel continued turning, compounding her pleasure as it slowly lowered her back to earth before raising her aloft yet again.

Her thoughts were full of Norman, of course, and what could be done about Ethel. If she followed the family's time-honoured tradition of denial, she'd just look the other way and pretend everything was fine, but it was painfully obvious how well that had worked out.

So instead she surrendered to the moment, letting the wind tug at her clothes and ruffle her hair, smiling to herself at the simple pleasure of going around and around. And all the while, a muffled cacophony drifted from the pier: the sound of slot machines and fairground rides blurring together in a constant reminder that life is at its best when lived with joy.

It was afternoon when she returned to the house, the sky growing yet darker overhead, but still no rain. She found Norman sitting in the kitchen with a mug of tea, listening to the radio.

'How was shopping?' he said, attempting a cheery tone.

She put a compact of eyeshadow on the table in front of him. 'Wear that and we can start driving again.'

Norman recoiled. 'I can't do that!'

'You don't have to put much on, and you don't need to do anything else, but you have to wear some.'

'For the life of me,' he replied, 'I don't understand why this is so important to you.'

'I'm not just doing it for your sake, Granddad, I'm doing it for mine, too.' Faced with his perplexed expression, she took a seat opposite him. 'How much do you know about black holes?' Norman looked so fazed by the question, she smiled. 'It's okay, most people don't know much about that stuff. I only mention it because you can't really *see* a black hole, you can only infer its presence from what's going on around it.'

'All right . . .' replied Norman, looking even more confused.

'Did it never seem odd to you that we haven't seen each other in twelve years?'

'I just thought your mother was busy,' he replied. 'That's what she always said on the phone. Is she not okay?'

'This isn't about her, it's about all of us. I mean, take Uncle Gerry. It sounds like you hardly ever see him, and I can't even *remember* meeting him before yesterday. It's like there's something in this family that's been eating it up from the inside.'

Norman's face dropped. 'You're saying I'm a black hole?'

'Granddad, don't take it too literally. This is just about things hiding in plain sight.'

'You really do like science,' he said, making it sound like he hadn't believed her until now.

'I also happen to have excellent taste in eyeshadow,' she replied, pushing the compact across the table. 'I chose the colour especially for you.'

Norman opened it gingerly, his eyes lighting up as the powder came into view: a pale pink, redolent of spring days and cherry blossom.

'It is very pretty,' he said.

Florence smiled. 'It would destroy my reputation forever if anyone knew I'd actually walked into a shop and bought that colour. Even the woman behind the till looked confused. But I think it will look great on you.' She waited, expecting some response to her proposal, but Norman just sat there, staring at it. With a sigh, she stood up. 'Look, there's some reading I should get on with. I'll be upstairs, but please at least think about it.'

She was nearing the top of the stairs when Norman came out to the hallway.

'All right,' he said, his voice fizzing with nervous energy. 'I've thought about it. And I agree.'

# 10.

Norman closed his bedroom curtains before putting on the eyeshadow, as though his every movement was under constant surveillance. 'You can go and set yourself up in the car,' he said, calling out to Florence. 'I'll be down in a jiffy.'

This, it transpired, was not entirely true. While it was fair to say that Norman was punctual to a fault, Ethel clearly had a different grasp of time. Florence had been waiting outside for what felt like an eternity when Norman finally emerged from the house, hurrying towards the car with his head down.

It was only when he was in the passenger seat, locking the door behind him for good measure, that Florence was able to see his face – nothing but the faintest hint of pink eyeshadow to suggest that this was Ethel rather than Norman.

'*That* took you twenty minutes?' she said.

'We should get going,' he replied. 'I don't want Sally to see me.'

'There's nothing to see. I'm sitting next to you and I can't tell the difference.'

'Do you not like it?' he said, checking his reflection in the mirror.

'There's nothing to like or not like. It's literally nothing.'

'Tell that to the blokes you find down the pub. They wouldn't say it's nothing. Did you notice what this shade is called? It's *Candy Girl Fantasy*. That's definitely not nothing.'

'Okay, fine,' she said. 'It's *barely* anything.'

'Which is how my leeks were once upon a time and look at them now.'

Florence started the engine. 'By the way, I've put your wig in the glovebox.'

Norman looked scandalised. 'I'm not going to wear my wig!'

'And you don't have to. I'm just saying, maybe while we're out driving sometime, you'll feel comfortable pulling it on for a while. If it's in the glovebox, you at least have that option.' She reversed them out into the street, Norman raising a hand to shield his face from view as they drove past Sally's house. 'Granddad, she can't see anything.'

'Oh, you'd be very surprised at the things Sally notices.' He glanced back at her house, as if expecting her to come charging out and chase after them. 'I was thinking we could go out to the dual carriageway. You can practise driving at speed.'

'And conveniently not run the risk of bumping into anyone at all,' replied Florence.

Norman shrugged, stealing yet another glance at himself in the mirror. 'Practice is practice.'


While Florence drove up and down the same few miles of road with a growing poise and confidence, Norman pored over his reflection in the mirror, agonising over every detail, checking and re-checking it so many times, it wasn't the makeup he saw anymore, but rather the curl of his lashes, the hint of his cheekbones, a faint echo of someone he used to be.

Above them, the sky grew darker and darker, so blackened and glowering, it looked less like the onset of rain than Judgement Day. Florence had already turned the headlights on when the downpour began: a few fat drops splodging across the windscreen, a fleeting moment of climatic flirtation before the whole sky fell at once.

'Please tell me this is normal,' she said, slowing to a crawl, the windscreen wipers struggling to keep up with the onslaught.

'Yes, yes,' replied Norman, unconcerned. 'It can get quite inclement in these parts.'

'Granddad, this isn't *inclement*, it's apocalyptic.'

'That's the thing about living by the sea, I suppose. Sometimes all the water is where you want it to be, and sometimes it's not. There's a lay-by up ahead. You can pull in there and wait it out if you want.'

Florence needed no encouragement, turning on the hazard lights and inching along until they'd reached the relative safety of the lay-by.

'Jeez,' she said, as she finally pulled to a stop and turned off the engine, nothing now to distract them from the sound of the rain hammering on the roof.

Norman peered up at the leaden sky, no break in sight. 'I dread to think what this is doing to my leeks.'

He was still staring up at the clouds when Florence spoke. 'What was your life like before you met Gran?'

'I didn't really have one,' he replied. 'I was only twenty when we met. I'd just finished my National Service the year before.'

'That still leaves one year where you were, you know ... free to do whatever you wanted.'

If they'd been having this conversation at home, Norman would wander off and make a cup of tea at that point, or perhaps go outside and check on his veg – anything, really, to change the subject – but there he was, trapped in a car with a nosy teenager, unable to even step outside under the pretence of stretching his legs.

'Well,' he said, trying to make it sound like nothing of significance. 'I used to go up to London sometimes.'

Florence jumped on this remark with all the enthusiasm of a bloodhound. 'That sounds interesting. We should go together, you can show me your old haunts.'

'I didn't really have any. I only knew a few people.'

'Okay,' she said. 'So what happened to them?'

Norman peered out of his steamed-up window, beginning to think that being out in the rain would be a welcome escape. 'We lost touch, that's all. You'll see it for yourself as you get older, sometimes friends drift apart, that's just how it is.'

'Did Gran ever meet them?'

Norman sighed. 'Is this more black hole research?'

'I'm just asking about your past, that's all.'

'Just like you *only* bought me some eyeshadow. No ulterior motive at all.'

Florence fell silent, so that for a few moments the only sound was the rain. 'If you hadn't noticed,' she said, a hint of irritation creeping into her voice, 'I'm trying to help.'

'And thank you,' he replied. 'But I don't need it.'

This was evidently the wrong response.

'Excuse me?' she said, angling herself to face him, the colour of her hair adding to Norman's sense that he was staring down a warship in full battle mode. 'Have you seen the state of this family?'

'I can tell you this, it's in a much better state than it would have been if I'd come out as Ethel.'

'But you don't *know* that,' she replied. 'Maybe everything would have been better.'

Norman gasped in disbelief. 'Are you mad? Imagine what your mum and Gerry would have thought when they were young. How ashamed they would have been.'

'Or maybe they would have grown up thinking you have great taste in nail polish. You'll never know.'

'You make it sound so simple,' he replied. 'I can assure you, it's really not.'

'But why?' she said, even more insistent. 'If you keep asking *why, why, why,* you eventually get to *why not?*'

Norman snorted. 'Trust me, we're a long way from that. One look at the newspapers should make that obvious.'

'Oh, please, that's just manufactured outrage, as if the world doesn't have enough of that already.'

'Manufactured or not,' he said, 'it's still outrage, isn't it?'

Florence said nothing, and Norman found himself hoping that the conversation had finally run its course.

But no.

'Don't you think it's strange?' she said, the words coming at him on a fresh new wave of annoyance. 'No one would have a problem with a woman dressing like a man. It's like being a man is the gold standard for everything.'

Norman struggled for something to appease her. 'Maybe people just think womanhood is something special and sacred.'

'Yeah, right,' she said, mockingly. 'Which is why women get paid less than men, get fewer opportunities than men, and get abused more than men.'

Norman stared at her. 'Is this even about me any more?'

'Yes. Because you don't question the status quo. Even when you can see it doesn't work, even when it's *hurting* you, you still don't question it. It shouldn't need a teenager to point that out.'

'I don't see why everything has to be about me,' he replied, sounding more defensive than he'd expected, but unable to stop himself. 'There are still lots of things I don't know about your life. Like why you visited out of the blue. Or why you've dropped out of university.'

'What?' she said, incredulous. 'Who said I'm dropping out?'

'You did. You said you were on your way there and then you changed your mind. You said you're not going back.'

'I said Mum *thinks I'm at uni*. It's still the first week of September. Term doesn't start until the end of the month.'

'Oh,' he replied, already feeling foolish. 'I thought it was sooner than that.'

'Sure, when I was in *primary* school. I'm not seven any more.' She exhaled angrily. 'This is exactly my point. I'm beginning to wonder if anyone in this family actually pays attention to anything.'

Using her sleeve she began clearing the condensation from her side window, venting her frustration in swipe after swipe.

'But, in that case, I'm confused,' said Norman. 'Why did you leave your mum's so soon if you didn't need to?'

'Because life at home sucks,' she replied, still irritated. 'Because this family is so far beyond damaged, it's almost a joke. And don't tell me you can't see it. Don't tell me it's normal that you all avoid each other for years on end.' She started swiping at the windscreen as well, seeming to need the act of eradication. 'I knew there was a reason why this family's the way it is. And since nobody else could be bothered to do anything about it . . .'

'Ah,' replied Norman, comforted that at least something now made sense. 'So that's why you came. It was to learn my secrets.'

She looked at him, her expression more serious than normal. 'No, Granddad, I came to learn the *family's* secrets.'

# 11.

By the time the sun was setting, Florence and Norman had reached an unspoken truce, comfortable companions once more. They were sitting in the living room – Florence reading a textbook, Norman listening to the radio – when she had an idea.

'How about I paint your nails before dinner?' she said. Norman looked at her as though she'd just suggested he go jogging naked. 'Nail polish isn't a big deal any more. Even guys do it.'

'What, like straight blokes?' he replied, his alarm turning to confusion.

'Yes, Granddad, times change. I bought you some dark red polish at the same time I got the eyeshadow.'

'But I can't paint my nails, other people will notice!'

'You can wear gloves when you go out,' she replied. 'To be honest, I'm surprised everyone isn't already wearing gloves in this place, it's that cold every day.' Norman still looked unconvinced. 'Look, worst case scenario, you can just take it all off tomorrow morning. You'll still have the rest of this evening to admire my handiwork. It can be our special secret.'

Norman's eyebrows began to rise. 'Do you really think the colour will suit me?'

'It'll look *amazing*,' she replied, jumping from her seat. 'Give me two seconds.'

She bounded up the stairs and grabbed the nail polish from her room, returning to the lounge to find Norman looking as excited as she felt.

'I've never done this for someone else before,' she said, as she positioned herself in front of him, his hands splayed out between them.

Norman sat, transfixed, as she began to apply a deep garnet hue.

'See,' she said, 'this is the kind of thing I meant earlier. It's not like I expect you to run for Mayor as Ethel, I just want you to feel comfortable doing small things that make you happy. If you're not happy, the people around you can't be happy either.'

'It is a beautiful colour,' he replied, his smile confirming their truce.

When she'd finished all his nails, Norman sat taller, smiling wider, carrying himself with a new-found grace.

'Goodness, aren't they gorgeous?' he said, holding up his hands like precious artworks. 'Your grandmother would have loved this colour. Not on me, mind you, but ...' He wiggled his fingers, admiring his nails from every angle. 'They look lovely, thank you. And just in time for supper.'

Although his nails suggested a sophisticated siren, the menu was still firmly Norman: two cans of chilli con carne from the cupboard. After Florence had opened them for him – 'I don't want to chip my nails, do I?' – he heated up the contents in the same old battered saucepan as always, though Florence noticed how he occasionally stopped stirring to admire his hands, smiling to himself each time.

They'd just sat down to eat when the doorbell rang, Norman freezing as the sound chimed through the house.

'Don't worry,' said Florence. 'I can get it.'

'No, it's not that, it's just ... well, it's dark out, isn't it?'

'So?' she replied, growing suspicious as he remained there even as the doorbell rang a second time.

He stood up with a marked reluctance, pulling on his gardening gloves as he headed out to the hallway. 'You just can't be too careful after dark.'

Florence grew more alarmed. 'Why? What happens round here at night?'

His voice drifted back. 'I've heard some real horror stories.'

'Like what?' she said, panicked now, but Norman was already at the front door.

Florence braced herself for the opening bars of a violent home invasion, but instead it was Sally's voice she heard.

'Good evening, Norman, is this a bad time?'

'We're just eating supper,' he replied.

'Then I'll be quick. Might I pop in for a moment? You don't want to let the cold in.'

Sally's footsteps grew closer – a different kind of home invasion, but disconcerting nevertheless. Moments later, she entered the room, a cake tin in her arms. It was only then, in the bright lights of the kitchen, that she noticed Norman's gloves.

'What on earth are you wearing those for?' she said.

Clearly at a loss for words, Norman stared at his hands, the gloves dirty and weather-beaten. Then finally –

'It's, er, for my ... neuropathy,' he said. 'It comes and goes.'

Sally nodded to herself. 'I *knew* something was wrong when I saw your bedroom curtains shut this afternoon. It's so unlike you.' She didn't notice Norman's alarmed expression, was too distracted by the sight of their dinner on the table. 'Do you really have to wear the gloves even to eat?'

'It does help,' he replied, sounding less and less sure of himself. 'The pain in my fingers, it, er, can get quite bad.'

'Gracious, then it's just as well I made you a cake.' Sally proffered the tin. 'It's a Victoria sponge, since you liked it so much the other day.'

Norman's face lit up, all other fears momentarily swept away by the temptations of sugar and animal fat. Until he noticed Sally was waiting, clearly hoping for a more detailed discussion of her concerns and suspicions: Norman's symptoms, for instance, and their specific connection to the afternoon's curtain-related anomaly.

Norman kept his gaze firmly on the cake tin.

'Well,' said Sally, eventually. 'I should let you get back to your tea before it goes cold. I can see myself out.'

She didn't look at Florence as she bustled from the room, moving with the air of someone familiar with the house.

'Thanks again for the cake,' said Norman.

Sally's voice echoed back from the hallway. 'You're very welcome. I hope you're feeling better soon.'

Seconds later, the front door slammed shut, silence returning to the house, but the air seemed to roil in her wake.

'She knows,' said Norman, his expression sinking.

'Oh, come on,' replied Florence. 'She's not got X-ray vision.'

'I wouldn't put it past her.' He looked at the tin again. 'Mark my words, that's not a cake, it's a Trojan horse.'

# 12.

When he woke the next morning, Norman did something he would never normally do: he remained in bed, staring at the curtains. They were tightly drawn shut and yet still daylight bled around the edges of the polyester jacquard, determined to enter the room. In earlier days it would have felt like shameless sloth to still be in bed, but these were very different times: in less than a week, Ethel had somehow transitioned from a deep secret to a terrifying Hydra; every time he'd tried to lop off its head, another two had appeared.

When he finally got up and tiptoed downstairs, he kept all the curtains drawn shut, the entire house consumed by an uncharacteristic gloom.

He was using a tiny gap in the living room curtains to peer out into the street when Florence came downstairs.

'What are you doing?' she said.

Startled, he span around to face her. 'Nothing.'

'If you're still worrying about Sally, you really need to get over it.'

'Shouldn't you still be in bed?' he replied.

'And shouldn't you have opened the curtains by now?'

Norman tried to strike a dismissive tone. 'There's nothing wrong with doing things differently sometimes.'

'You should get that tattooed,' she said. 'Maybe on your hand, so you can see it every day.'

'Actually,' he replied, 'I've been thinking about what you said yesterday.'

'About wearing makeup in the car?'

'No! Visiting London. It's been so many years since I was up there last. I think you're right, it might be nice to see how everything looks these days.'

'Okay . . .' she said, sounding suspicious.

'I was thinking, we could take the ten o'clock train.'

She laughed. 'You want to go *this morning*?'

'Of course, why not?' Before he could even stop himself, he was peering back out into the street, wanting to see if Sally was already up. 'It would be nice to get away for the day, don't you think?'


They'd barely boarded the train when Florence plugged her ears with the smallest headphones Norman had ever seen, visual confirmation that for the next hour or so he'd hear nothing from her other than the faint, metallic rattle of whatever she was listening to.

She momentarily unplugged one ear. 'You don't mind, do you?'

'No, no, you listen to your music,' he replied, trying to hide his disappointment. 'I'm quite content to just look out the window. It's been a long time since I made this journey.'

Within seconds, Florence's eyes were closed, her head subtly nodding to some unknown rhythm, and Norman found himself feeling more alone than he'd anticipated. He watched as they pulled away from the platform, less the beginning of a train ride than a forcible rewinding of history: reliving his early visits to London; not going there often, but as often as he dared.

It was funny to think that Florence was the same age that he'd been when he started making those trips, the two of them alike in so many ways: venturing into adulthood, unsure of the terrain. But then came all the things Norman didn't want to remember from those days. The mistakes he hadn't yet admitted – to Florence, to anyone.

He closed his eyes, wishing it all away, but the clackety-clack rhythm of the train made it impossible, the sound cutting across an entire lifetime. With his eyes shut, he was right back there in the past, nothing between him and the final time he'd made that journey, the night everything changed forever.

Feeling something touch his knee, he opened his eyes. It was Florence, one ear unplugged again. 'Is everything okay?' she said, looking concerned.

'Oh, I'm fine,' he replied, trying to regain his composure. 'I was just remembering some things from the past, that's all.'

'Anything you want to talk about?'

He forced a chuckle, but it rang hollow. 'Don't mind me. I'm just getting sentimental in my old age.'

'Okay,' she said, looking unconvinced. 'Just remember, if you need to talk, I'm literally sitting *right here.*'


From the moment Norman suggested the trip, it was obvious to Florence that they weren't visiting London, they were running away from Clacton. And in trying to evade the scrutiny of his neighbours, he had now run headlong into some other problem, sitting there on the train looking like the world was coming to an end. He denied it, of course, but that was Norman in a nutshell: denial came with the territory.

Florence pondered this as she went back to her music: how a dangerous no-man's-land seemed to exist between Norman and Ethel, two parts of his life that had been at war for so long, it was impossible to get a good view of one without dodging live fire from the other.

She discreetly kept an eye on him for the rest of the journey, but whatever had been troubling him, he appeared to press it all down out of sight, so that by the time they were pulling into Liverpool Street station, he was back to his usual self.

'I have an idea,' he said. 'You mentioned that things weren't so good at home with your mum. While we're in town, we could pop over there and say hello. It might cheer her up a bit.'

Florence scrambled for a response. 'She's, er, gone away. She sent me a text yesterday. She's visiting a friend in ... Newcastle, I think she said.'

Norman looked taken aback for a moment. 'That's a long way from home.'

'Yeah ...' replied Florence, hating the lie but feeling even less enthusiastic about telling the truth. 'As far as I can work out, it was, you know, all very spur of the moment.'

'Oh, well, next time, eh?'

'And let's look on the bright side,' she said. 'It gives us more time to check out your old haunts.'

'There's only a couple of places I can show you. As much as anything, this is just a chance to see how much London has changed.'

Florence hooked her arm in his, ready for their big adventure. 'I can't wait to hear all about it.'

Together, they crossed the station concourse, their measured pace at odds with the throng of people around them.

'The difference is already amazing,' said Norman, gazing up at the glass roof. 'You've got to remember, London was still a dark and damaged place back in my day. The buildings were soot-stained, the air was thick with coal smoke. The war had been over for ten years, but the scars were plain to see.'

This sense of wonderment continued as they made their way down into the Underground – *The ticket barriers! The trains! The other passengers!* – until finally they made their way back to street level at Covent Garden.

As the piazza came into view, Norman stopped dead in

his tracks. 'Bloody hell,' he gasped. 'Would you look at that!' Confused, Florence followed his gaze, nothing to see but shoppers, diners, buskers on a balmy September day. 'This place was a massive market back in my time. Crates of fruit and veg stacked up everywhere you looked. Stallholders yelling at the top of their lungs. And such a stream of trucks coming and going, you'd get mown down if you didn't have your wits about you.' Still looking dazed, he wandered closer, past a string quartet in the middle of a Shostakovich recital. 'It was all potatoes and runner beans back then. I never imagined the place could look this fancy. So much for everything getting worse in old age.'

'We can stop for a drink, if you want,' said Florence.

Norman recoiled. 'No, no, no, it's enough to make my brain hurt. Don't get me wrong, it's lovely, it really is, but I feel like I need to lie down in a darkened room just to get my head around it.'

Moving at a glacial pace, they made their way through the market hall, Norman awestruck at every detail, peering wide-eyed into each of the shop windows as they passed, marvelling at the home décor boutiques and cupcake parlours, not a root vegetable in sight.

'It's like visiting a different planet,' he said, as they finally emerged at the other end of the building. 'It's amazing how much can change in a single lifetime. It makes me wonder how the place will be when you're my age.'

'Hotter,' she replied. 'And possibly under water.'

'Oh, yes, I forget that you young people worry about things like that.' He patted her hand dismissively. 'I'm sure everything will be fine.'

They'd just wandered down a side street, the sound of Covent Garden's buskers growing fainter with every step, when Norman pointed to a pub in the distance.

'That place up there,' he said. 'I went to it once or twice. I'm amazed it's still here.'

'Was it a place for cross-dressers?'

Norman glanced at the other passers-by, seeming worried that someone might have overheard. 'Of course not, it was just a pub.'

'Okay,' she replied. 'So why *that* one and not a pub in, say, the town where you lived?'

Ignoring the question, Norman approached the place in silence; its façade a profusion of Victorian etched glass and gilded woodwork.

'It looks much neater than it did back then,' he remarked.

Florence stopped to get a better look, her arm pulling free of Norman's as he continued walking.

'Do you not want to go in?' she said.

Again, Norman appeared suspicious of eavesdroppers. 'It's nice to be on the move, don't you think? I can tell you more about the place while we walk.'

He stood there offering his arm, waiting until Florence reluctantly joined him. They were some distance away when he finally spoke.

'It wasn't just a pub,' he said. 'It was a place for – for *men*, let's say.'

'Granddad, it's okay to say gay bar.'

Norman chuckled nervously. 'Not when you're a straight man, especially at my age. I shouldn't have even been there, of course, but I didn't know where else to start. I was only nineteen at the time. That was the thing back then, everything was out of sight or in the shadows. If you wanted to find a place for something out of the ordinary—'

'Straight men in dresses, for instance.'

'Well, yes, your only option was to feel your way and try to meet the right people. There were some coded personal ads in the classifieds, but it wasn't like I could have the replies sent to my parents' house. I thought it might be easier if I just came up to London and tried my luck. Literally, as a matter of fact. I assumed that a pub surrounded by theatres might be a good place to start. Thespians and all that.'

They turned on to Charing Cross Road, ambling northwards.

'So, did you go to that pub as Ethel?' said Florence.

Norman laughed. 'Lord, no! I was just hoping to meet someone who could point me in the right direction. Looking back, I was probably quite naïve about it. Lots of the punters didn't really approve of men like me. They had enough problems with straight men in everyday life, I think they resented me being there just because I like to wear a dress sometimes.'

Florence waited for him to say more, but he looked distracted.

'So, you never met anyone there?' she said.

He looked at her with that vague sense of alarm that seemed to accompany all of his revelations about Ethel. 'Well, there was someone . . .'

# 13.

For the second time in less than forty-eight hours, Norman regretted his honesty. Words like 'Ethel' and 'cross-dressing' had re-entered his public vocabulary for the first time in decades, their mere presence in dialogue indicating that his carefully constructed lie was falling in ruins around him.

Heart pounding, he was wondering how he could change the subject when, instead, he took a deep breath and reminded himself that the time for running was over; that in setting free the past, he was also liberating himself.

And so he disinterred yet another word from long ago. *Suzie.*

'Suzie was a tranny,' he said.

Florence let go of his arm. 'Woah, Granddad, people don't use that word any more. It's, like, super taboo.'

'Fine,' he said. 'Suzie was a transsexual.'

'Transgender.'

'You know what I mean,' he replied, waiting for her to take his arm again. 'She hadn't had the surgery back when I knew her, but she lived very openly. That took real courage in those days.'

'I think it still does,' said Florence.

'It was an unlikely friendship, of course. You've got to remember, most cross-dressers are straight; it's very unusual to mix with, you know . . . other people.'

Florence laughed. 'Gay and transgender, you mean.'

'Exactly,' he replied, realising only then that he'd stopped worrying if passers-by overheard their conversation. 'I suppose that's what made the friendship so special: me, a straight bloke from Clacton who likes to wear a dress sometimes, and Suzie . . .' He smiled at the memory. 'She was larger than life, a bird of paradise. To be honest, I still don't know why she took a shine to me, but I'll always be glad she did.'

They came to a stop at Cambridge Circus, multiple options fanning out before them. 'Suzie introduced me to another place in Soho, not far from here, but there's no point showing you. The building was demolished donkey's years ago.'

'Another pub?' said Florence.

'More of a speakeasy, really. Without Suzie, I never would have known about it.' He chuckled to himself. 'That place was an eye-opening experience, to say the least. You had to knock at a small side door to get in and then it was down a few steps into a . . . well, it was much like the whole city at the time: crowded, smoky. There was certainly no reason for a cross-dresser to be there, but Suzie knew such an interesting collection of people, I was spellbound.'

Florence squeezed his arm. 'Thank you for telling me all this. It means a lot.'

'It's nice to have the opportunity,' he replied. 'These are things that even your grandmother didn't know.' He blushed at the memory. 'I had some of the other punters in the bar coming on to me, of course – touching my bum, that kind of thing – but it was all well intentioned, it never bothered me.' They crossed the road and headed down a side street, away from the heavy traffic. 'There's only one other place I can show you. It's someone's house, but it's not far from here, we can walk.'

He smiled to himself, the memory still clear of when he'd first taken that route almost seventy years before; when *he'd* been the one tagging along, unsure of where they were or where they were heading.

'Are we going to a friend's place?' said Florence.

'Something like that,' he replied, certain that he'd asked Suzie the same question all those years earlier, getting a similar reply. 'Rex was his name. He was a proper character. I sometimes think he didn't have friends so much as an audience.'

Just as Norman had ventured years before, they headed north, brushing the edge of Soho Square and across Oxford Street into the quieter backways of Fitzrovia. After zig-zagging through several more streets, Norman stopped opposite a terrace of Georgian houses. 'That was the place over there. The one with the bay trees by the front door.'

'It looks very posh,' said Florence.

'Well, I suppose it is, but it didn't look that smart back then. This whole area had none of the spit and polish you see now. It was very fringe in those days.'

Florence stared at the house, not admiring it so much as perplexed. 'It's odd to think of you knowing someone like that.'

Norman laughed. 'That's exactly what my parents would have said if they'd known; worrying that I was getting above my station. Though, I suppose if they'd understood the full situation, that would have been the least of their concerns. Rex and Suzie were good friends.'

'Did they live together?'

'Goodness, no! I doubt there's a house in London that would have been big enough for those two. Suzie had a bedsit up in Hampstead. Not a posh bit of Hampstead, I might add. She was many things, but rich wasn't one of them.'

Confused, Florence turned to him. 'I don't get it. What happened to these people? Why did you stop seeing them?'

Norman looked away. 'We lost touch.'

'But why? It sounds like they were good friends.'

Still avoiding eye contact, he let his gaze linger on the house.

'That's just life, isn't it?' he said. 'Things don't always work out the way we expect.'


Evasive Norman was back, though Florence still couldn't tell if it was intentional. After a lifetime of keeping secrets, perhaps it had become second nature to sidestep difficult truths.

They crossed over to Rex's house, a shiny bronze plaque by the front door declaring it to be a doctor's surgery.

'It's been like this for years,' said Norman. 'First it was a solicitor's place, and then a dentist.'

'So, you did come back sometimes?' she said.

Norman looked caught out. 'I was somewhere nearby at the time. I thought I'd just give the place a look to see if Rex was still around. That was a few years after I'd last seen him.'

'That's when you saw it was turned into offices?'

'Not exactly. He was definitely still living here that first time, because I recognised the piano in the window. But somehow it had been so long since we'd seen each other – imagine me pulling up in a bloody great lorry. And the thing is, it wasn't really him I wanted to see, it was Suzie. We'd lost contact and Rex was the only link. The next time I passed, the piano was gone, the whole house empty. After that, I sometimes drove by for old times' sake, just to see what was becoming of it.'

He fell silent, still doing his best not to look at her.

'Have you never wanted to find him?' said Florence.

'I thought about it, of course, but it was different in those days. If someone wasn't in the phone book, you were basically at a dead end. Anyway, I think he *wanted* to disappear. I think they both did.'

Florence frowned. 'Why would they want that?'

'I'm sure they had their reasons,' he replied, the answer sounding more evasive than ever. He stepped closer to the front railings, gesturing to a small basement courtyard. 'That would have been the staff entrance back in the old days. When I met Rex, it was already converted into a separate flat. There was an old bird living down there, and Rex had the rest of the house for himself. She was so deaf, I doubt she heard a single bomb during the war. It gave him a fair amount of freedom in the kind of parties he threw.'

'And in all these years, you've never thought of just knocking? For all you know, he never sold up, he was just renting the place out.'

Norman shook his head, as though the very notion was preposterous. 'No, it never felt right.'

'Then why did you keep coming back?'

It took him a few moments to respond. 'I suppose I wasn't really looking for Rex, I was looking for me. This was the first place I ever felt totally free to be Ethel.'

A middle-aged woman peered out from the ground-floor window, doubtless wondering why an old man and a grey-haired teenager were standing outside a doctor's practice they couldn't afford.

'We should probably get going,' said Norman. 'But I'm glad you've seen the place.'

Although he smiled as he said it, they were just a short distance down the street when Florence saw him glance back, an unmistakeable look of sadness in his eyes.

# Twenty-eight years earlier

## 1994

The official word was that Gerry and his wife, Maureen, had been 'having a few difficulties'. In truth, this was like saying Britain and Germany were only having some teething problems at the Battle of the Somme. What in earlier years had seemed like a well-matched marriage – a plain and bookish man wedded to an equally plain and bookish woman – had somehow transformed into violent trench warfare, so that even *trying* to help came with the unnerving sensation that one might die in the process.

Norman had always assumed that most marriages hit a rough patch around the seven-year mark, but Gerry, as precocious as ever, had managed to get there in four; he and his wife realizing that they hated each other at the same time she became pregnant with twins.

And yet, against all odds, they remained together after the birth, spending the next two years in an eerie standoff that Betty and Norman chose to see as a good sign. Or at least that's what they kept telling themselves month after month, even repeating the fantasy as they drove over to Gerry and Maureen's house in St Albans, summoned there for the first time in several years for Sunday lunch.

'They wouldn't invite us if things hadn't improved,' said Betty, gazing out the car window so absentmindedly, Norman couldn't decide if she was speaking to him or just thinking aloud. She was smoking a cigarette at the time, the eddies and curlicues of that grey fog filling her silence with a voice of their own.

'The way I see it, Gerry's marriage is a bit like the Channel Tunnel,' said Norman, knowing full well that Betty was still spell-bound by its recent opening. 'To imagine we've gone from Europe at war to something as big and beautiful as that. It makes me think that anything's possible.'

Smiling, Betty stubbed out her cigarette, the air instantly

beginning to clear. 'The world's changing, isn't it? You can't help but be hopeful.'

'Exactly,' replied Norman. 'And let's not forget that Gerry and Maureen have two lovely little girls now. That's sure to have brought them closer.'

Their arrival in St Albans gave further reason for hope. Gerry and Maureen's neighbourhood was even more aspirational than they remembered: the windows in every mock-Tudor home suggestive of a Laura Ashley catalogue; every car in every driveway seeming to out-polish the next. As Norman and Betty drove through that suburban idyll, it seemed inevitable that the calm and order were symbolic of a much greater truth: the marriage *must* be doing better.

First impressions of Gerry and Maureen certainly confirmed that belief, their bodies visibly filling out as though in preparation for years of middle-age stasis.

'The girls are asleep,' whispered Maureen by way of hello, saying it in such a voice of disbelief, anyone would think this was the first time they'd been quiet in two years.

After a hushed round of handshakes, hugs, and the removal of coats, everyone tiptoed to the living room where Maureen had laid the coffee table with small bowls of sun-dried tomatoes and stuffed olives – things so inconceivable to Norman, he could only assume they were decorative.

Perhaps someone else would have noticed that the atmosphere was a little stiff as Gerry poured the wine – that Maureen, for instance, hadn't taken a seat so much as braced for impact – but it was the same undercurrent of tension that had defined the entirety of Norman's life, and so he took his glass of wine, blithely raising it in a toast.

'Cheers to the two of you and your young family.' He realised that Gerry and Maureen looked less enthusiastic. 'Don't worry, we don't need to clink glasses or anything. We don't want to wake the girls, after all.' Deciding it was best to lead by example, he took a sip of his wine. 'The house is looking lovely, by the way. It feels like a proper home.'

'We're selling up,' replied Gerry, addressing the words to his glass rather than anyone in particular.

Norman glanced at Maureen, who at that moment also appeared more interested in her wine, before turning back to Gerry with a rising sense of panic. 'Do you plan on staying in the area?'

After a few seconds of tense silence, Maureen spoke. 'The girls and I are moving to Australia. My sister moved out there a few years ago.'

Betty's jaw dropped, only two words bubbling free. 'Bloody hell.'

'Well, quite,' said Gerry, lobbing the comment in Maureen's direction, but she batted it back with a practised skill.

'It's really not that far,' she replied.

'True, it's only the other side of the planet!' said Gerry. 'By the time we're an inter-galactic species, it will literally qualify as just around the block.'

Still feeling dazed, Norman turned to Maureen. 'Are you really sure it's what you want?'

'The flights are already booked,' she replied, trying for a smile that she couldn't sustain. 'We're leaving in a few weeks' time. For a while, I thought it might be better to wait until the girls are older, but if we leave now they won't remember any of this. It seems kinder that way.'

Judging by Betty's expression, it took her a few moments to understand the full implications of that statement; that Maureen wasn't just talking about the erasure of a semi-detached house in St Albans, she was also proposing the eradication of everyone in it.

Her face paling, Betty fumbled in her handbag for a cigarette. 'Does anyone mind if I smoke?'

Maureen only shrugged, clearly no longer caring what happened to the house or its contents.

Betty hadn't even got the cigarette to her lips when she started to cry, at first a soft whine but it quickly escalated into a loud wail, not so unlike the air raid sirens that Norman remembered from his childhood.

From upstairs, there was the high-pitched cry of a baby, followed a split-second later by another, their infant misery booming through the house in stereo. Maureen sighed and left the room with her glass of wine still in hand, so that Norman wondered whether the alcohol was for her or the children.

Next to him, Betty had already dissolved into a snot-nosed, puffy-eyed mess, struggling through her tears to light her cigarette as though it was the only thing left in the world that offered any solace.

Gerry downed his glass of wine before refilling it almost to the brim and guzzling half of that, too.

'So, that's all our news,' he said, tersely. 'How are you both?'

'Well, I mean, we're fine,' replied Norman, certain that compared to Gerry and Maureen, he and Betty now qualified as the poster children for domestic bliss. 'Are you really sure there's nothing that can be done?'

Gerry shook his head. 'I know all this must seem a surprise, but I can assure you, it's been a long time coming.'

'But Australia!' said Norman. 'Trust me, you don't want to look back in years to come and wish you'd done things differently. Regrets can be a terrible burden.'

Gerry took another generous mouthful of wine, staring at Norman more critically. 'You make it sound like you speak from experience.'

Norman faltered, aware he and Gerry were venturing into dangerous territory. He glanced at Betty beside him, but she was far too distraught to be following the conversation.

'Well,' he said, hesitantly. 'We all have regrets of one kind or another.'

# 14.

Given that even a crossword was enough to leave Norman needing a cup of tea, it was obvious that stopping for a drink was now a top priority. Florence found them a café nearby, though when they got there Norman appeared confused.

'It looks like an office, they're all on laptops,' he said, lingering in the doorway. 'Are you sure we can just walk in?'

'Trust me,' she replied. 'It's fine.'

'Really, you could tell me there's a typing pool in the back room and I'd believe you.'

Florence rolled her eyes. 'Granddad, even if this was an office, there wouldn't be a typing pool.'

They hadn't even made it to the counter when he caught sight of the water dispenser, slices of lemon and cucumber floating in it, sprigs of mint, too.

'Would you look at that,' he said, sounding so amazed, several people looked up to see what was happening. 'It's like a liquid salad, isn't it? Throw some lettuce and a chopped egg in there and you'd have lunch.'

Blank faces stared back.

'Tell you what,' said Florence, worried about what he might say or do next. 'Why don't you go and sit down. I'll bring the tea over.'

She watched as he made his way across the room, still getting occasional looks from the other customers – a fascination reflected right back at them by Norman, who wandered through the room with the look of someone visiting a zoo for the first time.

He was still studying the room when Florence joined him with their drinks.

'I'm at least three times older than everyone else here,' he said.

'Yeah, it feels a bit like I'm back at uni,' she replied.

Norman took his first invigorating sip of tea, sighing happily to himself. 'Do you miss university?'

'Sure, from an academic perspective. I'm less keen on some of the other students, but someone's got to be the misanthrope, right?'

Smiling, Norman tutted at her. 'I don't believe you could be a misanthrope even if you tried.'

'Oh, you haven't met the people I'm at uni with. It's like half of them are convinced that their entire lives are social media content, and the other half have just given up and gone full goblin mode.'

'I don't even know what you're studying,' said Norman.

'It doesn't really matter. It's kind of complicated.'

'Try me,' he replied.

'No, really . . .'

'Come on!' he said. 'I might be old, but I'm not a total fool.'

'Fine, it's theoretical astrophysics, with a focus on quantum field theory and supersymmetry.'

In the silence that followed, Norman just stared at her. 'I have no idea what you just said.'

'Yeah,' she replied, feeling awkward for him. 'I could explain, but I honestly don't think it would help much.'

Norman blanched. 'I told you to be a hairdresser!'

'Which was a lovely suggestion. I mean, it's an art, isn't it? I'm sure it takes real skill to do it well. But yeah, I'd rather be a physicist.'

'A *physicist*?' he replied, awestruck. 'Like Einstein and that bloke in the wheelchair?'

'Stephen Hawking. Well, yeah, I guess you could say that, but it's a big field.'

'It's funny, I'd never really thought of a physicist looking like you.'

Florence laughed. 'And how, exactly, does a physicist look?'

'Well, a shirt, of course. And a sleeveless V-neck. Maybe a tweed jacket.'

'Okay, so a *man*,' she said, still laughing. 'A man trapped in the 1950s.'

Norman blushed. 'Do I sound very out of touch?'

'Yes, but it's okay, I love you anyway.'

Smiling to himself, he took another sip of tea. 'I'm so pleased we came to London,' he said. 'It's turned into a lovely little outing.'

'*This* is the version of you that you need to show Mum and Gerry.'

His smile faded. 'You're not going to tell them about me are you?'

'Of course not,' she replied. 'That would be just as bad as never telling them at all. This is something that can only come from you.'

Norman sighed. 'All this talk of the past today, it has got me thinking about Betty and the kids. I can see now that I probably wasn't the easiest person to live with. That's the thing when you're trying to keep an important secret. I wouldn't say I was a curmudgeon necessarily . . .'

'You may as well,' said Florence. 'That's the word Mum uses about you.'

His face fell. 'Really?'

'But just because that's what you *were*, it doesn't mean that's what you *are*. It's one hundred per cent up to you where you take things from here.'

'The trouble is, when it comes to being Ethel, nothing is ever quite as simple as it sounds.'

'Look, it might be easier to embrace that side of yourself if you had more to wear than just a black sequinned dress. You know, something for those times in life when you're not in a scene from *Downton Abbey*.'

Norman blushed. 'Do you really like the dress that much?'

'Granddad, that wasn't my point. I think we should go shopping.'

Left to his own devices, Norman would have settled for some quiet charity shop, preferably in a near-empty neighbourhood, with a blind person working on the till. It was only as the hubbub of Oxford Street came into view that he realised Florence had other ideas.

'Just for the record, this isn't the kind of place where I'd go shopping for myself,' she said, striding towards a department store teeming with shoppers. 'But unless you have a hidden love of goth jewellery, there's no point taking you where I'd like to go. This place will have everything you want.'

Norman felt the panic rising in his chest. 'Do you not think we should find somewhere quieter?'

'No,' she replied, not slowing her pace. 'No one knows who you are. No one cares. You just need to keep telling yourself that.' Norman followed her through the doors, into the perfumed, brightly-lit embrace of the makeup hall. 'We could also get you some new cosmetics while we're here.'

He gazed around, intimidated by its polished perfection. 'Maybe not today. One step at a time, eh? To be honest, all my other shopping trips have been furtive affairs; quite military, in fact. In and out as fast as possible, preferably under the cover of darkness. I've never had the confidence to go into a proper shop like this.'

'And look at you now,' she said, getting on the escalator a few steps ahead, ascending in front of him like a messianic figure.

When they reached the womenswear department, Norman tried his best to keep close to her, convinced that if he strayed too far someone would tell him to leave. But keeping pace with a teenager was easier said than done, Florence darting here and there whenever she spotted something new.

'How about this?' she said, holding up a satin blouse, the fabric seeming to shimmer in the light.

Norman momentarily forgot all his concerns. 'Ooh, it's lovely.'

'Yeah, it feels age-appropriate and yet it's got that kind of naughty edge I think you secretly like.' She started gathering up a few. 'You should try a bunch of colours, just to see how they look.'

'Do you think they'll let me try them on?'

'Oh, please,' she replied, so shocked at the question, she didn't bother to reply. 'I wish we'd brought your wig, too. It'd be useful to see how it all looks together. Actually, that's something else we should do while we're in London, get you some more wigs.'

Norman noticed one of the sales assistants making a beeline for them, weaving through the racks of clothing like a seasoned predator. 'Can I help you?' she said, still some way off.

'I want these for my grandfather,' said Florence, 'but I'm not sure what size would be best.' She beckoned him over, Norman too shocked to resist. 'See,' she said, holding the blouse up to him. 'I'm thinking this one, but then I think it should be even bigger, if you have it.'

To Norman's mind, it felt like the silence that followed lasted at least three years. The woman stared at him, her serious expression at odds with the jaunty music playing overhead.

'I think we should start with that one first,' she said, nodding at the blouse in Florence's hands. 'The cut is more generous than it looks. We don't have anything bigger in that colour, but I think we have a larger size in powder pink.' She turned back to Norman, nodding this time. 'I think the pink would really flatter your skin tone. Let me see if I can find it for you.'

# 15.

His makeup was still a work in progress, but in every other respect Norman was reborn. Whereas Ethel's wardrobe used to be more exhibit than exhibition – one solitary black dress representing a lifetime of shame – now it was a gateway to a wonderland of colours and fabrics. Florence had been insistent that he should get something for every whim, but even she'd struggled to explain when he might need a metallic pink bomber jacket. And yet he'd said yes because it brought him pleasure every time he looked at it. Magpie-like, he didn't care whether it had purpose or value; it was enough to marvel at it and watch it sparkle.

For the last couple of days he'd spent breakfasts and dinners as Ethel, feeling more and more comfortable with the experience – not just with wearing a wig and outfit in Florence's presence, but in having the curtains closed at times of day that Sally would undoubtedly find suspicious. It had become something of a thrill, in fact, knowing that all that stood between him and the outside world were thin sheets of fabric hanging across his windows; that only he and Florence were privy to Ethel the nurturing homemaker, Ethel the go-getting businesswoman, Ethel the athleisure queen.

Emboldened, for breakfast the next day he chose a sleeveless jumpsuit tied at the waist in a large bow, completing the look with a blond wig, yet another acquisition from their shopping spree.

'Wow,' said Florence, as he descended the stairs. 'You look great.'

He did a twirl for her. 'It's got a quiet confidence, don't you think?'

Florence nodded approvingly. 'We are what we wear.'

They were in the kitchen beginning their slow ritual of tea and toast when the doorbell rang, followed moments later by the unmistakeable sound of Sally's voice. 'Yoo-hoo, it's only me!'

Norman went stiff, his long blond bangs perfectly framing eyes wide with panic. 'Bloody hell,' he hissed. 'What am I going to do?'

'Go upstairs,' said Florence. 'I'll answer it.'

'I'm eighty-six. I haven't been able to climb the stairs that quickly for at least ten years.'

The doorbell rang again.

Panicked, Norman moved to the living room as fast as he could and sank on arthritic knees to hide behind the sofa, dismayed that his confidence had so quickly disappeared and that his jumpsuit was incapable of fixing it, even in a fetching aquamarine.

Crouching on all fours, he listened as Florence answered the door. 'Hey, Sally.'

'Good morning. Is your granddad about?'

'He's ... er ... in the loo,' said Florence. 'Can I help?'

'Is it possible to get my cake tin back? I'm busy baking again.'

'Yeah, of course, I'll get it for you.'

Norman listened as Florence went out to the kitchen, Sally remaining on the front doorstep. But then there was the unmistakeable sound of Sally stepping inside and closing the door behind her. 'It's a bit nippy out there,' she said, calling through the house. 'You don't want to let the cold in.'

Now that Sally was indoors, Norman knew well enough that nowhere in the house was safe. It didn't help that he could hear the sound of running water in the kitchen, Florence evidently deciding to wash the tin before giving it back. Such a never-ending sound of running water, he could only assume that she was applying a physicist's eye to the task: wanting it clean and spotless at an atomic level.

Sally spoke again, her voice getting closer to Norman, perhaps standing in the open doorway to the living room. 'Why are all the curtains shut?' she said.

'What was that?' replied Florence, shouting over the sound of the tap.

'The curtains,' said Sally, louder. 'Why are they all closed?'

'Oh, yeah, I've, er, started Granddad on a new exercise pro-gramme. He feels less self-conscious this way.'

Sally murmured in response, clearly stepping into the lounge at that point – Norman could hear her padding across the deep-pile carpet, aimlessly moving around the room. She was getting closer and closer when Florence finally returned.

'Sorry for the wait,' she said. 'Here you go.'

'Now that I think of it,' replied Sally, 'maybe I should wait for your grandfather to come down. I have some important news for him.'

There was a moment of awkward silence.

'The thing is,' said Florence, 'I'm also working on his diet, trying to get him to eat more healthily. Between you and me, I think the fibre has really clogged him up. I reckon he could be up there for ages.'

There was another pause, presumably while Sally grimaced.

'Well, put like that,' she replied, 'maybe it is best I get going. But please tell your grandfather for me, I'm convening a special session of the committee this afternoon. I have a *very* important announcement to make. My place at two sharp.'

Norman listened as the front door opened and then, with a reassuring clunk, closed again.

'It's all clear,' said Florence.

Norman called back to her. 'What do you mean, "eat more healthily"? I eat just fine.'

Florence came into view, smiling at the sight of him sprawled on the floor, his wig hanging precariously. 'Granddad, everything you eat comes out of a tin.'

'It's healthier that way, they're hermetically sealed. I've heard about all that "eating clean" stuff. You can't get cleaner than a tin.'

She laughed. 'Are you going to get up?'

'I'm stuck,' he replied. 'To be honest, I didn't even know I could get into this position any more. I know for a fact I can't get out of it.'

He reached for her hand and tried to stand up, but soon realized it would be more complicated than that. What followed was a protracted process of pulling and tugging that left both of them breathless by the time Florence helped heave him into a chair.

'I presume you heard about the meeting,' she said, panting.

'Oh, I dread to think what her special news is.'

'Maybe she's decided to move away,' replied Florence, with a laugh.

Norman straightened his wig. 'I suppose there's only one way to find out . . .'


Every last trace of Ethel was gone when Florence and Norman crossed the street to Sally's house, a stiff wind blowing in from the North Sea.

'I've been thinking about your old friends in London,' said Florence, bracing herself with her arms in an attempt to keep warm. 'I can try finding them if you like.'

Norman looked unconvinced. 'I doubt you'll have much luck. You can't just lose touch with someone and then find them seventy years later.'

'Why not?' she replied. 'Invisibility these days is like a super-power: most people don't have it.'

'Well, true,' he said, as he pressed Sally's doorbell, the muffled sound of a Westminster chime playing behind her uPVC double glazing. 'I sometimes forget how much the world has changed. I daresay you could just look it up on Twitter or something.'

'That's not really how it works, but yeah, let's just say I'll check Twitter.'

As the door opened, Sally looked taken aback that Florence was also there, but said nothing, instead focusing all her attention on Norman.

'Come in, come in,' she said. 'The others are already here.' After the requisite shoe removal – and the reveal of Norman's toenail – she herded them straight through to the living room, where Ernie and Horace were eating Black Forest gateau.

Ernie shouted through a full mouth. 'Norm!'

Sally tutted. 'Really, Ernie, if you're not careful you'll spit crumbs.'

'I hear you've started exercising,' said Ernie. 'It's obviously working.'

Norman froze, all eyes on him.

'You *are* looking better,' said Sally, sizing him up much as a farmer might assess a cow. 'You only started, what? Two days ago?'

'And already looking younger,' said Ernie, still chewing on his cake. 'You'll have to tell us your secret.'

'Yes,' said Sally, growing more animated. 'I know you don't want anyone to *see* what you're doing, but maybe you could just *talk* us through it.'

'We could all start doing it,' added Ernie.

'I think,' replied Norman, struggling over the words, 'all that really matters is that you find something you love to do. I have Florence here to thank for that.'

Sally nodded approvingly. 'It's just as well you've started keeping fit. After that neuropathy scare, you can't be too careful, can you? It could be your heart next. Or worse, your brain.'

Looking uncomfortable with the scrutiny, Norman gestured at the cake stand, Sally's Black Forest gateau standing proud in layers of cream, cherries and chocolate. 'That looks lovely.'

'Actually,' said Sally, 'I've made something else I want you to try.' She bustled from the room while Norman and Florence took a seat. When she returned, it was with two slices of a different cake, dense and squat. She winked and lowered her voice as she handed one to Norman. 'It's got prunes in it!' She handed the other to a horrified Florence. 'I'm sure you'd prefer the healthy choice, too.'

With these important details sorted, Sally retreated to her usual seat, pausing for dramatic effect before she addressed the room. 'You're probably all wondering why I've called this meeting. It is my great honour to announce that I have been contacted by the local newspaper, which wants to write an article about our work.'

'Wahey,' said Ernie, his lips smeared with chocolate. 'We're going to be famous crime busters!'

Sally frowned at his enthusiasm. 'Apparently, we won't be able to say it quite that way in the article. Now that we're reporting *everything* we see in the neighbourhood, the official crime rate has actually increased by seven hundred percent. But as I pointed out to the reporter, you can't solve crime unless you catalogue it first, so I'm confident that we really are making the town a safer place. And let's face it, numbers aren't everything, are they?'

'We should ask the reporter about that woman in Frinton,' said Ernie, not addressing anyone in particular so much as throwing the comment out there to see who'd bite first.

Naturally, it was Norman who took the bait.

'What woman?' he said.

'The one who almost got eaten by spiders,' replied Ernie. 'The poor thing was so tightly wrapped in silk when they found her, it took firemen over an hour to cut her free.'

'That can't be true,' said Norman, his voice rising in confused disbelief. 'I mean, it's Frinton. Nothing ever happens in Frinton.'

Ernie responded with a shrug. 'Be careful what's under your sink, that's all I'll say on the matter.'

'Moving on . . .' said Sally, a little too loudly. 'Norman, during my discussion with the reporter, she also expressed *great* interest in your leeks. I think the photographer will want to take some photos of your patch while they're here.'

Ernie's jaw dropped. 'They're sending a photographer, too?'

'Of course,' replied Sally. 'We're doing something important for the community. They want to give us the credit we deserve.' She looked at each of the men in turn. 'That does mean, though, that we should all make more than the usual effort on the day. We want to look our best, after all.'

Ernie waved his cake fork at Norman. 'It's all right for you, you're already looking fresher. Look at the rest of us, we're haggard old wrecks.' He glanced at Sally. 'No offence.'

She gave him a stiff smile. 'What with schedules and whatnot, they won't be able to meet us for a week or two, so do with that what you will.' She turned her attention back to Norman and Horace, blushing now, unable to hide her excitement. 'This really is a tremendous opportunity. It's a chance for all of us to put our best foot forward and show who we really are.'

# 16.

Breakfast the next morning was with Norman the hardcore gardener rather than Ethel. Somewhere in the depths of his wardrobe, Norman kept a set of clothes that were even older and more threadbare than the rest, seeing out their final years on the frontlines of his horticultural ambitions.

'There's a fair bit to do out there,' he said, as he and Florence sat at the kitchen table with their tea and toast. 'I've been neglecting things for the last few days.'

'You and me both,' she replied. 'There's a bunch of reading I should get done today.'

'I've got to get everything looking its best, haven't I? What with the press coverage.'

Florence smiled at the way he said it, as though his leeks were paparazzi gold dust. 'Your vegetable patch is going to be famous,' she said.

'It already is,' he replied, with a playful hint of indignation. 'Maybe not in the way you young people think about fame.'

'You mean your leeks don't have ten million TikTok followers?'

Norman looked confused. 'I've won a few awards over the years. Dare I say it, there are some who think of me as a Grand Wizard of the vegetable arts. People keep a very close eye on me come harvest season.' He took another bite of toast, chewing on it thoughtfully. 'Except Sally, of course. From now on, all she's going to be watching me for are signs of dementia.'

'I thought we already were,' replied Florence, deadpan.

'The thing is,' he continued, 'the newspaper people are bound to ask how I get my veg so big. I need to think of an interesting answer that doesn't give all my secrets away.'

'What kind of secrets are we talking about?' said Florence, unsure if she wanted to know the answer.

Norman munched on his toast, seemingly happy to talk on this subject forevermore. 'Oh, I have a few tricks up my sleeve. Late at night, when no one's around, I often go out there and wee on them. And if ever I see a good bit of roadkill while I'm out, I like to bring it home with me and mulch it into the soil.'

Florence cringed. 'Jesus, no wonder you don't eat any vegetables. I'm not sure I want to eat any after that.'

She looked down at her toast, suddenly glad that the jam wasn't homemade.

'It's all science, isn't it?' said Norman, still chewing away happily. 'Though, granted, my science isn't as complex as yours. I'm not even going to ask what you'll be reading about today.'

'Yeah, it's hard to explain, even for me.'

'But, from now on, that's exactly how I'm going to think of it: physics is just your vegetable patch. No different to mine, except you grow really complicated things.'

'And mine doesn't involve roadkill or urination,' she said.


By the afternoon Florence had retreated upstairs, using the blank canvas of her bedroom ceiling to ponder the complexities of what she'd learnt. She was still lying atop her bed when there was a gentle knock at the door. 'Are you sleeping?' said Norman.

'No, come in.'

He poked his head into the room. 'Is everything all right?'

'Yeah, you know, I'm just thinking.'

'Of course you are. It's a wonder your brain hasn't caught fire by now.'

She smiled. 'How's the vegetable patch?'

He came further into the room, no longer wearing his gardening gear, but instead an old rain mac buttoned up to his chin. 'The leeks are looking very photogenic. And don't ask me how, but I've got a very good feeling about next year's cabbages. Anyway, now that I'm done, I thought I might pop out for a while.'

Florence propped herself up on her elbows, unsettled by the idea that he was going somewhere without her.

'I've been thinking,' he said, 'about what you mentioned in London; about buying some new makeup. Well, why not? "Seize the day" and all that. I mean, I'm not going to London, obviously, but I thought I might drive over to Colchester, they have some big shops there.'

'Do you want me to come with you?'

'No, I think it'll be good to confront my fears.' He gestured at his mac. 'I'm wearing that lovely satin blouse under here.'

Florence nodded approvingly. 'Hybrid Ethel, I like it.'

'Well, wish me luck,' he replied, blushing. 'I'll be back by six.'


It wasn't the full-scale temple to beauty – and Mammon – that the place in London had been, but Norman still felt intimidated as he walked into the over-lit department store.

'I dread to imagine the electricity bill,' he muttered to himself as he wandered the glaring aisles of its makeup hall, endless mirrors seeming to bounce the light every which way, offering constant opportunities to see his wrinkles and receding hairline from a new angle.

A young woman in a white lab coat called to him as he passed her counter. 'Can I introduce you to our new range?'

Norman stopped, shocked that a beautiful young stranger was talking to him.

'I'd love to,' he replied, not even caring what he'd agreed to;

happy to talk about anything, just to stop feeling like the odd one out. 'I'm such a fish out of water in this place. I must be at least sixty years older than everyone else here.'

'Don't you worry about that,' she replied, warming to him. 'Everybody's welcome.'

'I'm afraid bright lights and mirrors are a bit like time and gravity: they're not your friends after a certain age.'

'I wouldn't know it to look at you, my love. Are you shopping for a gift?' Before Norman could get the words out, she was speaking again. 'I promise I can make you the world's favourite granddad if you give me a chance.'

'No, it's ... well, I do have a granddaughter, but actually I want something for ...' He held the words in his mouth, the closest he'd ever come to saying them aloud. 'I want something for my sister. She's getting on, as you can imagine, but she's young at heart.'

'Then take a seat,' she said, gesturing at a stool better suited to glamorous cocktails, or perhaps falling and breaking a hip. While he made himself comfortable, she began to pore over glistening bottles of potions, a temple to the mysterious alchemy of feminine beauty. 'A lot of older women use our products. Can you tell me more about your sister? Would you say her skin tends to be oily, normal or dry?'

'Pretty oily, I'd say. I mean, she's the spitting image of me, the poor thing. Same skin, cheekbones, the lot. I'd like to get her something that makes her feel more glamorous, but that's probably just like putting lipstick on a pig, isn't it?'

The girl laughed. 'If my brother said that about me, he'd get a punch.' She pulled a mirror closer, his reflection magnified and illuminated; an eighty-six-year story written in the wrinkles of old age. 'I love the way the blue in your eyes catches the light. Are your sister's eyes like that, too?'

'I suppose so,' he replied, staring at his reflection; not a magnification of his shortcomings and deficiencies at all, but rather proof that there was still some life left in him, still some hope. 'I'd never really noticed my eyes, but now that you mention it ...'

'I think she'd look amazing in this eyeshadow,' she said, putting it on the counter. 'Especially if we keep the foundation very neutral and match it with the right lipstick.'

'That sounds lovely.'

'Everyone deserves to feel beautiful, that's my attitude. Whoever they are and whatever their age.' She began picking up some other products. 'I don't suppose you know anything about her current skincare routine?'

'I'm sure it's very basic. A dab of Pond's at night, that sort of thing. And I daresay her makeup brushes are pretty useless. I should probably get her some of those, too.'

'By the way, she's welcome to come in for a free session. I might be able to show her some tricks she doesn't know.'

Norman blushed. 'She's a bit shy, that's the trouble.'

'Then tell her from me, I promise to be gentle.'


When he got back to the car, Norman was feeling so exhilarated by the experience, he *had* to try the makeup on straight away; it seemed feasible that his heart would give way from excitement if he waited until he got home. Using the car's rear-view mirror wasn't the best circumstance, but it also seemed par for the course: after the last eighty-odd years, he'd long since made his peace with awkward, furtive moments of self-expression. Between the gloom of the multi-storey car park and the weak glow of the car's dome light, it was hard to tell if he was using too much or too little, but still he persevered, finding solace in each small brushstroke.

'It's not Marilyn Monroe,' he said to his reflection, a work in progress. 'But we do what we can, eh?'

If Florence had been there with him in the car, he would

have told her how he once met Marilyn in the flesh. Though it was only now, replaying the memory, that he realised it already sounded wrong. 'Once met' implied that they'd bumped into one another and had a friendly chat, whereas Norman had actually stood around in Leicester Square for hours and hours, waiting for Marilyn to arrive for a film premiere.

'Over sixty-five years ago and I still remember it like it was yesterday,' he told an invisible Florence. 'I daresay we were half delirious by the time Marilyn turned up, but I can remember the atmosphere in the crowd as she got out of the car. She had such *charisma*, such star power, we were in thrall to the sight of her. We were only just out of the war years and yet there she was, looking so glamorous it was like she'd come from a different galaxy. Which I suppose she had, in many ways.'

He paused, the words transporting him back to that moment: hundreds of camera bulbs lighting up the gloom of Leicester Square – all the more remarkable that little more than ten years earlier everyone had been huddled in basements and Tube stations while bombs fell from the sky.

'I never knew about her problems back then – the abusive husband and all that sadness she carried inside. That was the thing about movie stars in those days, they were a mystery.' He continued applying mascara, the recollection of Marilyn helping to steady his hand, reminding him that every brushstroke can be an act of transformation; not just a beautification, but an armouring, a readying for battle. 'I only saw her for a few seconds before they hurried her indoors, but I thought about it for weeks afterward. Months, even. I mean, listen to me, I'm still talking about it all these years later.' Feeling that he'd applied enough makeup, perhaps too much, he took his brunette wig from its hiding place in the glovebox. 'I suppose that's the thing about life,' he said, as he pulled it into place. 'Some experiences are so magical, they stay with you forever.'

He stared at Ethel in the mirror, a fully realised woman, in full view of anyone who might walk past. Granted, the car park was so gloomy, they might need a torch to see her properly, but it still felt like an important milestone.

Hands trembling, heart pounding, he started the engine and headed for the exit, slowly advancing towards the outside world until finally he was there on the cusp of it, a place of pedestrians and traffic, nowhere to hide on Colchester's daylit streets.


Emboldened by the anonymity of being in a different town, he spent longer than planned just driving around: long enough to repeat *Diamonds Are A Girl's Best Friend* numerous times; long enough for the sun to go down, the last of the daylight draining away. But all the better, he thought, to sneak home like that – without the wig, of course, but Sally and the other neighbours would never notice his makeup in the dark.

He'd just started heading back when he decided that it was a day worth raising a toast to. For everything it had been, and everything that life may yet become. Just a few minutes later, he spotted a shop glowing on a darkened street. The neighbourhood wasn't the nicest, but the store was the kind that would likely be forced out of business by the supermarkets. As one underdog to another, it felt like an appropriate match.

As he parked, some small inner voice kept telling him to stay in the car, that he needed that metallic bubble of anonymity.

'No, thank you,' he said, looking himself in the mirror. 'I've spent eighty-odd years listening to that voice. Eighty-odd years of living in fear. No more.'

The shop was quiet inside, the greying proprietor behind the till engrossed in a book as Norman marched towards the wine.

He was checking the chilled bottles when he first heard the voices outside – young, spirited, too loud to be sober. Turning back to the wine, Norman caught sight of himself in the chrome edges of the fridge, his heavy-handed makeup looking cartoonish beneath the shop's harsh strip lights.

The man behind the till was still looking worried by the noise outside when Norman put his bottle of wine on the counter. In that respect, Norman at least provided a distraction: standing there face to face, any concerns the man had melted away, instead he just stared at Norman, open-mouthed. Deciding that Marilyn had probably experienced this reaction many times – possibly even from Norman back on that day in 1956 – he gave the man the biggest smile he could muster, mentally imagining a storm of camera bulbs flashing as reporters called his name.

The young men were some way off as Norman left the shop, the two of them swaggering down the street, early twenties if that. Although he tried not to look at them, they clearly got a good look at him. There was the inevitable laughter as he walked back to his car, but he was hopeful that that might be the worst of it.

'Fag,' one of them shouted, the word sounding angry and raw. Ignoring them, he kept going, the car just a few yards up ahead, but then there was more shouting, their voices growing louder, closer. 'Did you hear me? You pervert.'

In all his years as a haulier, Norman had only once been in a crash; a car in the opposite lane veering into his path, no way of avoiding it. It had all happened in a matter of seconds, but still he saw each passing moment in perfect clarity: the look on the other driver's face, the awful inevitability of it seeming to unspool before him.

Norman remembered that experience as he heard the young men sprinting towards him, turning to look as they lunged forwards: a slow-motion symphony of spittle-flecked words, their mouths twisted in rage. And then the carrier bag was slipping from his fingers as they punched him to the ground, Norman unsure if the sound of smashing was the bottle or him, every kick a dull explosion somewhere deep inside, first once, then twice, and then again and again and again.

# Thirty-five years earlier

## 1987

Of all the cross-dressing get-togethers that Norman attended while travelling around the country, none were as good as Barry's. Not, it should be mentioned, because of Barry himself, who was far too uptight to be much fun, but rather because Barry knew how to throw a party, his pernickety nature finding its perfect expression in food, lighting and music.

'For the vol au vents, I didn't know whether to do coronation chicken or chicken à la king, so I did both,' said Barry, inadvertently proving Norman's point. 'I think my wife would be very impressed if she knew.'

'Remind me again,' replied Norman. 'Where's she gone?'

'Norfolk. Her bridge club is competing in some tournament or other. They've all been very fired up about it, like Vikings going off to pillage a new land.' He stood back from the buffet table, smiling at his handiwork as he smoothed down the creases in his cocktail dress. 'I should have made more sausage rolls, but never mind, it's too late now.'

He was turning the bowl of potato salad an inch, nodding to himself at this improved perspective on the chopped chives, when he noticed two men coming up the front path. Norman also turned to look, but Barry's net curtains were more like cataracts than window dressings, the world outside reduced to a milky blur.

'If you'll excuse me,' said Barry, slipping from the room.

In his absence, Norman stood there, wondering if there was some unspoken rule about when it was acceptable to start eating. In any other setting, he'd just go ahead and help himself, but Barry was the type who'd know at a glance if even a single chipolata went missing.

Out in the hallway, the sound of the doorbell coincided with

Barry opening the front door, speaking in hushed tones as he hurried the men indoors. After some muffled conversation, Norman heard the newcomers traipse upstairs.

Barry returned moments later. 'It's Roger and Eric,' he said. 'They're just getting changed.' He glanced at the buffet table, perhaps checking if anything had happened while he was gone. 'I didn't expect them to come together, but you know how Roger gets after a few Babychams, he'll be in no fit state to drive.'

In the minutes that followed, Barry continued moving around the room, touching up the placement of flowers and coasters and dainty bowls of sugared almonds, each a muted rainbow of pastel shades. And all the while, Norman stood there in his dress – its shoulder pads worthy of American football – trapped in a preparty purgatory, wondering how much longer it would be until he could start eating.

From upstairs, there was the sound of heavy, cumbersome movements, nothing to suggest the feminine transformation that was supposed to be taking place.

Barry winced at the noise. 'You can be sure that's Eric,' he said. 'I do wish he'd make more of an effort. I know you come here in a lorry, but at least you're good enough to park it several streets away, and let's face it, you brush up very well. Whereas Eric is as ladylike as a pallet of bricks.' On cue, there was the sound of thunderous footsteps on the stairs before Eric entered the room, his outfit suggestive of a sex worker who'd fallen on hard times. Barry leant closer to Norman, lowering his voice. 'Really, I dress like this as an homage to my wife, to everything I love about her. If Eric is the same, that poor woman is truly beyond God's help.'

More people arrived, each of them disappearing upstairs as a married, middle-aged man before returning as a woman reborn. At some point, this gathering of near-strangers – brought together by Barry's discreet classified ad in the local newspaper – became an actual party: alcohol began to flow and Barry finally allowed people to touch the buffet table. Being a stickler for decorum, he was doubtless hoping that his guests would strike a genteel pose while eating – balancing plates on dress-covered knees; dabbing demurely at their lips with his perfectly folded napkins – but not everyone shared his view of femininity. Instead of the Swiss finishing school that Barry had envisioned, the party took on the air of a boarding school for troubled girls, some of the guests clearly aspiring to better things while others simply embraced their damage.

Eric was inevitably one of the latter, getting into a heated discussion as to why he was the only one in the room using his real name rather than a feminine alter ego.

'Because I'm not a woman,' he said, legs spread wide while he tore at a chicken drumstick. 'I'm a man in woman's clothes.' Given that he was talking to someone who'd introduced himself as Marjory, his words fell on deaf ears.

Eric became more strident. 'The way you lot go on, anyone would think we're bloody fags.'

Norman noticed how people recoiled at the prospect; how there could be nothing worse than to be thought a homosexual or, God forbid, a transsexual: a roomful of men in dresses, no one seeing the irony that they themselves were as judgemental as the society that judged them.

Roger came to the rescue, swaying across the room with a cocktail in hand, smudges of lipstick on his face and glass. 'Now, now, ladies …' He nodded at Eric. 'And cross-dressing gentleman …' He paused to down the rest of his drink, the faintest hint of a slur in his voice. 'The best thing we can all do is get absolutely shit-faced pissed. I'm going to make cocktails for all of you.'

He staggered to the drinks tray, was picking up a bottle of brandy when Barry swooped in. 'Belinda, darling, what are you doing?'

'Brandy and Babycham,' he replied. 'It's called a Legover. It's all the rage in Blackpool these days.'

'I'm sure you could say the same of chlamydia,' said Barry, 'but that's no reason to try it.' He led Roger to a dining chair placed against the wall, the suburban equivalent of a drunk tank. 'I'll make you a cup of tea, how about that?'

'Why can't I have a Legover?' he whined.

Barry became more insistent, his inner matron in full flow. 'Belinda, if nothing else, think of your wife. How are you going to explain it to her when you stumble home three sheets to the wind?'

Mention of wives had a more sobering effect than intended, not just on Roger but everyone else, too. Despite Bananarama playing in the background, the mood in the room took a decided downturn. Norman's thoughts inevitably drifted to Betty, who at that moment probably pictured him sitting alone in some dreary roadside caff, a plate of egg and chips in front of him. Whereas he was in suburban Peterborough, nibbling on a vol au vent next to a middle-aged man called Marjory.

Betty was the one alone, that was the real irony of it. For so many years, Norman had justified his work because he needed to look after the family, but now the kids had both grown up and moved on – and yet there he was, still away from home for days at a time, something that only made sense if one thought of Ethel as being part of the family, too.

He tried to picture what Betty might be doing at that precise moment. Reading seemed most likely. In recent years, she'd thrown herself into books; had made a particular habit of dipping into the encyclopaedia and sharing titbits with Norman whenever he was home, each one seeming oddly symbolic of a deeper truth that neither of them were willing to admit. She'd been explaining tectonic plates when he last saw her, marvelling at how the planet was covered in invisible fault lines, and ever since then Norman had been haunted by the thought that the same could be said of the family; that they'd all pulled away from one another, the distance growing so imperceptibly, Norman had only realised what was happening after he found himself viewing them across a vast unbridgeable gulf.

Roger's drunken voice cut through Norman's thoughts. 'I don't want to talk about wives,' he shouted, getting emotional. 'As God is my witness, I tried to include mine, but she doesn't want to see me dressed as Belinda. *She* was the one who chose secrecy, something that cannot exist in the absence of lies.'

'Oh, who cares,' said Eric, loading up a plate with devilled eggs. 'The way I see it, ignorance is bliss. For all we know, our wives are keeping secrets, too.' He didn't appear concerned by this bombshell statement, even chuckling to himself as he considered the possibility. 'And let's be honest, if their secrets are equal to ours, we're all in trouble.'

# 17.

Never mind the tinned food and the occasional act of eating things off the floor, as far as Florence was concerned the real problem with Norman's lifestyle was its Luddite quality. As someone who spoke of mobile phones as if they were still a new and unproven technology – a mere fad that would pass soon enough – he might as well have been living in the Middle Ages: as soon as he was out of sight, he was out of reach. Inasmuch as Norman didn't like driving after dark, it was clear that something had happened, but in the total data vacuum that was his life, it was impossible to know what.

As one hour turned into two, Florence tried comforting herself that, if there really was a problem, Norman would at least call the house. Or ask someone else to. Because that was the kind of man he was. Until, that is, she tried the landline and found that it was dead.

Worried that a house in darkness might seem like an easy target, Florence started turning on more and more lights, not only in the rooms she was using, but all the others, too, leaving the curtains open in each, not because she wanted to, but because closing them would surely cancel out the act of turning on the lights in the first place. Except, by the time she was finished, the entire house was glowing like a new arrival from outer space, and Florence saw how people turned to look as they passed, not just people on foot but even in vehicles, everyone appearing to notice the house as if for the first time. And so she began to worry that this was only inviting a much worse outcome: that instead of saying the house was occupied, she was now broadcasting to the world that a young female was alone.

She was waiting in the living room window, the only spot that brought her comfort, when she noticed that Sally was doing the same, staring in her direction. Florence briefly considered going over there and sharing her concerns, but even if she and Sally liked each other – which clearly they didn't – Norman had left the house in women's clothes; this was no time to involve a nosy neighbour. So instead Florence raised her hand in a wave – not a gesture of warmth so much as a statement of presence; a reminder to Sally that the watcher was also being watched. In response, Sally merely drew the curtains, her window going dark.

# 18.

The pain was welling up from so deep inside, it seemed conceivable to Norman that he'd torn the very fabric of himself in two. It didn't help that he was stranded on a hospital gurney, his makeup – which hadn't been the best to start with – now smudged and whorish, a fitting match to his ripped blouse. Occasionally, a nurse would stop by to tell him that he'd be moved to a bed as soon as one became available, and each time Norman thought that he should say something about his appearance – make light of it, perhaps, something to break the ice – but he'd waited a lifetime to express himself like this; if he made a joke of it now, the cuts and bruises would surely be the least of his problems. And anyway, hadn't Marilyn been through all this before? Maybe that's what she would have told him if they really had chatted in Leicester Square: life can be hard, but all injuries fade in time.

As the hours passed, the visits from nurses became less frequent, Norman slowly transitioning from being a new arrival to a piece of that landscape, another scratched doorframe, another scuff mark on the wall, another flickering light.

Desperate to quiet his fretting mind, he tried to focus on the sounds around him: the purposeful walk of staff, somehow finding the energy to keep going hour after hour; the often-timid gait of visitors, perhaps afraid of what they might find when they reached their loved one; the well-oiled wheels transporting patients to who knows where – a place of so many possibilities, so few of them nice.

He was staring at the ceiling listening to yet more footsteps – heavy, faster than usual, a cadence he hadn't heard before, perhaps a doctor late for a shift – when they came to a stop beside him.

He looked up to find Gerry standing there, a lifetime of secrets laid bare in an instant.

'Father,' he said, his tone sounding more strained than usual. 'What happened?'

'It was just some kids,' replied Norman. 'It's nothing.'

'That's clearly not true. The nurses tell me you'll be staying for a while.'

'Only for a bit, just to keep an eye on things.'

Gerry was desperately trying not to look at the smudged makeup; trying to tiptoe through a minefield in which there was no clear ground any longer, only mines laid edge to edge.

'Does this mean you're gay?' said Gerry, every muscle in his face so rigid he could have been made of stone.

'I'm not gay, Gerry. I just like to dress as a woman. Sorry, if this is hard for you.'

'Finding my bashed-up father in hospital dressed like a hooker? Telling me he's a cross-dresser. Why on earth would that be hard?'

'You can call me Ethel if it makes it easier.'

Gerry snapped at him. 'No, it does not make it any bloody easier.'

'For what it's worth,' replied Norman, 'your mother did know. I mean, she didn't approve—'

'Really? How surprising.'

'But now that she's gone,' said Norman.

'*Barely* gone, you do realise that?'

'The thing is, I'm almost gone, too. I'm not trying to hurt anyone, Gerry, I need you to know that. I'm just trying to stop myself hurting.'

There was the sound of more footsteps, a nurse joining them.

'Mister Cartwight?' she said. 'I'm here to take you upstairs for your CAT scan.'

'But I'm only waiting for a bed,' he replied, unsure what a CAT scan was, but certain that it didn't bode well.

'We'll be doing some tests while we sort out a bed for you. It's nothing to worry about.'

Since that's what everyone tended to say when they didn't want to alarm the patient – *You'll be dead in days, but it's nothing to worry about!* – Norman only began worrying more.

'Will you come up with me?' he said to Gerry.

The nurse cut in. 'You won't be able to join us, but you're welcome to wait downstairs. I can ask someone to let you know when we're done.'

'It's probably best I go and see Florence,' replied Gerry, looking relieved at the chance to get away so soon. 'She must be sick with worry by now.'

'She knows about me,' said Norman. 'About the makeup and – she knows everything. She's been wonderful.'

Gerry looked embarrassed that the nurse was listening. 'I'm sure she'll come and see you tomorrow. Is there anything you'd like her to bring you?'

'My clothes are a bit torn up. I'll need something fresh to go home in. And I wouldn't say no to a mirror and some makeup remover. Which at least puts it in perspective, eh? Here's everyone else dealing with matters of life and death, and my biggest problem is some streaky mascara.'

Gerry wasn't ready for levity, had possibly never been ready now that Norman came to think of it, and as soon as that thought had formed in his mind he wanted to kick himself for not seeing it sooner: how Gerry had so rarely smiled, even as a child, and for all these years Norman had just written it off as bookishness, as though intelligence inevitably precluded joy.

He was already turning away when Norman called to him. 'It was lovely of you to come, Gerry. It's always lovely to see you. I should have told you that a long, long time ago.'

# 19.

Norman was dead, that was all Florence could think when she saw Uncle Gerry arrive. Why else would this family come together except at a time of tragedy? She watched as he got out of his car, his serious demeanour broken only by a look of confusion that every window in the house was ablaze with light, the whole place glowing like a homing beacon.

He'd just started up the front path when Florence opened the door. 'What's happened?'

'Don't worry,' replied Gerry. 'He's fine. He's in hospital, but—'

'Hospital?'

'He got into a – a spot of difficulty, let's say. Some drunken teenagers, as far as I understand it. But I've just seen him and everything's under control. You'll be able to go and see him tomorrow.'

'You should come in,' she said.

Gerry looked awkward. 'It's probably best I don't. I've got a long drive home, you know how it is. I really just wanted to make sure you're doing okay.' He looked up at the house, the windows appearing to shine brighter from that angle. 'So, everything's all right?'

'I like light,' she replied.

He nodded as only a parent could. 'Father asked if you could take him some fresh clothes tomorrow. The ones he has are a bit torn up.'

'Clothes?' she said, putting more than usual emphasis on the word.

'Yes, some clothes. Something to travel home in.'

Florence looked at him more carefully. 'So, nothing he has is wearable?'

'Well, I didn't *inspect* what he has.'

'But you got a reasonable look?'

Gerry sighed. 'I do know about him, if that's what you mean. He was slathered in makeup for a start. And yes, the silky blouse was something of a giveaway.'

'He's ripped that blouse?' said Florence, with a gasp. 'What a shame, he's only just bought it.'

Gerry took a deep breath, the subject seeming to need a manual override. 'If you could take him some fresh clothes, I'm sure that would be much appreciated.' He took some money from his wallet. 'And here ...'

'You don't need to do that.'

'Just in case,' he replied, holding it there until she took it. 'I've written my number down for you as well. I don't suppose you already have it. No one could accuse us of being a close family, could they?'

'I'll text you, so you have my number as well.'

'Do,' said Gerry, brightening. 'And if you could update me tomorrow, to let me know how things are.' He took a step back, eager to be off. 'I'll pick him up when he's ready to come home, but you're in charge in the meantime.'

'Isn't he getting out tomorrow?' she replied. 'I thought you said everything's fine?'

'Oh, they're just doing some tests. I get the impression it's all pretty routine, but I don't think Father sees it that way. I daresay by the time you get there, he'll have convinced himself he's dying.' He seemed to notice her surprise. 'Maybe you haven't seen that side of him yet. But I suppose that's the thing about him, isn't it? None of us have ever known the totality.'

He began walking away, was about halfway down the front

path when he paused, the physical distance seeming to make intimacy easier.

'Actually,' he said, smiling, 'I think a mirror and some makeup remover would also be appreciated, if you have them.'

# 20.

Florence had grown so accustomed to being behind the wheel of a car – thinking of herself as a full-fledged driver even though the law still disagreed – it was a rude shock to find herself walking to a bus stop the next morning. After she'd waited for the bus, shared it with too many other people, and ridden all the way to Colchester on a circuitous route that added at least an hour to the journey, it was clear that her new circumstances were existentially wrong, an evolutionary reversal akin to quadrupeds returning to the sea.

She arrived at Norman's bedside ruffled by the experience. 'I can't believe I'm about to say this, but I really miss driving.'

'Good morning to you, too,' he replied.

'Yeah, sorry,' she said, sweeping in to give him a peck on the cheek. 'How are you feeling?'

'Well, it's not been the best time of my life, but there's no point being a sourpuss, is there? I daresay it's difficult for the nurses as well, though they all manage a smile and a kind word.'

'Your landline doesn't work, by the way.'

'Oh, I keep forgetting about that. I've been meaning to get it fixed for a while. I just thought, if there was something important in the meantime, people would send a letter.'

Florence sighed. 'I'm going to pretend I didn't hear that.'

She began to settle, cat-like, turning this way and that as she deposited her coat here, her bag there; a slow, methodical unpacking of the outside world until finally she sat down on the edge of his bed, a bag of sweets in her hand.

'Are they for me or for you?' said Norman.

'Both,' she replied, offering him some. 'There's a bit of everything in there.'

Norman peered inside. 'Emphasis on the everything.'

'Actually, in theory, they're all yours. Uncle Gerry gave me some money in case you need anything.'

'I need a new blouse,' he replied, popping a fruit pastille in his mouth.

'Yeah, I'm not sure that's what he had in mind. And now, of course, there's a few quid less.' She gestured at the sweets like a courtroom exhibit, proof of criminal activity. 'I figured if he wants to do an audit of the money, we could just pretend they were all for you.'

'I wouldn't worry about that,' said Norman. 'I suspect he's got bigger things on his mind after yesterday. Though it's ironic, really; all these years, I've been so scared of the family knowing, and now Gerry finds out just as I stop.'

Florence looked at him with a puzzled expression. 'What do you mean by that?'

'I'm not going to try being Ethel again, not after what happened.'

She took a lollipop from the bag, nestling it in the side of her mouth, her words becoming pebble-like, smoothed and rounded by the new oral mass. 'The last I knew, you were going shopping in an old rain mac.'

'I did go to the store and I got myself some lovely new makeup. Which cost a small fortune, by the way. I'd never realised being a woman was so expensive.' He picked a toffee from the bag, appearing to take comfort in unwrapping it, revealing the soft, chewy treasure beneath. 'I was so happy about things, I decided to put some on right there in the car. I was feeling very glamorous by the time I finished. Though, in retrospect, I'd probably slapped it on a bit too thick. Together with the blouse and whatnot, well, I was asking for it, I suppose.'

'No, you weren't,' replied Florence, the lollipop doing nothing to blunt her indignation. 'We should all be safe to walk the streets, no matter what other people think of how we look. What did the police say?'

Norman looked away, talking to his toffee wrapper rather than her. 'Well, you know how it is. What with budget cuts and all. They're so busy looking for, I don't know, bank robbers and terrorists, they don't have time to worry about old people like me.'

Norman fiddled with the wrapper.

'You did report it, didn't you?' said Florence.

'I thought about it.'

'The police aren't psychic. You of all people should know, you have to actually *tell* them when something happens.'

'I didn't see the point,' he replied.

'You were the victim of a crime!'

Norman sighed. 'But it wouldn't change anything, would it? Unless they're going to buy me a new blouse.'

'Yeah, Uncle Gerry mentioned you'd torn yours.' She paused, aware of the enormity of that statement. 'I mean, it wasn't like "Dad's ripped that lovely new blouse of his", but, you know, his words pointed in that direction.'

'It was a good deal nicer than this thing,' said Norman, picking at his bedgown, its colour and cut seemingly chosen to demoralise.

'Here, I've brought you some clothes.' She handed Norman the bag she'd brought with her, watching as he peered inside, his look of curiosity turning to alarm.

'I can't wear this in here,' he said, pulling out the metallic pink bomber jacket.

'You're not supposed to. It's for going home in, not for hanging around a hospital ward.'

'But Gerry will be picking me up.'

'Good,' replied Florence. 'If a picture says a thousand words, I reckon that jacket is a whole book. A book he needs to read, by the way.' She watched as Norman caressed the fabric. 'Look me in the eye and tell me you don't love that jacket.'

'It is pretty, isn't it?'

He touched it again, with a tenderness that belied his true feelings, while Florence psyched herself up to strike a non-chalant tone.

'And everything else is all right?' she said. 'I mean, there isn't something you've conveniently forgotten to mention?'

He put the jacket down, his eyes widening in fear. 'Why would you ask that? I'm fine.'

'It's just Uncle Gerry said something about tests.'

'They were only routine tests,' he said, almost barking the words at her. 'They probably do the same for everyone.'

A new voice came from the foot of the bed. 'Is this a bad time?'

They turned to find a young female doctor standing there; ginger hair and freckles atop a white ward coat.

'No, not at all,' replied Norman, his expression saying otherwise – his entire appearance, in fact, redolent of a small woodland creature frozen in the path of an oncoming truck.


Inside he might be a trembling mess, but it was a comfort to know that he could appear calm for Florence's sake. He would never admit it, but he'd lain awake most of the night, dreading this moment. During those long hours, lying there in the hospital's ersatz darkness – an institutional twilight, the low background hum of machinery seeming to parallel his state of mind – he'd had plenty of time to analyse the way the nurses had spoken to him after his test: trying to shield him from the terrible truth; the doctors probably drawing lots in the staff room to decide who'd have the messy task of telling him the bad news.

The doctor moved closer. 'How are you feeling today, Mister Cartwright?'

'I'm fine,' he replied, convinced more than ever that this was the beginning of one of *those* conversations: the friendly doctor making small talk and chitchat before revealing that they'd found terminal cancer and expected him to die within days. Hours.

'I just wanted to update you on your test results,' she said.

Norman turned to Florence, eager for her to be somewhere else, anywhere else. 'You should go and buy us some more sweets.'

'Why?' she replied through a full mouth. 'We've already got enough to start a shop.'

'Then get us something we don't have.'

'How about a diabetic coma?' she replied, still no hint of movement.

'A cup of tea. I'd love a cup of tea.' He saw her glance at the unfinished cup on his bedside table. 'That one's gone cold. I'd like a *hot* cup of tea.'

'Fine,' replied Florence, dragging herself from the bed.

'With lots of milk,' he called after her. 'And three sugars.'

'Your doctor is standing right beside you,' said Florence. 'You should at least pretend to be more virtuous.'

Norman waited until she was well out of earshot, finally giving the doctor a nervous smile. 'I thought it better we do this alone.'

'If that's what you prefer,' she replied.

'Look, I've had plenty of time to think this through. Whatever the problem is, you can just give it to me straight. I'd rather hear the truth, no matter how bad.'

The doctor's smile vanished. 'In that case, I'm very sorry to tell you, your tests do reveal something quite important. They indicate that you're old, and at the current time I'm afraid we have no cure for that.' Norman stared at her, certain that he'd misheard. 'For your age, Mister Cartwright, I'd say you're in relatively good health. All the more so since you drink your tea with three sugars.'

Norman stared at her, still shocked. 'You really didn't find anything bad?'

'You mean other than all that bruising?' she replied. 'I suspect everything was working better seventy years ago, but that's not an unexpected result.'

Norman smiled. 'It certainly felt much better seventy years ago.'

'Of that I have no doubt.' She rifled through her notes, nodding to herself. 'As long as you have someone to come and collect you, you can be out of here in a couple of days. And rest assured, as soon as we have a magic pill for old age, I'll be putting your name on the list.'

# 21.

Norman's pink jacket was safely stowed back in its bag when Gerry came to collect him. Nevertheless, Gerry approached with a strained smile, giving the clear impression that he'd been rehearsing for this moment and yet still found himself lacking.

'Good morning,' said Norman, sitting there in his grubby old rain mac. 'Thank you for doing this.'

'It's not as if we can just leave you here, is it?' He smiled at the neighbouring patients as he spoke, so that anyone would think he was taking Norman away for their sake. 'Are you all packed?'

'And raring to go,' replied Norman, wincing in pain as he picked up the bag.

'Here, let me,' said Gerry, taking it from him.

They set off for the elevator in silence, slowly making their way out to the lift lobby and down through the building. As they finally emerged into daylight, Norman stopped to take a deep breath.

'Is everything all right?' said Gerry, speaking for the first time.

'It's funny how we take things for granted, isn't it? This air, it feels like a drug.' He took another breath, invigorated by its freshness. 'I hadn't realised how much I'd missed it until now.'

Gerry's expression softened. 'After an experience like yours, I daresay some recalibration is required.'

'Like an old gas pump,' said Norman. 'A bit rusty and worn at the edges, but still up to the job.'

Although this provoked a smile, Gerry didn't become

chattier. In the silent drive across town – trapped together in a family hatchback, the air heavy with all the things they weren't saying – Norman's over-riding thought was that he'd never been a passenger in Gerry's car before; that life had turned full circle from the time when he'd been the one driving Gerry home, a silent young boy bruised and scuffed up by school bullies.

'That's where it happened,' said Norman, as they pulled to a stop behind his car. He pointed to the spot in the road, nothing to suggest what had taken place – no broken glass, no blood stains. An act of senseless violence neatly erased, at complete odds with his own memory of it.

'It doesn't bear thinking about,' said Gerry. 'I'm just glad it wasn't worse.'

He waited while Norman heaved himself from the car, the pink jacket slipping into view as he took the bag from the back seat. Both men stared at it, its metallic fabric glowing despite the overcast day.

Norman tried to push it back out of sight; this needless reminder of the things he was not yet brave enough to do.

'Florence picked it out for me,' he said, struggling to hide it from view. 'I should have stopped her. I mean, imagine what it's like when the sun shines, I'll be blinding people.'

The jacket remained poking from the bag, refusing to fully disappear from Norman's life. Momentarily distracted, he smiled to himself as his fingers touched the fabric.

'The colour suits you,' said Gerry, looking as taken aback as Norman that he'd said it. 'And it's bold, isn't it? I don't think anything bad has ever come from being bold.'

'Well, put like that . . .' replied Norman. He felt himself blush, and even Gerry seemed lost for words, neither of them sure where to look.

'Anyway,' said Gerry, clearing his throat. 'Would you like me to follow you home? Just in case.'

'No, no, I'll be fine,' he replied, not noticing that he winced in pain as he said it. 'Give me a day or two, I'll be right as rain.'

There was no way to know when Norman would get home. Gerry had sent Florence a message to say he'd dropped Norman off at his car, but that was only useful information if Norman could be trusted to drive straight home – and, as one hour turned into two, it was clear that he couldn't.

Left with no other choice, Florence returned to her perch in the living room window, waiting such an eternity for Norman to come into view, when he did eventually pull up in the driveway she didn't know whether to be relieved or mad.

She was outside before he'd opened the car door. 'Where have you been?' she said, her transformation into middle-aged worrier now complete. 'I was going out of my mind.'

Moving more gingerly than normal, he began the slow process of extricating himself. 'I stopped at the shop on my way back. I was craving those chocolate biscuits, the buttery ones that melt in your mouth.'

'I could have got them for you,' she replied.

'But browsing the shelves is half the pleasure. It just took much longer than I expected, everything hurts.'

'That's because you're not supposed to be out shopping.' She started gathering up his bags. 'If the hospital wanted you to be running around, they'd have put you on a treadmill.'

'I can't sit around all day,' he said.

'Yes, you can. I'm here to look after you.' She walked with him, the two of them slowly progressing to the front door. 'I've already got it all planned. Lunch, dinner, the lot. I even got some extra for today, just in case Gerry joined us.'

'That would have been nice,' replied Norman, 'but I don't think he's quite ready to sit down and eat with me yet. Though to be fair, that's been the case for years. Long before he knew about Ethel.'

Florence was helping him through the front doorway when they heard the unmistakeable sound of Sally calling to them as she hurried across the street. 'Norman?' she said, her voice more fraught than usual. 'What on earth happened?'

'I was visiting Colchester,' he replied, not a moment's hesitation. 'I fell down a flight of steps.'

'What steps?' she said, her voice rising, a maelstrom of confusion and concern. 'Where in Colchester are these steps? At the very least we need to write a letter to the council.'

He suddenly sounded less sure of the lie. 'I think someone is already looking into that ... I just need to rest up for a day or two. Florence will be looking after me.'

Sally's eyes darted to the pink jacket sticking out of the bag, its metallic fabric sparkling in the light.

'Florence bought it the other day,' said Norman. 'Do you like it?'

Sally just stared at it, seemingly more confused by the jacket than Norman's injuries.

'I thought I might start experimenting with colour,' explained Florence, the words sounding preposterous coming from her mouth. 'But look, I should really be getting Granddad inside ...'

'Yes, yes, of course,' replied Sally, still appearing unsettled, as though life no longer made sense. 'Do let me know if you need anything. Anything at all.'

As she drifted away, Florence helped Norman across the threshold and closed the door behind them, order restored to their small universe.

'Ah,' said Norman with a happy sigh. 'Home sweet home.'

'So, do we have a deal? You do nothing for the rest of the week, and I'll run around like some medieval serf.'

Norman looked at her, evidently considering the possibility.

'What's for lunch?' he said.

'It's a surprise.'


Norman soon learned a fundamental truism: doing nothing at home is much nicer than doing nothing in hospital. There weren't lots of lovely nurses to chat with, but in every other sense it was a relief to be back in his own bed, surrounded by the reassuring clutter of everyday life. Even the draughty windows were a pleasure, a constant reminder that there was a big wide world outside and he was still a part of it.

Florence revealed herself to be a surprisingly good carer. There were extra pillows on his bed, and the radio was within easy reach so there need never be a dull moment. She'd even dug out one of Betty's old vases and filled it with flowers, the gesture making Betty feel present, too.

He was still admiring the flowers when Florence entered the room with a tray. 'Lunchtime,' she announced, lowering it onto his lap. 'It's just cheese on toast and some soup. Nothing special.'

'Don't be silly,' he replied. 'The cheese on toast looks lovely. Did you make it yourself?'

'Well, I sliced the cheese, if that's what you mean. Strictly speaking, the rest was done by thermodynamics.'

Norman tried a spoonful of soup. 'It's beautiful.'

'I definitely can't take any credit for that. It's from a tin.'

'But it takes skill to choose a good one, doesn't it? Not to mention heating it to the right temperature; not too cold, not too hot. Lots of people fail at things like that.'

They sat in silence, Norman eating under her watchful eye.

'I've found that friend of yours,' she said. 'Rex.'

Shocked, Norman stopped eating. 'How on earth did you manage that?'

'Let's just say it wasn't Twitter.' She handed him an address. 'He's in a place called Farnham.'

'I know it. Or know of it, at least. It's a bit posh, if I remember correctly.'

'If you want to write to him,' she said, 'I can sort it all out for you. I would have suggested we drive over there, but I'm heading back to uni the week after next.'

'We still have time,' he replied. This was met with a look of incredulity. 'I'll be fine in a day or two, your cooking alone will see to that.' Wanting to prove his point, he took another spoonful of soup. 'Honestly, I'm feeling better by the minute.'

Florence sighed, a smile on her face. '*Maybe* we can talk about it next week. For now, the only thing you're doing is resting.'

# 22.

In the days that followed, Norman made visible progress, his bruises deepening into purples and blues like late-stage supernovae exploding across his body, one era coming to an end so another could begin. It was harder for Florence to tell how he was actually *feeling* because he seemed determined to downplay all her concerns. She occasionally caught him wincing at some movement or other, but he would always claim it was his arthritis or his age or the approach of bad weather, as though his joints had barometric abilities. Certainly nothing to do with having been attacked.

It was after a few days that she noticed the biggest change in him: a studied nonchalance, so well-rehearsed she could only imagine he'd been practising it all week. 'I was thinking,' he said, as she cleared up after lunch. 'Maybe we could drive over to Farnham tomorrow.'

Florence stopped what she was doing, all the better to watch his body language. 'You haven't left the house in days,' she said. 'What makes you think you're up to a drive like that?'

'I feel fine,' he replied, raising his arms as proof of his total mobility. Perhaps feeling that a stronger sales pitch was needed, he stood up from the table, his face set like concrete, incapable of registering pain. 'See,' he gasped, trying not to wince. 'I'm in rude health.'

Florence glanced out the window, the skies over Clacton looking cold and leaden. 'I know it's not great weather for it, but we *could* go for an ice cream by the beach today.'

Norman's face lit up. 'That's a lovely idea.'

'But this is a probationary thing, do you understand? We'll go for ice cream and see how we get on. Bigger decisions can wait.'

Despite the overcast sky and chill wind, Norman and Florence arrived at the seafront to find that they were not the only ones eating ice cream; a motley band of strangers briefly united in that most English of all traditions: pretending that it's warmer than it actually is.

'It's nice to be back,' said Norman, as they settled on an empty bench. 'When I was in hospital, it felt like I might never get out. I would have paid all the money in the world just to come and sit here with an ice cream.' He was about to attack his cone when he stopped. 'I never asked you how your Mum got on in Newcastle.'

Florence hesitated. 'Oh, yeah, it was, er, fine, I think.'

'That's nice,' he replied, not appearing to notice anything unusual. 'I've been up that way plenty of times over the years.'

Down on the beach, three men started shouting out to sea, their drunken words unintelligible. The ice-cream eaters turned as one and watched as they staggered towards the shoreline, one man carrying the remains of a six-pack, another wrapped in the flag of England.

Norman seemed unnerved by them. 'See, that's why I'm never dressing as Ethel in public any more.'

'Don't say that,' said Florence.

'No, I mean it.' He watched them while he licked his ice cream. 'I was lucky to get off so lightly last time. There's no point tempting fate, is there?'

There was more yelling on the beach, the men's words lost to the wind.

'Losers,' muttered Florence.

Norman took a more sympathetic tone. 'Back in the old days,

young men like that would have been working at this time of day, but there just aren't the opportunities any more. It sometimes seems like you need a PhD just to work at the supermarket.'

Florence rolled her eyes. 'Granddad, that's totally not true.'

'But you know what I mean,' he replied. 'I often think this country has demonised the working classes; if you can't be a banker or a lawyer, you just get shunted to one side and forgotten. It's no surprise young men like that end up feeling lost and angry. It's funny, there are some houses up the coast that are crumbling into the sea and everyone's up in arms about it, but no one seems to care that the economy fell off a cliff years ago.' They watched as the men gave up shouting, instead collapsing onto the sand to focus on their beer. 'I did tell you, didn't I, how much Betty loved the encyclopedia? She was always dipping into it and sharing something new. I remember her getting very worked up by Eskimos having so many words for snow.'

'They're called Inuit these days,' said Florence.

Norman nodded, another piece of information destined to be forgotten. 'As far as Betty was concerned, it was just proof that they had too much time on their hands. She didn't mean anything bad by it. I think she was worried about their mental health as much as anything. If they had all that time to think up so many words for snow, they surely had time to dwell on their problems, too. It's never good to dwell on things.'

'Granddad, where is this going?'

'The Eskimos? Nothing. Nothing at all. It was this other time I wanted to tell you about. I remember it as clear as day: me and Betty were watching one of those crime dramas on telly. A bit of a nail biter, actually. There was this middle-aged man drowning – screaming and thrashing around so much, it probably would have taken less effort to just swim to shore. But I remember really feeling for the bloke, because he started to see his whole life flash before him, and it turned out he'd always loved someone, but now he'd never have a chance to tell her. And right then, just as I thought I might get a bit weepy, Betty said "That's not how people drown." Just like that, so matter of fact I wondered if she'd even been paying attention to the story. He was still going under when she explained that she'd read it in the encyclopedia, that in real life people drown quietly. Apparently, the body goes into a sort of paralysis. People don't raise their arms or shout, they just quietly sink. I can't tell you how the show ended, but that titbit has stayed with me. I've often thought you could say the same thing of this town, maybe the whole country: people drowning in plain sight, while everyone else goes about their daily lives, none the wiser.'

'That's pretty profound,' replied Florence, still eating her ice cream.

'Betty was good at finding things like that. I've tried looking through the encyclopedia since she passed, but it's not the same.' He smiled at the sound of gulls crying overhead. 'She used to love sitting here with an ice cream.'

'By the way, I've made my peace with going to Farnham,' said Florence. 'If you think you're ready, that's all that matters.'

'Physically, yes,' he replied. 'In every other sense, I doubt I'll ever be ready. The thought of seeing Rex again is a bit daunting, to be honest.'

'Remind me, how long has it been?'

Norman sighed. 'Oh, a long, long time. I was only twenty.'

'So, around the same time you met Gran?'

There was something about the question that seemed to trouble Norman. Florence watched him, familiar now with his dissemblance.

Eyes fixed firmly on the horizon, he stood up. 'We should probably get going, eh? It's starting to feel a little nippy out here.'

# 23.

Even though they hadn't been on any driving lessons in recent days, Norman was impressed by the way Florence handled the journey to Farnham, her driving finally beginning to reflect the confident, self-assured adult he knew her to be. That's not to say, however, that the entire journey was plain sailing. They were nearing Farnham when she stalled on a busy roundabout, the driver behind them instantly voicing his anger in a blare of horn.

'Oops,' said Florence, as she calmly put the car back in first gear.

'Not to worry,' replied Norman. 'The most important thing is not to get flustered.' Tired of waiting, the driver behind swerved around them, slowing down just long enough as he passed to yell something and flick a finger. Norman tutted as the man sped off. 'And definitely don't let someone like *that* get to you.'

Florence looked unfazed. 'Granddad, that man's tiny dick is not my problem.'

Unsure how to respond to that, but certain that a pep talk wasn't needed, Norman let her get on with things; noticing, for the first time, that her jewellery – something he'd struggled over when they first met – actually gave her the air of a warrior.

'I never asked any more about that boyfriend of yours,' he said, once they were on the move again.

'*Ex*-boyfriend,' she replied.

'But you never told me why you broke up.'

'Oh, God, more a case of why did we stay together so long? I'll start by saying this: a man should never quote Maya Angelou in the hope of getting laid. And definitely not when he thinks Maya Angelou is a white woman from France.' Although Norman didn't know what she was talking about, he could tell by the brittleness of her smile that it wasn't the main reason. Sure enough, it began to fade. 'The thing was, he had this habit of belittling me. I mean, it was super, super subtle; I didn't even notice it at first. I don't even know how to describe it, really. It was, like, these tiny, almost invisible put-downs. Like a constant pick-pick-pick that I didn't catch on to for . . . months.'

'What a terrible person,' said Norman.

'Yeah, but really good at hiding it. A really nice terrible person.' She began to look more comfortable with the subject; the simple act of talking about it helping to soothe the memory. 'The thing is, it wasn't really *him* that shook my confidence, it was the fact that I found myself in that position at all. I mean, I know there are plenty of douchebags out there, but I'd just always assumed I'd be able to spot them coming from a mile off.'

'And still he wanted you to meet his family? That's what I don't understand.'

Florence shrugged. 'I guess some people have different standards for happiness. For all I know, that's the kind of marriage his parents have. Or, you know, maybe he just really is a bell-end. Either way, I deserve better than that.'

She said it so matter-of-factly, it took Norman a moment to process the enormity of what she'd just said.

'I think that's the nicest thing I've ever heard,' he replied, welling up with pride.

She flashed a smile at him. 'We all have to stand up for ourselves, right?'

'That's the kind of thing Suzie would have said. I hope I can introduce you one day, I really do. Rex was older than the rest of us, so if he's still around, Suzie must be.'

'Who knows,' she replied. 'You might have her details in a few minutes. We're almost there.'

'Oh, don't, I'm on tenterhooks, I don't know where to put myself.' Needing a distraction, any distraction, he looked out at the neighbourhood, as impeccably groomed and well-to-do as he'd expected. 'Betty was always suspicious of gardens that are too neat,' he said, trying to chase away his nerves with mindless chatter. 'She used to think it was just a cover for all manner of excesses. No one's going to look at flower beds like that and think the owner is indoors smoking opium, but who's to know? If you can afford a good gardener, it stands to reason you can afford the drugs. Rex will have a neat garden, I can promise you that. Possibly a few opium pipes, too. He'll probably have an entire opium den in the basement and a four-storey pleasure palace atop that.'

'Or not,' replied Florence, pulling to a stop outside Rex's house: not the Georgian pile of yesteryear, but rather a bungalow. An expensive bungalow, its garden as meticulous as any of the neighbours', but a bungalow nevertheless.

Norman's face sank. 'When you think of that house of his in London. And now to end up here . . .'

'What's wrong with it?' said Florence. 'I'd love to live in a house like that.'

'He is getting on, of course. I suppose a bungalow is much more practical at his age.'

'Granddad, it's a beautiful house. Even the front gate looks expensive.' She looked down at her clothes. 'I'm suddenly feeling very under-dressed. I feel like I should have made more of an effort.'

'Oh, you don't need to worry about things like that with Rex. If he's anything like he was when I knew him, you could turn up in pearls and a fur coat and he'd still judge you.' This did nothing to calm her concerns, but at least she got out of the car, trailing behind Norman as he walked up to the front door. 'The important thing is to spend enough time making small talk first. I don't want him to think that I've only come to ask about Suzie.'

'Even though you basically have,' she replied.

'Well, yes, I suppose so. But Rex was a good friend, too.'

They stood in silence as he rang the bell, a solemn *ding-dong* booming through the house.

'I feel like I'm about to start a new school,' said Florence.

Norman nodded. 'In many ways, you are.'

From inside, there was the sound of slow, heavy footsteps growing louder and louder, until finally the door opened to reveal a man of advanced years, his entire bodyweight seeming to balance on a thick wooden walking stick. For a few seconds, he and Norman stared at one another.

'Hello, Rex. It's been a while.'

The man's eyes grew wider. 'Heavens above. If it isn't Ethel Cartwright.'

# 24.

Rex led them through the parqueted hallway, each small step accompanied by the thud of his walking stick and the slow shuffling of feet.

'Please forgive the smell in here,' he said. 'My new housekeeper is excessively literal. She can't believe something's clean unless it smells like a chemical spillage.'

'Have you lived here long?' said Norman, still appearing unsure of himself.

'Oh, who knows any more. The decades blur after a while.' They reached the living room. In one corner, a grand piano, a sea of silver-framed photographs on top. 'Please, make yourselves at home,' he said, crumpling into a well-worn armchair, a glass of water beside him. He watched as they took a seat on the sofa. 'I see the family resemblance. You've evidently been keeping yourself busy.'

'Two children, three grandchildren,' replied Norman. 'Florence here is the youngest.'

Rex lit up. 'The baby of the family! How splendid.'

'She's a physicist,' added Norman, proudly.

Florence laughed. 'Sorry, I think he wants to tell everyone that.'

'Then you have no choice but to bask in the attention,' replied Rex, giving her such a disarming smile, it was impossible not to like him.

Norman gestured at the piano. 'You still have it, after all these years.'

'And I *still* don't know how to play, that's the madness of it. I got it for Ronnie. You remember Ronnie, don't you? Tall, German, impossibly handsome.' He turned back to Florence, becoming enlivened in her presence. 'The fact that Ronnie was German was *utterly* scandalous when we first met. We were just out of the war, the country was in ruins.'

'But why?' she replied. 'It's not like all Germans were the enemy.'

'But that's the thing, he was. He'd been held in a POW camp near Portsmouth. When the war ended, he decided to stay. Quite a few did. I mean, many of them had nothing to go back to, but it was more than that. It was a chance to start again, I suppose. To live a different life. And for the most part, they were made to feel welcome, that was the beautiful thing. It's just some people didn't feel that way. Like my mother, for instance.'

'She didn't like Ronnie?' said Florence.

'Oh, my dear, she *hated* him. She'd always dreamt that one day I'd just butch up and marry some young Sloane called Patricia or Caroline or whatever, so being with a man was always going to be a bit of a problem, but the fact that he was *German* ...' He took a sip of his water. 'To be fair, I could understand it to some extent. She'd lost her husband in the Second World War, and two brothers in the First. But that was precisely why I thought it was all right. We can't hate forever, can we? Otherwise we just keep repeating the same mistakes ad infinitum.'

Florence glanced at Norman, his expression so blank, it was hard to tell if he was dazed by meeting Rex or simply biding his time until he could ask about Suzie.

'Did your mother come around in time?' she asked Rex.

'Lord, no!' he replied. 'She never met him, not once. I think she took it with her to her grave, this dense little knot of hatred. I can't tell you how many times she threatened to disown me in favour of my sister, though of course I inherited everything in the end. You have to marvel at the English upper classes: being a sodomite and sleeping with the enemy was still considered better than being a woman.' He reached for his glass of water, then stopped. 'Gosh, my manners. Can I offer you a drink?'

'A cup of tea would be nice,' said Norman.

Rex gave him a withering look. 'Really, Ethel, why can't you make an old man's life easier by having a martini?'

'It's a bit early for that, isn't it?'

'I'm reliably informed,' replied Rex, 'that even Her Majesty the Queen – may she rest in peace – was on her second gin by noon. And you know what they say, imitation is the sincerest form of flattery.' He picked up his glass and took another mouthful. 'Not to mention, I'm almost ready for a refill.'

Norman stared aghast. 'I thought that was water.'

'Good Christ, no. The beauty of gin is that you can trust its purity. Unlike tap water, which, lest we forget, has come dripping from every orifice of every man, woman and child this side of the English Channel.'

'I can make us some tea,' said Florence. 'I'm driving, so no gin for me.'

'Well, if you insist,' replied Rex. 'The kitchen's out there on the left.'

Rex waited until Florence had left the room. 'My goodness,' he said, excitedly. 'Isn't she a total darling?'

'She is,' replied Norman. 'One of my better accomplishments. One of my few.'

'How did your family react when they found out about Ethel?'

Norman shifted in his seat. 'Well, I'm not really sure you could say they *know*, exactly.'

'Ah,' said Rex. 'Still in the closet, then?'

'Florence knows everything. She's been lovely. And my wife, Betty, I did tell her. Though whether she really *knew* it ...'

'Time passes regardless, that's the thing, isn't it? Happy, sad, accepting, resentful; the clock keeps ticking and we're all dead in the end.' He drained his glass and held it out. 'Would you be a saint and fix me another?' Norman looked at Rex as if he'd just asked him to perform a miracle. 'Ethel, making a martini is like riding a bicycle. Once you've learnt, it's impossible to forget, it's a basic fact of nature.'

'I'm not sure I ever knew in the first place.'

Rex glowered. 'I want it known that I consider that a terrible insult. It's *utterly* impossible that we were friends and I failed to teach you.' He hauled himself from his armchair. 'Though I daresay my nurse would be grateful that you're forcing me to move about.'

'I think she'd be less impressed that you're only moving to the gin.'

'She knows me better than that,' replied Rex. 'And movement is movement, surely? There's no point being a fascist about it.' He poured a hefty measure of gin into a cocktail shaker, adding the merest touch of vermouth – more of an anointing than an actual addition of liquid. 'I find it comforting to know that, even if dementia sets in, I'm more likely to forget my own name than how to do this. It really is that simple, Ethel.'

Despite his limited mobility, he finished mixing the drink and carried it back to his chair with a surprising ease.

'Cheers,' he said, taking a mouthful.

Norman tried to strike a casual tone. 'I was thinking of Suzie the other day. Are you still in touch?'

'Oh, my poor Ethel. I imagined you knew. I'm afraid Suzie's long, long gone. Dead for more than sixty years.' Norman felt the ground sway beneath him, Rex's voice becoming more distant. 'We tried to reach you at the time, but you'd disappeared. Needless to say, the family didn't want any of her friends at the funeral. Most of all me, of course.'

'But I don't understand,' he said. 'What happened? She must have died so young.'

For once, Rex looked lost for words. 'I'm afraid it was a sad, sad ending. I can tell you if you really want to know, but I think it's a much kinder thing to remember her as she was.'


The kitchen was decades beyond its prime: cupboards and work-tops that were doubtless top of the range in the 1980s had taken on a faded quality, not worn out so much as neglected: party-size serving platters sitting unwanted; tureens quietly gathering dust.

If the room had any purpose now, it was mostly palliative, Rex's carers having commandeered several cupboards for pills and bandages and the accoutrements of old age. There was no dust on those.

When Florence finally returned to the living room with two cups of tea, the change in mood was unmistakeable.

'I'm sure that will help,' remarked Rex, as Florence handed Norman a cup and saucer.

'What's wrong?' she said, alarmed by the slump of Norman's shoulders.

'It's Suzie,' he replied. 'It turns out she's been gone for a long time already.'

'Oh, I'm so sorry.'

He tried to put a brave face on it. 'Well, better to know, eh?'

This provoked murmured agreement from Rex and Florence, the room fading into a respectful silence while Norman sought solace in his tea.

Rex caught Florence's eye. 'How did you get on out there?'

'It was fine,' she replied. 'Everything is very well organised.'

'A little too organised, if you ask me. It's all order, but no soul any more.'

'It does feel like the kitchen isn't used much.'

'Exactly,' said Rex, bursting back into life. 'It's a tragedy, isn't it? But it's seen some riotous days in its time. I'm inclined to think that's the best any of us can say in the end.'

'Do you not cook at all?' said Norman, briefly resurfacing from his sorrow to make it sound like he was an enthusiastic home chef.

'Someone delivers a hot meal every lunchtime,' replied Rex. 'It's not exactly haute cuisine, but it does the job. After Ronnie died, my heart gave out – in every sense – and that's when the party stopped. My only visitors these days are the nurse, the housekeeper, the gardener, and so on and so forth.'

'There are more?' said Florence.

Rex gestured vaguely, as though even he'd long since lost count. 'What can I say? It takes a village. And I'm eternally grateful to them, that goes without saying. But dear God, they're all so boring. Suzie's sister used to visit quite often, but neither of us are especially mobile these days.'

Norman looked up from his tea. 'I never knew she had a sister.'

'None of us did. Suzie's family had cut her off years before, but after everything that happened, the sister reached out to me. It was guilt, I suppose, but over time we became close. Almost like family, really. She was one of the reasons I moved to this neck of the woods.'

Florence looked from Rex to Norman and back again, realising only now that there were important gaps in her understanding. 'What do you mean "after everything that happened"? Why did Suzie's family cut her off?'

'Because it was the fifties,' replied Rex. 'A different world to this one. As starchy and strait-laced as any before it. You have to remember, for the older generation, Queen Victoria was still in living memory.'

'Okay ...' she said, still confused. 'So, Suzie's family didn't approve of her being transgender?'

'They weren't really the kind of people to approve of anything. I'm not even sure they knew the full details about Suzie, not until we were arrested, anyway.'

Florence gasped. 'Arrested?'

'Has your grandfather not told you about that?' He turned to Norman. 'Really, Ethel, how could you fail to mention something so important?'

'What was that?' he replied, too mired in sadness to keep pace with the conversation.

Rex spoke more softly. 'I know your pain, Ethel. I felt it myself for the longest time.'

'I'd like to visit Suzie's grave,' he said. 'I want to pay my respects.'

Rex chose his words with more care than before. 'Her sister can sort you out with the details. She's in a nursing home not far from here. You may as well go and see her while you're in the area. Better that than make two trips.'

'Do you think it will be all right?' said Norman. 'She won't mind us turning up unannounced?'

Rex began to laugh. 'Good grief, no. Once you've met June, you'll realise that's *exactly* what she'd want you to do.'

# 25.

They hadn't even reached the car when Florence suggested they find somewhere for a cup of tea. Norman had only just finished one at Rex's, but Florence knew him well enough to understand that the drink itself wasn't the point; there was something therapeutic in the process, each new cup offering the promise of comfort. Norman appeared to need industrial doses of that right now: ever since learning about Suzie, there'd been a noticeable deflation in his posture; even now, he leant against the car as though needing it for support.

'I'm sure we can find somewhere nice,' said Florence.

'I don't know about that,' he replied, looking up and down that one residential street as if it was representative of all streets everywhere, an eternal purgatory of expensive cars and well-manicured herbaceous borders.

Deciding that Norman was in no frame of mind to be given options, Florence found somewhere online, first driving them closer before leading Norman on foot through the streets of Farnham as if she'd lived there her entire life.

'*Et voilà*,' she said, as the café came into view. It wasn't Florence's usual kind of haunt – shabby chic, unashamedly upbeat – but there was no point explaining this to Norman, who by that point didn't even seem to be aware of his surroundings.

She left him in peace until their drinks had been brought to the table, the teapot's mere proximity to Norman appearing to have an analgesic effect.

'How are you feeling?' she said.

'Oh, I'm fine,' he replied, the words sounding so much like a sigh, it was impossible for them to be true.

'Rex is a character.'

'Isn't he? It was strange to see him looking so old, but in every other way, he's exactly as I remember. That's another reason the news about Suzie hit me so hard. If Rex can still be just like the old days, it makes me think that Suzie would have been the same. It's a shame you won't get to meet her, she was a rare kind. I used to wish I had half her confidence. Not to mention her optimism. You could have given her lemons and all she would have seen was a bowl of fruit.'

The conversation trailed off, the reminiscence only seeming to make him sadder.

Florence spoke more gently. 'Did Rex say how it happened?'

'Not the details, but enough to know it was an unhappy ending.'

Under different circumstances, Florence would have stopped there, would have left Norman to his grief, but there were still unanswered questions.

'What was that about them being arrested?' she said.

'It was a police raid,' he replied. 'They were quite common back in those days.'

'But arrested for what?'

'I suppose it would have been gross indecency,' said Norman. 'But that didn't really mean anything. It was just a catch-all phrase for everything that was considered different to the norm. I suppose they both spent time in prison after that.'

'Wow,' said Florence. 'I can't picture someone like Rex in prison.'

'Or Suzie. Let's not forget, she would have been locked up with the men.' He added yet another spoonful of sugar to his tea, as though sweetness was something prone to dissipate. For a while, he just sat there stirring it, gazing into its ripples and eddies. 'The thing is,' he said, finally, 'I was supposed to have been with them that night. It was only a fluke that I wasn't there. To think I could have ended up in prison, too.'

'For cross-dressing?' she replied.

'It wasn't really *what* you did in those days, it was *who* you did it with.'

'That doesn't sound very fair.'

'Ah, well,' said Norman, with a sigh. 'None of us expected *fair*, that's just how it was back then. They were difficult times. It's one of the reasons I'd hoped that Suzie was still around. I wanted to tell her that she'd been a good friend. Wanted to tell her lots of things, I suppose. About Betty and the kids. About how life's been since I last saw her.' He stared into his tea. 'Though I suppose most of all I wanted to tell her that I'm sorry.'

Florence leant closer. 'Sorry for what?'

# Forty-three years earlier

## 1979

It was supposed to be a family holiday, but Norman couldn't shake the feeling that it was the end of an era. The end of multiple eras, in fact, all of which had somehow managed to converge on a single moment in time, giving the family's annual summer getaway the kind of deep profundity that one wouldn't normally associate with a holiday camp.

It didn't help that the 1980s were fast approaching and Norman found himself spending more and more time worrying about what they might bring – hadn't the twists and turns of the 40s, 50s, 60s and 70s already been enough? And yet here they were, marching towards yet another decade and the winds of change were already beginning to blow: the country had just elected its first woman Prime Minister – a *woman!* – and now the talk was of reining in the unions and pushing the country in a new, uncharted direction.

Closer to home, too, change was in the air. Gerry had just turned seventeen and although Norman didn't like to admit it, it seemed likely that this would be their last holiday together as a family. Gerry had already made no secret of not wanting to join them on this trip, seizing every opportunity to explain why he disliked the very notion of a holiday camp, let alone the one they'd chosen, which somehow managed to take everything he hated about the concept and condense it into several acres of unremarkable countryside. And yet every time that Gerry railed against this flagrant compromise of his dearest values, all Norman could think was that he'd been called up for National Service at Gerry's age; that he would have given his eye teeth to swap that experience for two weeks of fancy-dress parties and knobbly-knee competitions.

At least his eleven-year-old sister got into the spirit of things, seeing every experience as another step on her journey to a fairytale wedding with a handsome Prince Charming – until Gerry ruined that, too, by explaining in torturous detail that not only would she never meet a real prince at a holiday camp, the mere fact that she'd stayed at one would forever leave her tainted in the eyes of high society.

If such a thing was possible, even the camp itself seemed to know that the world was changing. With ever more holidaymakers tempted away by a fortnight in Majorca, there were noticeably fewer people than in earlier years. Their absence gave the place a strange air of finality, not helped by the frequent rain.

To her credit, however, none of this stopped Betty enjoying herself. In the same way that an asteroid slams into the planet regardless of how people are feeling, so too Betty arrived at the holiday camp determined to have a good time, and no amount of existential angst – from her children, her husband, or the world at large – was going to stand in her way. This was expressed in a daily ritual that was as simple as it was effective: after breakfasting on bacon and eggs that other people had cooked, and spending the morning at bingo while someone else made her bed, she would call in at the bar for a pre-lunch sherry, bookended by a post-lunch shandy. This was always followed by a round of crazy golf or an afternoon nap – sometimes even both – until, later still, after enjoying a dinner that had been conceived, cooked and served by others, the day would end with a graceful decline into a sea of rum and blackcurrant, preferably while the camp's live band played jitterbug and boogie-woogie tunes from her salad days.

Carried through those two weeks on a leisurely wave of inebriation, Betty became a softer, more relaxed version of herself, impervious to things that would have irritated her at home. Even the camp's inevitable Topsy Turvy Party – a night of drunken gender reversal – was simply a chance to have fun. Never mind that Norman would be spending the entire evening dressed as a woman, all that mattered was that every other man at the camp would be doing the same.

'What if I don't want to dress as a girl?' said Gerry, whose revulsion at the holiday had taken on new proportions ever since the Glamorous Granny Contest a couple of nights earlier. 'Why can't I just stay in the chalet and read?'

'Because we're on holiday,' replied Betty. 'You're obliged to have fun even if you don't want to.'

Cigarette hanging from her mouth, she busied herself preparing their outfits: for her, a man's pin-stripe suit and tie, while his sister would be dressed as a prepubescent brickie, the implication of it clear; the new Prime Minister might be a woman, but everyone knew that only a man could work in construction.

Given that Betty had chosen a pink polka dot dress for Gerry, his lack of enthusiasm was perhaps understandable, but it wasn't as if the experience had come as a total surprise; there'd been a Topsy Turvy Party every year that they'd stayed there.

Undeterred, Gerry turned to Norman for backup. 'Father, did we learn nothing from the Nuremberg Trials? Just because everyone else is doing it, that doesn't mean we have to join in.'

Norman was too busy putting on lipstick to give an immediate reply. In those few seconds, applying makeup while the whole family watched, he kept telling himself to be more heavy-handed than usual; to make it look like this was as unfamiliar and uncomfortable to him as a pink polka dot dress was to Gerry.

'Your mother's right,' he said, as he puckered his lips. 'It's just a bit of fun.'

Unlike my dress, he thought to himself. It was the same thing he'd worn for previous Topsy Turvy Parties: one of Betty's old maternity dresses that she'd taken in only slightly, so that the overall effect was of a middle-aged man drowning in a floral polyester sack. Every time he put it on, it was hard not to imagine that Betty had chosen it on purpose, wanting to make sure that he didn't enjoy the party too much. Lord knows what Suzie would say if she could see him dressed like that: participating in a public mockery of himself, and yet doing it wilfully because it was still the closest he could ever get to feeling accepted.

In the background, Gerry continued frowning – at his dress, at Norman, possibly even at the nature of life itself.

'Come on,' said Betty. 'You've got to get in the spirit of things.'

'Like Dad?' replied Gerry.

Betty hesitated, not helped by the fact Norman was applying mascara at that moment, smiling to himself at every tiny brushstroke. Worried that his makeup was still looking too practised, he clumsily daubed on some blusher, instantly replacing Ethel with a pantomime caricature.

'How do I look?' he said, turning to face them.

Betty regarded him through a veil of smoke, her expression giving nothing away. 'Believe you me,' she said, finally. 'You look utterly ridiculous.'

# 26.

'I don't want to judge a book by its cover,' said Florence, as they arrived at the old people's home. 'But this place looks kind of bleak.'

Norman stared at the squat, grey building. 'It is a bit joyless,' he replied, nevertheless feeling an odd kinship with it. Knowing, in fact, that if he was to be translated into an architectural form at that moment, he would look something similar. 'I'm sure it's better on the inside than out.'

This, as it turned out, wasn't entirely accurate. The place wasn't *bad* as such – the residents weren't chained to their beds or crawling in their own filth – it was more the absence of anything good. It was functional, practical; suited to the needs of its residents in the same way, say, that a baggage carousel is suited to luggage, simply moving it onwards to its final destination.

A nurse led Norman and Florence through one of the dayrooms, most of the people in there watching them pass in a mixture of interest and disappointment. They continued down a long corridor towards yet another lounge, this one dominated by the sound of a daytime soap opera. Only one person in the room was facing away from the television, her wheelchair angled towards a window overlooking the garden; a woman of such age and frailty, Norman felt young in her presence.

The nurse crouched beside her, speaking in the loud, slow voice that people so often use with the elderly. 'June, you have visitors.'

'I'm not . . .' Breathless, she pressed a mask to her face, a plastic

162

tube coiling down to a ventilator at her feet. After a long, rattling inhalation, she tried again. 'I'm not deaf, for Christ's sake.'

'That's lovely,' the nurse replied, still speaking too loudly. 'I'll leave you to it, then.'

As she hastened away, June sized up her guests. 'Who are you?'

'Rex gave us your address,' said Norman. 'I was a friend of Suzie's.'

June reacted to the name, possibly hadn't heard it said aloud in a long, long time. 'That must have been many moons ago.'

'I know,' he replied. 'Time flies, doesn't it?'

'Not in here.' She started to wheeze, and gave her chest a gentle thump. 'It's the fags that did it. Such a dirty habit.' She turned to Florence, hopeful. 'Do you have one, by any chance?'

Florence gestured apologetically. 'Sorry, I don't smoke.'

On the other side of the room, the soap opera cut to a commercial break, a roomful of elderly people now staring at an advert for adventure holidays.

'If you'll be my chauffeur,' said June, 'we can talk in my room.'

'Sure,' replied Florence, getting into position behind her wheelchair. 'Point the way.'

June did so literally, keeping her arm outstretched as they advanced across the sea of orthopaedic armchairs and onwards down another nondescript corridor.

Having seen the rest of the building, Norman was hopeful that June's room would be an oasis of sorts, but it had the same utilitarian air as everywhere else, only more cluttered: an entire lifetime reduced to a space barely big enough for a bed, a wardrobe and a chair. If all the bedrooms in the building looked like hers, the place wasn't a nursing home so much as a large bonfire waiting to be lit.

'My life has gone from a cow to an Oxo cube,' she said as Norman closed the door behind them. With a wheezing gasp, she somehow managed to stand upright. Florence rushed to help, but

June shooed her away. 'This is my only act of independence.' For a few seconds, she stood there, wavering in some unseen breeze, before taking a small step forward and collapsing onto her bed. Once settled, she beckoned Florence to come sit beside her. 'And you can have the armchair,' she said to Norman. 'Though you should be aware, someone probably died in it.'

'After a day like mine, it might be me next. I've only just heard about Suzie. I didn't know she was gone.'

'Ah,' replied June, sadly. 'Unfortunately, there was no happily ever after for Suzie.' Her gaze drifted around the room. 'I'm sure I have some pictures somewhere.'

'Really?' he said. 'I'd love to see them.'

'Me too,' she replied, appearing increasingly confused by the clutter. 'It's those damned nurses, moving things and meddling.' She pointed at a bookshelf. 'Could you pass me that box?' Florence only had to take two steps to reach it, carrying it back to the bed and putting it down beside June. 'I think this is the one.' She lifted its dusty lid and squinted at its contents, seeming more confused as she pulled out a sheet of paper and handed it to Florence. 'What does that say?'

Florence scanned through it. 'It's for a hospital appointment. Six years ago.'

'Then it's safe to say I've missed it.' She put the letter back, replacing the lid with a defeated air. 'See, it's the nurses. Worse than leprechauns. At least a leprechaun might get me some cigarettes.'

'It would be lovely to see a picture,' said Norman. 'We can help you sort through things.'

June waved the offer away. 'You'd never know it to look at it, but I've got quite a few things of Suzie's. When she died, my parents wanted to throw them all away.' She wheezed into her ventilator. 'I tried to save as much as I could, but you know how it goes.'

'We were good friends for a while,' said Norman. 'I never knew she had a sister.'

June looked saddened. 'We weren't close back then, though I wish we had been. Sometimes you only realise how bright a light was when it goes out.'

Norman allowed his gaze to linger on the stained carpet tiles before getting down to business. 'Rex said you could tell me where she's buried. I'd like to go and pay my respects.'

The atmosphere in the room shifted. June stared at Norman with a puzzled expression. 'Rex said that?'

'Yes.'

'He didn't tell you where Suzie's buried?'

'No,' he replied.

'And you *really* want to visit the grave?'

'I wouldn't be here otherwise. No offense.'

June hesitated, the air in the room unexpectedly tense. 'It's in Cornwall,' she said. 'Suzie's buried in Cornwall.'

Norman sat back, astounded. 'Why on earth is she buried all the way down there?'

'We spent every summer there as kids,' she replied.

'But it's miles away. It's the other end of the country.'

'Looking on the bright side,' said Florence, 'it would be good practice for my driving.'

'You don't need to drive the length and breadth of England to get that.' He turned back to June. 'I have to be honest with you, I doubt we'll ever go down there, but if you could tell me where in Cornwall she's buried, I can at least consider it.'

'For the life of me, I can't remember the name. And there's no point looking, is there?' She gestured at the room again, visual confirmation that some tasks were out of the question. 'But I can show you, if you'll take me.'

# 27.

Despite Norman's earlier sadness, the drive home was anything but quiet and mournful.

'Drive her to Cornwall!' he said, for what felt like the hundredth time. 'The madness of it. Hand on my heart, I doubt she'd survive a trip like that.'

'It's really not that far,' replied Florence.

'It's the very end of the country! It's the last stop before America.'

'Yes, but that doesn't mean it's *near* America.'

Norman looked unmoved. 'Did you not see, she practically died just moving from her wheelchair to her bed. Imagine if she died on the way to Cornwall. We'd not only have a dead body in the car, we *still* wouldn't know where Suzie's grave is.'

'Considering you both want the same thing,' said Florence, 'I think you're being very hard on her.'

Norman scoffed. 'Don't forget, you'll be the one having to help her to the toilet every thirty minutes. Who knows how much assistance she might need in there.'

'And I'd like to remind you, this is Suzie's sister we're talking about. If you don't want to do it for June, maybe you could consider doing it for Suzie's sake.'

This at least dampened his ire. 'I was hoping there'd be a stronger family resemblance. That it would feel like seeing Suzie in old age, but it wasn't like that at all.'

'You can hardly blame June for that,' said Florence. 'That's like when Mum complains I take after Dad in the looks department. Like I'm wilfully manipulating my genes just to stress her out.'

Perhaps aware that he was in the wrong, Norman shrugged the comment off. 'That's not what I meant. I just wish June had a bit more of Suzie about her, that's all.'

'And I'm trying to remind you, they're still family. This could be a great chance to learn more about Suzie's childhood. You'll be able to add some of June's memories to your own.'

Norman appeared to consider her point. 'Well, true,' he said. 'I hadn't thought of it that way. But we're still not going to Cornwall.'


Having learnt that a dear old friend was dead, it seemed wrong to Norman to have his favourite beef stew for dinner, and yet what was the alternative? Surely, by eating something he was less keen on, he would only be compounding the day's disappointments? Should he celebrate Suzie's life by cooking something he loved, or mourn her death by opening that one last can of pork casserole, the one with lumps of gristle and slimy mushrooms?

After choosing the beef stew – he would dedicate the pleasure to Suzie's memory – he emptied two tins into a saucepan and set about heating them up, staring at the gloop as it slowly began to bubble and steam. Florence was still in her room when he finally started plating it up.

'Dinner,' he shouted, calling up at the ceiling, waiting for the tell-tale creak of a floorboard to confirm that she'd heard.

Silence.

He went out to the hallway and shouted up the stairs. 'Florence, dinner's ready.'

And still nothing.

Deciding that there was no need to worry – she was nineteen, after all, not to mention up a steep flight of stairs – he returned to the kitchen. He was putting their plates of stew on the table when Florence joined him.

'Sorry,' she said, breezing into the room. 'I was on the phone to Mum.'

Norman brightened. 'Oh, yes? How is she?'

'Fine,' replied Florence, saying it as dismissively as always; not an answer, a brick wall.

Norman tried to let it go, but after a day like his, there was no energy left for artifice. 'Whenever we talk about your mother, I always get the feeling you're not telling me something.'

Seeming unperturbed by the question, Florence started eating. 'Look, you asked me not to tell her about you and I've respected that. But you need to understand that maybe there are things about *her* privacy that I also have to respect.'

Norman put down his fork. 'What has privacy got to do with it? We're family.'

Florence snorted. 'And that doesn't make you think *pot, kettle, black?*'

'But Ethel isn't the same! Ethel is something I do behind closed doors in my own home.'

'Which is what Mum might say about, I don't know ... wearing the same sweatpants for weeks on end. Even though they're covered in the stains of everything she's been eating for the last month.'

It took Norman a moment to realise what she'd just said. 'Are things really that bad?'

'Look, I've already said too much.'

'But things can't be that bad. You said she went to Newcastle recently.'

Florence looked guilty. 'I lied. Mum didn't go away.'

'Florence!'

'I said it for your sake. I didn't want your feelings to get hurt.'

This only confused him more. 'Why would they get hurt?' he said.

'Because she doesn't *want* to see you. Haven't you realised that yet? She's been avoiding you for years.' The words seemed to make her just as sad as they did him. 'Look, you do need to reach out to her, but you can only do it as *you*, the real you, not the person you've been trying to be all these years. She won't talk to that Norman. She doesn't like that Norman.'

He winced at her choice of words. 'That's a bit strong, isn't it?'

'Be honest, Granddad. Do *you* like that Norman?'

'Well, put like that . . .' he said, with a sigh.

Florence reached over the table and took his hand in hers. 'By all means, make contact with Mum. But only if you're ready to be honest.'

'The other Florence in my life,' he replied.

Even in her sadness, she smiled. 'Don't let her catch you saying that. She never uses her full name.'

'Oh, I'm used to that,' he said. 'She's been like that since she was a child. But maybe it's just as well, eh? It means I'll only ever have one Florence in my life. Just like I only have one Flo.'

# FLO

# 28.

Norman peered out through rain-soaked windows as they neared Flo's place, the council estate rising around them in bleak monolithic tower blocks. 'I don't remember it looking quite like this,' he said. 'Though I suppose it's better when the sun is shining.'

'Not really,' replied Florence. 'If anything, the rain washes away some of the grime.'

'How does it feel to be back?'

'Weird. When I left here I was dragging my bags to the bus stop, and look at me now.'

'Yes, behind the wheel of a car,' said Norman, albeit one with several new scratches and a missing wing mirror. 'You did a lovely job of that,' he added, as she pulled to a stop in front of Flo's block, his smile unwavering even as Florence forgot to put the car in neutral and stalled the engine. 'You should be very proud of yourself.'

Without the distraction of movement and windscreen wipers, the rain sounded heavier, Norman beginning to wonder if it wasn't an omen of some kind.

'Are you sure you don't want to come up with me?' he said, hopeful that she might change her mind.

'Totally,' she replied, a little too fast.

Feeling more reluctant by the second, Norman reached for the door handle. 'Okay, then. Well, wish me luck.'

He opened his door a few inches and slid an umbrella up

through the crack, its canopy unfolding in a protracted process of shaking and rattling. Yet even when he finally climbed out of the car, the umbrella offered less protection than he'd hoped, so that for a while he just stood there in the open doorway, unsure any more if any of this was a good idea.

'Granddad,' said Florence, calling to him over the sound of the rain. They both stooped to look at one another: Florence straining against her seatbelt while Norman cowered beneath his flimsy umbrella. 'This is the parent you were born to be. This is the parent Mum needs.'


Despite the building's size, there was no one in sight as Norman entered the lift lobby, its walls stained and scarred with successive layers of spray paint and other, more mysterious fluids. He rode up to the tenth floor in silence, accompanied only by the stale smell of tobacco and booze, the floor wet with what he hoped was rain.

Like her neighbours', Flo's front door was covered by a thick metal grille, so heavy and substantial it suggested that something much more frightening than mere criminals roamed these walkways.

After glancing around, Norman took a mirror from his pocket and hurriedly applied some lipstick; he still had enough aches and pains from his time in hospital to be terrified of bumping into yet more strangers while wearing makeup.

As soon as he was done, he rang Flo's bell, using the time that followed to compose himself: a deep breath, a pucker of the lips.

He was reaching for the bell a second time when Flo called through the door. 'Who is it?'

'It's me,' he replied. 'Your dad.'

'I'm taking a bath,' she shouted through the still-closed door. 'You'll have to come back another day.'

'Flo, we need to talk.' His words were met with such a silence, it seemed plausible that she'd already walked away, determined to sit it out in some other room. 'Please,' said Norman, louder now. 'There's something important I need to tell you. If you never want to see me after that, I promise, hand on my heart, I'll leave you in peace forevermore.'

The door opened a crack, Flo peering out from a gloomy hallway.

'I was the other woman in my marriage,' he said. 'I was always the other woman.'

The door didn't open any wider, but inasmuch as it didn't close, it still felt like progress.

Flo stared at him, her mouth open – though whether she was shocked by his words or his lipstick it was impossible to tell.

'I know I've got a lot of explaining to do,' he said. 'I was hoping we could talk about it.'


Flo hadn't been taking a bath, of course. Judging by the state of the bathtub, she hadn't taken one in weeks, the griminess in the bathroom – in the whole place – having progressed from something site-specific to a general ambience.

Norman considered this while he checked his reflection in the bathroom mirror, preparing himself for the conversation that lay ahead, while Flo sought refuge in the kitchen under the guise of making tea.

But at least I'm in, he thought to himself, still amazed that something he'd struggled for so many years to hide – the one thing he believed would drive the whole family away – had so far revealed itself to be the only thing that brought everyone closer.

Leaving the bathroom, he made his way back to the lounge, trying to move as quietly as possible, sure that he'd scarcely earnt the right of entry, let alone the right to make noise. It was only as he took a seat on the sofa, its cleanliness redolent of the bathtub, that he realised he and Flo had almost never been alone before. In Flo's early years, Betty had always been around, and then there was Florence. Not to mention all the other things that had slowly come between them: the words he hadn't said; the sadness she hadn't shared. In that respect, the griminess and disrepair of the flat was a fitting backdrop, the place having festered and rotted just like their relationship.

As he waited there on the sofa, he recalled when he and Betty had first visited, everything so fresh and new – from the paint to the carpets to the young Florence playing at their feet – it had seemed Flo's life was full of promise. The distant view of London, its skyscrapers reaching up through the haze, had lent the place a fairy-tale quality, only adding to the sense that Flo and her husband were on the cusp of something magical.

All these years later, it was a poignant memory: everyone so happy, no one had imagined that maybe that was as good as it was going to get, a fleeting apex before falling back to earth. Norman could still make out the distant skyline of London, its skyscrapers bigger than ever, but now the proximity only felt scornful; so near and yet so far.

Flo returned with two mugs of tea, handing one to Norman in a wary silence.

'Thank you,' he said, giving her a big smile. 'I've always loved a hot cuppa on a day like this.'

And still Flo said nothing, taking a seat on the opposite side of the lounge, as far away from him as it was possible to be without sitting in a different room.

'It's lovely to see you,' he said. 'I'm sorry it's taken me so long.'

'To tell the truth?' she replied, the words sounding harsher than he'd expected.

'Well, I was thinking more to come and see you . . .' He began to squirm. 'But yes, that too. I'm sorry it's taken so long to be honest with you.'

'Was it always like this?' she said. 'Even when we were young?'

'I used to keep some lipstick in my lorry, so I could wear it when I was alone.' Flo looked at him differently, still saying nothing, but paying attention in a way that Norman hadn't seen her do before. 'I had a few near misses, as you can imagine, but no one seems to suspect a man with smears of lipstick on his face. Most blokes were jealous, to be honest.'

'Mum, too, by the sounds of it.'

'She always knew,' replied Norman. 'I mean, she didn't want to talk about it. I daresay she never let herself *think* about it. But she did know.'

Flo said nothing to that, the distance between them still feeling like an impossible void.

'Florence has been lovely about it, by the way. It's been such a joy having her around. You've raised her well.' Flo flinched at the comment, unaccustomed to compliments. 'It can't have been easy for you, raising her alone.'

'It's not like I had a choice, is it?'

'Oh, I don't know,' he replied. 'You probably could have sold her to a glue factory.'

A faint glimmer of a smile appeared on her lips. 'Is that what you wanted to do with us?'

'Lord, no. You and Gerry are the only two things in my life I'm proud of. Though it might have briefly crossed my mind during your terrible twos.'

'Trust me,' she said. 'I know all about those.'

'But you just get on with things, don't you? All those times when nothing in life is how you want it to be, you somehow find a way.'

The conversation faded into another silence, but different this time: softer, more hopeful, and with it a sense that he and Flo were moving into unknown territory. And although he'd spent a lifetime running away from moments like this, had always found a way to keep too busy for honesty, now he just sat there, commanding himself to be still; to sink into it and be subsumed, so that finally they might discover what lay beneath.

'It would have helped to know about … about you,' said Flo.

'Would it?' he replied. 'I often wondered, but so many times it felt like the truth was even worse than the lie.'

Flo reconsidered. 'I suppose it must have been hard.'

'But harder for you, I can see that now. What with me being so distant all the time. Never being myself.' He noticed how she shifted position, less defensive than before. 'I can't tell you how sorry I am. How much I wish I could go back and do it all differently.'

As if on cue, they both turned to the window, two people whose capacity for emotion had just reached its limit.

'It looks like the weather's easing up,' said Flo.

'So it is,' replied Norman. 'I think it might brighten up in a bit.'

'It's about time we had some sunshine, isn't it?' She glanced at Norman, managing a weak smile. 'Can't all be rain, rain, rain.'

'I'll drink to that.' He raised his mug in a toast, certain that no matter what happened he would always remember this, the beginnings of acceptance; that he would cling to this memory and treasure it for the rest of his life. 'You might not believe it, but I've been teaching Florence to drive. She's getting quite good, actually.'

'She's a clever girl.'

'As I've discovered,' said Norman. 'It's too bad I only have a car rather than a rocket.'

Flo smiled. 'She might build you one if you're lucky.'

*Sinking deeper.*

'She's getting so good,' said Norman, 'I was thinking she

might be up for a really long drive. Maybe go somewhere nice for a few days, a little holiday.'

'I'd do the same if money wasn't so tight.'

'But that's the thing,' he said, surrendering, sinking fully. 'I know it might sound a bit mad, but maybe we could all go somewhere together. Maybe down to Cornwall for a few days. My treat.'

Flo cast her eyes down, tucking her legs beneath her and pulling her mug of tea closer than before.

He began to stammer. 'I mean, it's just an idea. Something to think about, eh?'

'Of course,' she replied, still not looking at him. 'It was good of you to come, but I've just remembered I have an appointment at twelve. I'll need to get going soon.'

Florence was still waiting downstairs in the car, pondering how strange it was that she was sitting in front of her mother's house but not going in – and how it was even stranger that her mother would probably find nothing strange about it – when Norman emerged from the building, wiping at his lips with what looked to be a tissue. It was only as he opened the door that she could see it was a wet wipe, its fabric smeared in traces of red lipstick.

She watched as Norman, looking defeated, sank into the seat beside her.

'Should I ask?' she said.

He groaned. 'To paraphrase Dickens, it somehow managed to be lovely and bloody awful.'

'Was the place very messy?' His pained expression was all the answer she needed. 'I try to stay on top of it when I'm around, but things go off the rails pretty quickly.'

'I made the mistake of inviting her to Cornwall.'

'What?' said Florence, incredulous.

'That says it all, really, doesn't it? When someone desperate for a holiday would rather stay at home than go with me.'

'Granddad, do you not think you were kind of getting ahead of yourself? You can't expect everything to suddenly get better just because you want it to be.'

Norman stared at the red-stained wet wipe in his hands, looking ever more disconsolate, until finally he looked up, as though only now realising that they were still parked there.

'We may as well get going, eh?' he said. 'There's nothing to keep us here.'

He said nothing after that, just gazed out the window distractedly as Florence steered them away from her childhood home, driving them through run-down streets that reflected the state of modern Britain, a parallel of her mother's life: the wasted potential, the missed opportunities, the wilful disregard as things deteriorated from bad to worse.

'Do you want to talk about it?' she said, as they accelerated on to a main road, the beginning of their sprint to freedom.

Norman looked pained. 'You can't tell me that your mother's whole life has ended up like that just because I lied about Ethel.'

'I never said it was *because* of Ethel,' she replied. 'I mean, it's probably a matter of confidence as much as anything. You spent years feeling bad about yourself. If Mum loved you when she was young, if she looked up to you, why wouldn't she internalise that? And let's not forget the secrets. There's really no difference between you hiding your struggles and Mum hiding hers.'

Norman didn't reply, but Florence could tell that the words were sinking in.

'Betty grew up not a million miles from here,' he said. 'It's funny when you think of it, isn't it? How times can change so much, but life has a habit of coming back to itself, like we're all going around and around in circles.' He started drumming his fingers on the door, still lost in thought. 'My parents weren't very communicative, either. People of their generation weren't, of course, but it often felt like there was more to it than that; some deep shame or sadness that blocked everything else up. That's how they stayed all their lives, right up until they died.' He sighed to himself. 'It's almost like a family tradition, isn't it? To struggle in silence.'

'Not any more,' replied Florence, her tone gentle and soothing. 'I know it doesn't feel good right now, but knowing how bad things are is actually a huge step forward. You can't start fixing the situation until you see it as it really is.'

He turned to her. 'Do you honestly think I stand a chance of fixing it?'

'Yes. One hundred per cent.'

His expression brightened, perhaps realising that today's disappointments were only the end of another round, not the end of the fight itself. As they sped onwards, his drumming of fingers became more musical, tapping in time to some tune in his head.

'I think we should still go ahead and plan the trip to Cornwall,' he said.

'If you're hoping Mum will change her mind, she won't, I promise you that.'

'But it's still a getaway for us, isn't it? One last hoorah before you go back to university. Not to mention, I can visit Suzie's grave. It could be a lovely little trip.'

'You're not worried about June?' replied Florence, smiling.

'Compared to the state of this family, I'd say June is the least of our problems.'

# 29.

Norman prepared for their trip with such military precision, Florence began to question whether they were merely visiting Cornwall or invading it. Believing the distance to be far greater than maps indicated, he rose earlier than usual on their day of departure, making enough fish paste sandwiches for a wedding reception. These would be enjoyed, he explained, in various lay-bys along the way, washed down with sweet milky tea from any one of several Thermos flasks.

While this meant there was no chance of starving to death if they broke down in the middle of nowhere, it also meant the car had acquired a distinctly fishy tang by the time they were collecting June from her nursing home.

Undeterred, she clambered into the car wheezing mechanically, half human, half machine, and promptly fell asleep, her whole body beginning to slump until eventually she was leaning at a precarious angle, held in place only by her seatbelt.

'Are you absolutely sure you know where you're going?' said Norman, as they drove off through the streets of Farnham. 'It's a long way.'

'I've got the whole route mapped on my phone,' she replied. 'Every inch of it. You can literally just sit back and enjoy the journey.'

This invitation to sloth was clearly something new to Norman. Before they'd even made it to the edge of Farnham, there was fidgeting and drumming of fingers.

'It's still a shame your mum couldn't make it,' he said, before correcting himself: 'Didn't *want* to come, I mean.'

'We were texting each other yesterday,' replied Florence. 'She didn't actually say it, but I got the feeling she appreciated the invitation. I know for a fact that learning about Ethel helped.'

Norman's spirits lifted. 'Well, that's something, isn't it?'

On the back seat, June lurched awake with a startled groan. She glanced around, confused, before wiping her mouth on her sleeve. 'Are we ...' She took a long inhalation on her ventilator ' ... nearly there?'

'We're still in Farnham,' replied Florence, laughing. 'Would you like anything?'

She shook her head and began fumbling in one of her pockets – an awkward, protracted process given her dexterity – until finally she pulled something free. Moments later there was the unmistakeable click of a cigarette lighter.

Norman twisted in his seat to find a crumpled cigarette hanging from her mouth.

'I found someone to bribe,' she said, looking thrilled.

'I'd really rather you didn't,' he replied. 'I've never much liked smoking, even when it was my wife doing it.'

June lit up anyway, puffing with remarkable skill for someone who couldn't breathe.

'For all you know,' she said, speaking to him through a grey haze, 'this cigarette is the only thing keeping me alive.'

'It's going to make the car smell, that's all.'

'Don't worry about that,' she replied, taking another puff. 'I can wind my window down.'

If she said anything after that, it was lost in a storm of loose ash and wind-ruffled hair, the whole car consumed by such a crosswind, even Norman gave up. Sighing to himself, he settled back in his seat, seeming to surrender to the realisation that this trip, like so much else in his quiet everyday existence, was fast taking on a life of its own.

'This is all going to seem worth it when I'm putting flowers on Suzie's grave,' he said. 'I just need to keep telling myself that.'

The journey was nothing like Norman had expected. There were no games, no tea breaks in sunny lay-bys. At the very least he'd expected more conversation, but even when June's window was closed, no one seemed inclined to small talk: June spent much of the time napping, while Florence looked more focused than usual on the act of driving. In the same way that Norman wouldn't see a tightrope walker halfway across a deep chasm and suggest they stop for a fish paste sandwich and a cup of tea, so too it felt inadvisable to break Florence's concentration.

When they were finally crossing into Cornwall, he was in a nostalgic frame of mind, remembering the many other times he'd travelled long distances. Mostly in the lorry, alone behind the wheel for days at a time, but once a year on a family holiday as well, generally sitting in traffic jams, the air in the car heavy with that particular scent of cucumber sandwiches sweating in Tupperware. On so many of those trips, Betty and the kids had asked to go on holiday to Cornwall the next year, and Norman had always given the same reply: that it's so far, they would regret the journey; that they were asking to cross the entire country when other people were going on holiday in the town they called home.

And now, all these years later, he was in Cornwall at last, but the family that had dreamt of it was gone: Betty was dead, Gerry avoided him at all costs, and Flo preferred to stay at home rather than spend any more time with him than necessary.

It was only their arrival at the hotel that snapped him from his thoughts, the place unexpected in its opulence. He wasn't paying – June had insisted on that – but still he felt a pang of guilt at the sight of it; would have happily stayed in a cheap caravan if they didn't have June's wheelchair to take into account.

Florence parked the car with a well-earned sigh. 'That wasn't so bad, right?'

'No, no,' he replied. 'You did very well.'

He glanced at June on the back seat, still looking so fresh he began to wonder whether, in earlier years, he'd been resistant to this trip for the family's sake or his own.

That thought grew stronger when he got to his room, where the bed alone had enough space for an entire family, and the bathtub was so big he could imagine floating about in it like some sea creature on a spring tide. With each new discovery – the bathrobes and towels, for instance, which were thicker than his carpet at home – he only wished that Betty was also there to experience it: how she would have marvelled that taking a shower didn't feel like a shower at all, but rather standing in the rain somewhere warm and peaceful; how she would have laughed for hours on the bed, lying on it crosswise and spreading herself out like a starfish. Life had offered so many opportunities for joy, he could see that now; so many chances to be happy, each of them a rare and special gift, and yet somehow he had let them all slip away.


When Florence knocked at Norman's door that evening, she expected many things: the faint sound of snoring, for instance, or to find that Norman had brought his radio and was now listening to *The Archers*. What she didn't expect was him to answer the door in a bathrobe, with a mud pack on his face.

'Is this a bad time?' she said.

'No, it's an excellent time. A really lovely time.' He padded across the plush carpeting and took a seat on his bed. 'I didn't expect this place to be so posh. I don't know where to put myself.'

'Yet you seem to be rising to the challenge,' she replied, laughing.

He touched his face as though having forgotten that it was caked in ashen mud. 'Do you have one in your bathroom, too? It's supposed to be youth restoring. Maybe next time you see me I'll look like a fresh-faced sixty-something.'

'June wants to buy us dinner at the restaurant downstairs.'

Norman raised his eyebrows, his mud pack cracking. 'She's very free with her cash, isn't she?'

'She's grateful, that's all.'

'And it's a nice offer, but I don't think I'll join you.'

Florence frowned at him. 'It's free. And it's food, which we all need to stay alive.'

'But think of the sandwiches in the car,' he said. 'Not to mention all that tea. It would be a shame to let it go to waste.'

'Granddad, take this from a scientist, it's already waste. Those sandwiches have been at room temperature for—' She checked her phone. 'Almost eleven hours.'

'But some bacteria is good for you, isn't it? That's what they were saying on the radio the other day.'

'The sandwiches aren't *fermented*, they're just bacterial. It's not the same thing.'

'Yes, yes, you're probably right,' he said, clearly intending to eat them anyway. 'But I still don't think I'll join you at dinner. I'd like a quiet night.'

'Jesus, we're not going clubbing! It'll just be the three of us. At a restaurant. In the middle of . . . fields.'

Norman touched his face. 'I want to give this mask a bit longer to work its magic. And I saw some bubble bath in there. I might give that a try next. Though the tub's so big, they should really provide a life vest.'

'Trust me,' she replied, 'if you eat those sandwiches, drowning will be the least of your problems.'

186

'Oh, don't you worry about me, I'll be fine.' He stood up, an unspoken signal that the subject was closed. 'Please thank June for the offer. And have a lovely evening. I'll see you both for breakfast in the morning.'


Given its location amid rolling farmland, the hotel restaurant turned out to be needlessly formal, the maître d' appearing unsure how to react to the arrival of an old lady on a ventilator and a grey-haired teenager in a black hoodie. In those intervening seconds of awkwardness, June took a long breath, her machine rattling mechanically.

'We're on honeymoon,' she said. 'A table with a view would be appreciated.'

Trying not to laugh, Florence pushed June's wheelchair as they followed him past well-heeled diners to a window table, its silver flatware sparkling in candlelight.

'I would have been happy with McDonald's,' whispered Florence, as a waiter handed them menus and then, with a theatrical flourish, laid starched napkins across their laps.

'I want you to order whatever you like,' said June. 'Go mad, it's my treat.'

'What are you having?' replied Florence.

'Oh, I don't really eat any more. I'm a bird; I'd rather just peck at some bread.'

'They're going to be thrilled with that. We have ...' Chuckling, she counted the cutlery. 'Four knives each. I think they're expecting us to eat more than a bread roll.'

June just shrugged. 'People's expectations are their own business.'

A different waiter appeared from nowhere, discreetly placing a basket of bread on the table, its contents barely visible in a nest of yet more starched white cotton.

'And there we go,' said June, flatly. 'That's me all sorted.'

Florence was still making her way through the menu – a document liberally smattered with French, even when describing a cheeseburger and fries – when June wheezed back into life. 'How's Norman doing? I never thought he'd say yes to this trip.'

'To be honest, he was hoping my mum would come,' replied Florence. 'I mean, he wants to visit Suzie's grave, of course, but I think the trip was also bait.'

'Your mum couldn't make it?'

Florence sighed, trying to think of the right response. 'I think she would love to come to Cornwall, just not with him.'

'Ah,' replied June, as she fumbled with a piece of bread. 'Another happy family. I know all about those.'

'But at least they're working on it. Coming out as Ethel has really helped.'

June froze.

'Oh, God,' said Florence, laughing. 'You don't know! Okay, ignore what I said, it's nothing.'

June's ventilator rattled into life, a new pronouncement in transit. 'Who's Ethel?'

'It would be much better coming from him,' replied Florence.

'I could be dead before I see him next. Even the anticipation could kill me.'

Florence tried to rationalise the ethics of the situation. It was one thing to tell someone like Sally or the maître d', but surely June was a special case? By keeping it a secret from her, wouldn't Florence just be affirming Norman's belief that it was a dark and shameful secret?

'Granddad is a cross-dresser,' she said. 'His alter ego is called Ethel.'

She watched as June processed this information, her face slowly lighting up. 'Good for him,' she said. 'It takes a real man to dress like a woman.'

'As far as I understand it, that's how he met your sister. He was up in London looking for his tribe, and then sort of stumbled into hers instead.'

'Isn't that often the way?' she replied. 'We start life thinking our tribe is one thing, but then we meet people who see us for who we really are.'

'The thing is,' said Florence. 'He's only just started being open about it. It's a . . . it's a work in progress, let's say. I think that's why visiting Suzie's grave is so important to him.' The light in June's face began to fade, but Florence was too busy reaching for her phone to notice. 'If you tell me where it is, I can plan the route for tomorrow morning.'

June beckoned a waiter over, eager to change the subject. 'You should go ahead and order,' she told Florence. 'You must be famished.'

# 30.

Norman was the first down to breakfast the next morning, the white table cloth and fancy napkins offering visual confirmation that his life was changing in unexpected ways. He'd been waiting some time before Florence arrived with June. If he was honest, he'd half expected Florence to come downstairs alone, pale-faced, announcing that she'd just found June dead in her room, but no, June was in her wheelchair, Florence pushing her at a ceremonial pace while she used her ventilator to take loud, tortured breaths. This evidently unnerved some of the other guests, most of whom looked to be on romantic getaways, but there was no point sugar-coating old age, was there? Much better, thought Norman, that those people come to terms with their mortality in a plush dining room with a nice view rather than wait until it's their turn.

'Good morning,' he said, as June came to a stop at the table. 'Did you sleep well?'

'No,' she replied. For an instant it looked like she was about to expand on this, but, perhaps realising the effort involved, changed her mind.

Florence took a seat opposite them. 'June's been telling me about the place we're going today. It's this famous cove with green rocks. It sounds amazing.'

'I'd like to get some flowers for the grave,' said Norman. 'Do you think we'll be passing a shop on the way?'

'I wouldn't do that,' June replied. 'There's not really a place for them.'

'But it's a grave,' he said, confused.

June took some time to respond, not catching her breath, but rather considering her words. 'You'll see when we get there.'

Norman and Florence glanced at one another, trying to understand what wasn't being said, but then the server was offering them tea and coffee and baskets of freshly baked temptations, not to mention the promise of a fried breakfast with all the trimmings, so that before Norman was even aware of it, his concerns had been swept away by a tsunami of five-star abundance.


By the time they got out to the car later that morning, the three of them had achieved an easy bonhomie, a blossoming familiarity that made the trip feel much more special than Norman had expected. That holiday mood grew even stronger as they neared the coast, the hedgerows giving way to glimpses of sea.

'And the grave is down here?' said Norman, spying a car park in the distance, but nothing else.

'Yes,' replied June, the word lacking any of its usual certainty. 'I might need to get my bearings, but it'll be fine once I'm out of the car.'

Naturally, this was easier to say than accomplish. After they'd parked, Norman manned the wheelchair while Florence helped June out, at first merely encouraging her before finally just tugging her free.

As June slumped into her chair, she looked dazed by their new surroundings; the air sharp, the sound of the Atlantic hurling itself on the shore below.

'It's exactly how I remember it,' she said, breaking into a smile.

Florence consulted her phone. 'The path down to the rocks is over there.'

'But I don't see a graveyard,' said Norman, sounding more concerned.

'Everything in its time,' replied June.

In the minutes that followed, they established beyond all doubt that their destination offered many things – a great view, a toilet, over-priced parking – but definitely no graveyard.

'You should go down to the beach,' said June to Florence. 'It's beautiful down there. Norman can look after things from here.'

Florence lingered. 'Are you sure?' she asked him.

He wasn't, but June continued to insist. 'We'll be fine. You go and explore. Shoo, shoo.'

Still looking reluctant, Florence left them.

'She's lovely,' said June, watching her go.

'I think the same thing every day,' replied Norman.

June pointed to a path along the coast. 'We want to go that way.'

Moving with some difficulty, Norman pushed her away from the car park. 'Is it looking more familiar to you now?'

'Yes, yes, just a little further. We can rest at that bench up there.'

When they reached it, Norman was so grateful to take a seat, it wasn't the view that hit him first, it was his breathlessness. It was only as he regained his composure that he realised the full grandeur of it, nothing to one side of them but ocean and sky.

'It's beautiful, isn't it?' said June, rheumy eyed. 'I have so many memories of this place.'

Norman glanced around, more confused than ever. 'But where is the grave?'

June didn't answer at first, just sat staring out to sea, the wind tugging at what little hair she had left. 'I lied. Suzie's not buried in Cornwall. She's back in Sussex.'

Norman opened his mouth to speak, but it wasn't words that came to mind, it was the mental image of June bouncing off the cliff in her wheelchair.

'Sorry,' she said. 'You must be disappointed.'

'Why would I be disappointed?' he replied, trying to sound calm. 'You've just told me that we came all this way for nothing.'

'This isn't nothing, Norman. Look at this place. This isn't nothing at all.'

They both remained like that, staring out to sea, the churning of the Atlantic a fitting soundtrack for Norman's emotions.

'Is the grave in Farnham?' he said. 'Were we right by it the whole time?'

June took her time to respond, still staring out to sea. 'She doesn't have a grave, not in the sense you mean. After she was cremated, our father tossed her ashes in the local dump.'

'No!' said Norman, with a gasp.

'He said that Suzie had lived like rubbish, so she should be thrown away like rubbish, too. He was a religious man, always saying that God doesn't make mistakes.'

'But Suzie wasn't a mistake,' said Norman. 'She was perfect.'

June appeared to drink in the sea air. 'She loved this place. I can guarantee you'll find more of her here than you ever will up there.'

'You could have told me when we first met,' he replied. 'Not just about the grave, but wanting to see Cornwall again.'

She turned to him. 'Do you honestly think you would have said yes?'

'I don't know. Maybe.'

'Norman, maybes are a luxury at my age.'

He took a deep breath and forced a cheery tone. 'Well, looking on the bright side, at least I didn't waste any money on flowers, eh?'

'You should find some and press them in a book,' said June. 'That's what Suzie would have done.'

'She would, wouldn't she? I'd forgotten about that.'

'Some of her books are more flowers than paper.'

'It's funny,' said Norman. 'She was always striding about town like she was late for an important meeting, but there wasn't a flower she wouldn't stop to admire. And occasionally pick, I might add, which didn't always go down so well if it was from a stranger's garden.'

They both smiled at one another, glad to have brought Suzie back to life, even if only for a moment.

'It's important to you, isn't it?' said June. 'To visit the grave.'

Norman hesitated. 'I want to pay my respects.'

She put a bony hand on his. 'In my experience, we only go in search of the dead for two reasons. Grief or guilt.'

'Oh, I suppose it's a bit of both, to be honest.'

'Trust me,' she replied. 'We all feel that with Suzie.' She kept her hand on his, seeming to need the contact. 'Things were really bad after the arrest. She never got back on track after that.'

'I think that's what I find so painful,' he said. 'When I think of her, I just remember her being so happy, so carefree.'

'More than anything, she was brave. She didn't want anyone to feel ashamed of who they are.' She held his hand, tighter than before. 'That's the best way to honour her memory, Norman. By living with courage.'

# 31.

Over the next couple of days, June showed them places from her childhood holidays – the beaches that she and Suzie had run along, the rocks where they'd sat and dreamt about what the future might hold – all of which brought Suzie back to life in ways that a mere gravestone never could. Spurred on by their shared recollections, it felt natural to Norman that he bring Ethel along for the ride as well: a touch of blusher here, some red lips there, even progressing to a jaunty silk scarf he found in one of the local gift shops.

Florence took it all in her stride, the ever-accommodating chauffeuse, happy to drive two sentimental oldies hither and thither across Cornwall as they followed June's memories along rugged clifftops and down narrow lanes. Despite Norman's dire predictions that the trip would kill her, June was invigorated by the change of scene, so that rather than needing to nap throughout the day, she spent most of her time gazing out the window, regularly winding it down so she could have yet another cigarette. Her contribution to Cornwall's picturesque countryside: a subtle trail of ash and carbon monoxide.

It was during one of their regular seaside stops that June decided the time had come for postcards. This turned out to be a more complicated process than Norman had imagined: June demanding to pore over all three racks of cards at the gift shop; requiring the higher ones to be handed to her one at a time, rejecting each one as too this or too that. Sunsets over the

Atlantic, for instance, were dismissed as a poetic misrepresentation of Cornwall's typical weather.

'The thing is,' replied Norman, 'I doubt you'll find any postcards of rain and mud.' He reached for another: the landscape in soft focus, patches of mist hanging low in the valleys. 'This is lovely.'

'That's what it's like to have glaucoma,' she replied with a grimace before pointing at a card near the top of the rack: a picture of a cow staring at them in stunned fascination. 'Give me five of those.'

'Are you sure?' he said, handing her one so she could take a closer look.

'Actually, no,' she replied. 'I'll take ten.'

Content with this arbitrary decision, they found a beachside table where June, with a cold can of beer beside her, began the laborious process of writing them out – such a tight tangled scrawl, it surely didn't matter what she said, the recipients would never be able to read it anyway.

'Everything is fantastic,' she said, muttering the words aloud as she wrote. 'Even the weather's good. I just wish . . .' She put her pen down so she could take a drag on her ventilator, a cigarette in the other hand. After some light coughing and a thump of the chest, she picked up her pen again. 'Where was I?'

'Wish you were here,' said Norman.

June scoffed. 'I just wish I could die here. Love, June.'

Seeming happy with this first card, she moved on to the next. Only nine more to go. She was putting pen to paper when she noticed Norman was staring at her, aghast.

'You two should go for a walk on the beach,' she said.

'We can't leave you alone,' he replied.

'I have beer, I have fags, I'll be fine. The worst that can happen is I drop dead,' she added, making it sound like a fun addition to their itinerary. 'Now, be off with you, shoo . . .'

Realising that he was expected to go for a walk whether he wanted to or not, Norman stood up. 'I suppose it might be nice to stretch our legs, eh?'

Not being an arthritic eighty-six-year-old, Florence merely shrugged. 'Sure, why not?'

While June got on with her postcards, they started out across the beach, the air sharp with the scent of salt and seaweed.

'It's lovely down here, isn't it?' said Norman, his silk scarf flapping in the wind. 'Cornwall's one of the few places I never visited back when I was driving the lorry. I can see now why everyone falls in love with the place.'

'It's been great,' replied Florence. 'It's hard to imagine being back at uni next week.'

'It's even harder for me to imagine you gone. I don't know what I'm going to do with myself.'

She laughed. 'You can sort out the heating in my room, for a start. I'll need it on my next visit.'

Arm in arm, they wandered over to a group of rocks at the base of a cliff, where pools of water lay stranded by the low tide. Peering into them, Norman realised they were each full of life, a variety of tiny creatures in an exile of sorts, patiently waiting for circumstances to turn back in their favour.

Florence used her phone to take a picture and then took another of the beach itself, stretching far into the distance. 'I might send that to Mum,' she said.

'That's a nice idea,' he replied. 'I was even thinking we could stop there once we've dropped June off.' Florence's expression darkened and she looked like she was about to say something, but Norman beat her to it. 'I don't mean to go and see her at home. Just a quick meet-up somewhere outside, maybe in the park or something. I saw a box of fudge in the shop just now, I thought that might be a nice gift for her. There was a lovely kaftan in there, too.'

She looked confused. 'Why would you want to buy Mum a kaftan?

'Not for your mother,' he replied. 'For me.'

'Ah, okay,' said Florence, laughing. 'I think it's a lovely idea. All of the above.' She took out her phone again. 'Here, let's take a selfie. I'll send that to her, too.' Before he knew what was happening, Norman saw his reflection appear on screen, Florence looking impossibly young and fresh-faced beside him.

'I think she'll like your scarf,' said Florence. 'Say cheese . . .'

# 32.

Their time in Cornwall came to an end, as all things do. Although their journey home was a literal rewind of the outward route, it struck Florence that they weren't coming back the same way at all; that the trip had reshaped them in ways she did not yet fully understand. This was especially true of Norman, who'd not only bought the kaftan he'd seen in the shop, but had also decided to wear it for the journey, sitting there in the front seat like he'd just jetted in from the Hamptons.

'What a lovely trip,' he said as they reached the outskirts of Farnham.

Florence checked on June, fast asleep on the back seat. 'It's funny, of all the mental pictures I have from the last few days, it's not beaches or cliffs or anything like that, it's how June looked this morning as we left Cornwall. Did you notice?' She lowered her voice. 'She was staring out the window like she knew it was her last time.'

'Well, let's be honest,' replied Norman, 'it probably was.'

'But it was heart-breaking. I wanted to tell her I'd take her back any time, every month, if necessary, just so she doesn't have to feel like that.'

'But there's always going to be a last time, isn't there? Nothing can change that. Maybe it was better this way; at least she had a chance to say goodbye. You begin to realise how rare that is as you get older.'

He pulled down the sun visor and checked his reflection in

the vanity mirror, looking first one way and then another as he judged the state of his makeup.

'You look great,' said Florence.

'I want to look my best for Rex, eh? I'm glad June wants to go there. I've been thinking of him and Suzie since our last visit. I feel guilty, that's the truth of it.'

'You don't have anything to feel guilty about,' she replied – and then glanced at him, concerned. 'Do you?'

The words appeared to require effort. 'It's the way things ended when I last saw them,' he said. 'The night they were arrested.'

'I thought you said you weren't there?'

'Only after a fashion. My train was late, that's all. I'd just turned on to Rex's street when the paddy wagons turned up.' He stopped speaking for a moment, the memory still raw after all those years. 'As soon as I saw them, I knew what was about to happen. I just hung about and watched it all from a distance.'

He looked so sad by then, Florence wanted nothing more than to stop the car right there in the middle of the road and give him a hug. 'I can't imagine how difficult that must have been,' she said, desperately wanting the words to soothe him. 'Surely, there was nothing else you could have done?'

'Oh, who knows?' replied Norman, sounding more and more burdened. 'I saw them as they were being led out, that was the worst of it. Suzie looked right at me and I didn't do anything. I didn't even smile and wave, I was too scared to give myself away. I just stood there while they were hauled off. After that, I went straight back to Liverpool Street and took the next train home. I never saw them again.'

The only consolation Florence could offer was to listen.

'When I got back to Clacton,' he said, 'I just put my head down and got on trying to live the life everyone else expected. I've carried the shame of it all these years. I mean, I was already ashamed of wanting to dress like a woman, but that's nothing compared to the shame of abandoning my friends.'

'I'm sorry you had to go through all that,' she said. 'Even worse that you had to deal with it on your own.'

Norman began to recompose himself. 'No, I'm sorry, I shouldn't have put all of that on you. It's not fair. Secrets can be such poisonous things.'

'Then imagine what an important day this is,' she replied. 'Because it's not a secret any more.'


June woke up long enough to get from the car to Rex's sofa before falling asleep with a lit cigarette in hand.

'Would you be a darling?' said Rex to Florence, gesturing at the cigarette's slow descent. 'If she didn't live in a nursing home, I swear she would have burnt herself to death years ago.' Florence plucked it from her fingers with just inches to spare. 'I'll take it,' he said. 'June's family to me, I don't mind a bit of her spit.'

Norman watched as June slumped further in her seat and began to drool. 'I'd imagined she was really looking forward to this.'

'What are you talking about?' said Rex, indignant. 'She's having a lovely time.'

'She's fast asleep,' he replied.

'Which I take as a great compliment. To my mind, it's no different to having a dog: it only falls asleep in your presence if it trusts you.' He took a puff of her cigarette, nodding with pleasure. 'I don't know why other people's always taste so much better.'

'When you sent us to June the first time,' said Norman, 'did you know she'd lead us on a wild goose chase?'

'It did occur to me,' he replied. 'This is Suzie's sister, after all; apples don't fall far from the tree. But why shouldn't an old lady have one last adventure? I'm sure you got something from the experience, too.'

'I'll say this, visiting Cornwall was a lot better than going to the local dump.'

Rex shuddered. 'Imagine that a family member could do something so foul and monstrous. It's always made me grateful that I don't have any family left. But then you bring your darling granddaughter into my life.' He smiled at Florence with such warmth, such charisma, she could understand how Norman must have felt all those years before, a shy young man stumbling into the royal court of King Rex. 'Please don't stand on ceremony,' he said. 'Ethel only looks this stiff because of her arthritis, whereas you are in the prime of life and should make yourself utterly, utterly at home.' He gestured at the photographs on the piano. 'I'm sure you were being much too polite last time. You should go and see what I looked like at your age. I only wish there were some pictures of Ethel in there, too.'

'That would be something, wouldn't it?' said Norman. 'I can't remember how I looked back then.'

'Like you'd just arrived in the big smoke, so fresh off the bus you still had hay seeds in your hair. And let me tell you, it was a beautiful thing.'

Florence pored over the photos, a lifetime of memories curated with a sharp eye, their polished silver frames yet another testament to Rex's invisible army of helpers. Parties were a common theme, Rex appearing in many incarnations, from urbane young sophisticate to the blue-blooded elder of his later years. But it was a picture of another man that caught her eye; his jawline and cheekbones so sharp, they lent new meaning to the word chiselled.

Rex called to her, a sly tone in his voice. 'I see you've found Ronnie.'

'How do you know who I'm looking at?' she replied.

'Because that's how everyone used to look when they first saw him. He was so elemental, like he was built from great blocks of humanity, all right angles and sharp edges. Naturally, it was a body that lent itself to nudity.' He scooped an olive from his martini, the first time Florence had seen him eat solid food. 'I've so often found it's the wrong people who like to be naked, but I can say with total confidence that Ronnie was the exception to that rule.'

'It looks like you've had a fun life,' she said.

'It has been fun. Though I can assure you that everyone in those pictures, and I do mean every single one, they'd all been hated and abused at one time or another; they all understood rejection and pain. What I loved about them was they still managed to find joy in life. Suzie's in there, too.'

'Really?' said Norman, springing from his seat.

Rex laughed. 'I don't think you'll need my help finding her.'

Norman hovered over the photos for mere seconds before snatching one up. 'You didn't mention it before.'

'You didn't ask. You didn't look. You hardly stayed long enough to notice them.'

Norman stared at the black and white picture: Suzie laughing for the camera, champagne flute in hand. 'You can bet that dress was red,' he said to Florence. 'She loved red.'

'I can't remember when it was taken,' added Rex. 'Before everything went off the rails, obviously.'

Norman smiled at the picture, reunited with his old friend at long last. 'It must have been around the time I knew her. She looks exactly the way I remember.'

'Then the sad thing is, she was probably gone just a year or two later. Such a tragic loss of a young life.'

'How did it happen?' said Norman, still holding the picture. 'I know you don't want to tell me—'

'I suggested that for your sake, not mine.'

'And thank you,' said Norman, 'but I want to know. I need to know.'

Rex took a fortifying sip of gin. And then another. 'Well, prison was a daunting prospect, as you can imagine.'

'What was the sentence?' said Florence.

'Twelve months. For nothing at all, I might add. That was the scale of the madness in those days, they didn't even need proof of a crime; it was enough that they arrested someone else and found your name in his address book. You were guilty merely by association. The irony is, the night they raided the house, we weren't doing anything licentious, it was just a quiet supper with friends. I might have overcooked the fish, but that hardly warrants a year in prison.'

'Were you all sent to the same jail?' said Norman.

'Ah, well, that's where it all began to go wrong. The rest of us decided to take our chances, but Suzie opted for treatment in lieu of the prison term. Hormone therapy mostly, but there were sessions with emetics as well. They had her in a dreary room somewhere, throwing up in a bucket for hours on end, as if that was going to make her straight. She visited me once in prison; I swear it was like watching a flower die, the way she'd changed, all the joy gone. Then they started her on electroconvulsive therapy to cope with what they said was depression, and it was like the last of her light was snuffed out. I was still locked up when she jumped in front of a Tube train. The doctors just claimed it was proof she really did have a mental problem, but we all knew her better than that. She would have sparkled into old age if only they'd treated her as a human being.'

Norman gently put the picture back on the piano, Suzie smiling up at him from some long-gone moment. 'I've wanted to apologise to you. For a long time, actually.'

'You have nothing to apologise for,' replied Rex, waving the words away.

'But I do. When you were arrested, I was so worried what would happen if I got too close to you and Suzie. Worried that everyone would find out about me.'

'Then how wonderful, Ethel, that you're telling me this in a kaftan.'

Norman still sounded distraught. 'But I wasn't there for either of you, especially Suzie. You'd both been so kind to me, and I failed you both.'

'Ethel, they were dark and terrible times. We all did whatever we had to. I can promise you, you didn't fail anyone. Not me, not Suzie. In fact, if Suzie was still around, she'd be thrilled for you, I know that for a fact. There would be laughter, there would be drinks.' He held out his empty glass. 'Speaking of which, would you be a doll and get me another?'

Florence stepped forward. 'I can do it.'

'No, thank you,' replied Rex. 'Tasks like this help keep dementia at bay.' He waved the glass in Norman's direction. 'I want you to make me an Angle Grinder.'

The request seemed to distract Norman from his sadness. 'I know the tool,' he said. 'But I have no idea what the drink is.'

'Then how lucky for you that my housekeeper has an entire recipe book in the kitchen. Don't come back until you've found it.' He waited until Norman, looking perplexed, wandered from the room. 'There's no such drink,' he said to Florence, a sparkle in his eye. 'And no such book, for that matter. I presume that will keep him busy for a while. Tell me, how is he doing, really?'

Florence tried to be diplomatic. 'There's some baggage to sort through, as you can imagine. Things are bit patchy with my mum and uncle.'

'Would we really be human if we didn't get relationships wrong sometimes? I'm inclined to think it's a much greater failing to expect perfection.'

Norman shouted from the kitchen. 'I can't find it.'

'Look harder,' yelled Rex. 'It must be in one of the cupboards.'

'I'm telling you,' said Norman, 'it's not here.'

Rex shouted even louder. 'Either you're implying my house-keeper is a thief or I'm senile. I advise you to choose your next words wisely, Ethel Cartwright.' He winked at Florence, invigorated by the sport. 'I meant what I said to your grandfather,' he told her. 'They were awful times, really. We all lived in fear of one kind or another. One slip up and your whole life could be ruined. Just look at poor old Alan Turing; even the great and the good lived on edge, no one was safe. I can't tell you how many people I've known over the years, men and women, who just couldn't do it any more. Who tried to settle down to a "normal" married life. But imagine how toxic that is, how it ripples out and maims everyone it touches, all because we demand people live a lie.' He took a drag on his cigarette, exhaling with a contented sigh. 'I think that's what I love about your grandfather. He's finally figuring out that he doesn't need to be anyone but himself; that there's room for him in the world just the way he is. Imagine, some people go to their graves having only lived the lives other people chose for them.'

Norman returned, looking apologetic. 'Maybe it's just me, but I've searched high and low.'

'Never mind,' replied Rex, gracious and soothing. 'You can mix me a Dubonnet and gin instead.' Norman moved to the drinks table and opened a bottle. 'No, no,' said Rex, bossy again. 'Don't do it in here.'

'Why on earth not?' he replied.

'Because I can tell that you're going to *labour* the process, and the only kind of labourers I'm willing to watch are handsome men a fraction of your age. Go and do it in the kitchen.' He waited as Norman clumsily gathered up the bottles, turning to Florence as he finally left the room. 'Am I very evil?'

'Yes,' she replied, laughing. 'Fortunately, I think he quite enjoys a challenge.'

'A fitting approach to life. Which you have ahead of you in delicious abundance.'

'It doesn't always feel very delicious,' she said. 'I'm still trying to figure it all out.'

'Oh, life is a vast blank canvas, my dear. And it's totally up to you what kind of picture you paint. Never let anyone tell you otherwise.'

Out in the kitchen, there was the sound of glass banging on glass, loud enough to be alarming. Seconds later, Norman shouted through the wall. 'Don't worry, everything's fine.'

Rex waited, poised for the sound of more destruction, but calm returned. 'Gosh, I love that man. It reminds me how much fun we used to have in the old days.'

Moments later, Norman returned, handing Rex his drink. 'I hope it's all right. I never claimed to be a bartender.'

'I'm sure it's perfect, thank you.' He took a sip. 'It's a little heavy on the gin, but quite frankly the same could be said of my entire life.'

While Rex took several more mouthfuls to confirm his findings, Norman watched June, still asleep on the sofa, her body slumped at an alarming angle, but her face a picture of peace.

'She looks so happy,' said Norman. 'It'll be a shame to wake her up.'

Rex looked confused. 'Why on earth would you want to wake her up?'

'I don't mean right now,' he replied. 'But we'll have to when it's time to leave.'

'No, she can stay longer, we have someone for that; a taxi driver we've been using for years. In fact, it'll be the perfect outcome.

He'll need to come in and manhandle her in front of me. His forearms are a joy to behold.'

'Are you sure?' said Norman.

'Absolutely, you'll make an old man very happy. I suspect an old woman, too, but she denies everything, of course.' He smiled at the sight of her on the sofa. 'It's amazing to think how the years have flown. I first met her just after Suzie died, over sixty years ago. And here we are, still together, two old fogies falling apart at the seams.' He glanced at Norman. 'You'll understand when you get to my age.'

'I'm eighty-six,' he replied.

'Ah, I remember those days. So many good years still ahead of you.' He lit another cigarette, the air around him greying. 'Gosh, what I would give to be in my eighties again. To be back in Italy for one last autumn of blue skies and glorious food. To wander in the garden and pluck figs ripe from the trees.'

Norman, who'd probably never had a fresh fig let alone been to Italy, looked unsure how to respond. 'There might still be a way,' he said.

Rex smiled at his optimism. 'Ethel, darling, look at me. My time is drawing to a close, I've made my peace with that. It was one of the many things Ronnie and I agreed on: one should always know when it's time to leave a party; only dirty slappers stay until the bitter end. Not that I'm expecting to drop dead just yet, so I sincerely hope you'll be my guests on more occasions to come.'

'That would be lovely,' replied Norman.

'You couldn't keep us away if you tried,' added Florence.

He beamed at them. 'Please know you're always welcome. Though I want you to remember this, Ethel: if the Grim Reaper does come calling for me, please don't be sad. I'd say it's been a good life, all told. For you and me both.'

# Forty-nine years earlier

## 1973

Life was beginning to feel Victorian. Not at home, of course – young Gerry and Flo had not yet been pressganged into working as chimneysweeps – but in so many other ways, it seemed that the world as Norman knew it was regressing to something unimaginable, teetering on the edge of a dark and deep precipice. What had started earlier in the year as an oil embargo of western nations had snowballed into something much bigger, the whole country beginning to fracture and disintegrate. After months of petrol pumps running dry, now there was talk of extended power cuts, the worst possible way to slide into a long, cold winter.

Over the years, Norman had lost count of how many times Betty had told him that he spent too much time working – though never, he noticed, complaining about the money he brought in every month – so it should have come as a silver lining that his hours on the road had been cut way back.

Betty's expression over breakfast suggested otherwise.

It probably didn't help that what should have been a gentle start to the day was a fraught, cacophonous affair: five-year-old Flo appearing to be trapped forever in her terrible twos, while Gerry, at the ripe old age of eleven, had recently acquired an aloof quality, as though he'd decided Norman and Betty weren't his kind of people.

Under the circumstances, Norman's morning paper was less a source of news than a survival strategy; a chance to be physically present at the table while conveniently removing himself in every other sense. Which was surely the ultimate testament to the challenges of everyday family life: that news of miners' strikes and predictions of nationwide anarchy were a welcome escape.

'My oh my,' he said, reading one of the news stories. 'Now

they're talking about introducing a three-day week for business.'
He made eye contact with Betty over the top of the paper, a soldier peering out from the trenches. 'The government claims there
won't be enough electricity otherwise. Some shops are saying
they'll use portable gas lamps so customers can see.'

'Whatever next?' she replied, still trying to feed Flo some
cornflakes. 'I never thought I'd live to see the day when I need a
torch just to go shopping.'

'And it's not going to do much for my hours, is it? Who's going
to need deliveries if everything's closed?' He noticed how Betty
paled at the thought – the prospect of the country falling into
total economic ruin seemingly nothing compared to the horrors
of him spending even more time at home. 'Though looking on
the bright side, maybe it will mean more people holiday here in
Clacton next summer. I swear if we lose any more tourists to
Benidorm, the whole town will disappear.'

'I've heard people raving about that place,' she replied, her
tone suggesting that she might, too, if only she had the chance.
'Apparently, it's so popular these days, it's full of high rises.
They're calling it the Manhattan of Spain.'

'But I doubt they have a pier,' said Norman, disapprovingly.
'And I daresay you can't get a decent cup of tea there for love
nor money.'

Noticing that Betty appeared irritated by the comment, he
ducked back inside his newspaper, taking refuge in an article
about the IRA. Moments later, the loud clang of a spoon hitting
the floor suggested that Florence still didn't like cornflakes, followed by Gerry speaking in a voice too cultured to be a child of
his age or his bloodline. 'Mother, may I be excused?'

Norman peeked over his newspaper again and watched in
envy as Gerry left the room in search of some quieter corner of
the house, somewhere unscarred by breadcrumbs and spilt milk
and fractious toddlers.

It had all sounded so simple when Norman and Betty had first talked of having a family of their own. 'Raising children' didn't sound so different to growing some vegetables in the garden – tomatoes, say, or runner beans: something that needs training at first, but then takes on an orderly life of its own. Instead, Norman had discovered that family life was a living, breathing thing with an unknowable mind; that rather than being the father-as-gardener that he'd first imagined, parenting was more akin to being a lion tamer, every day forced to enter the cage afresh with no training or safety equipment.

'Have you noticed the new people at number forty-three?' said Betty.

Norman lowered his newspaper yet again.

'I've seen the bloke once or twice,' he replied.

Betty shook her head. 'I suspect he's a real brute. The other day he was bellowing at her in the street, almost busting a lung, and she was just cowering in front of him, like she was used to it.'

'Gracious,' said Norman, unsure what else he could say about people he didn't know.

'I bumped into her at the grocer's the next day. She's called Sally.'

Flo shut down the conversation with an attention-seeking scream, Betty appearing wearied by the sound.

'I have an idea,' said Norman, putting his newspaper down. He hurried into the front room, where Flo's doll was sitting on the sofa, its long blond hair draped over one shoulder. Picking it up, he returned to the kitchen, the sight of it in his hands instantly entrancing Flo. 'I knew that would do the trick.'

As he often had in recent years, he sat down beside her, the two of them doting over the doll; rearranging her hair, adjusting her clothes. It had become such a secret pleasure for Norman, he wasn't even sure any more if he did it for Flo's sake or his own.

In the background, Ethel Merman came on the radio,

declaring that everything was coming up roses. Betty immediately reached for the paper, raising a wall of black and white newsprint between them. Having mentioned Ethel Merman when he'd told Betty about his cross-dressing, she'd become something of a sore point ever since – not helped by the fact that her star was shining so brightly, she was a ubiquitous reminder of something Betty wanted only to forget.

Trying to keep Flo distracted, Norman continued playing with the doll, combing its hair and adjusting its dress, so engrossed that he didn't notice Betty lower the newspaper. He was giving the doll a ponytail when he realised that Betty was watching him, a look of abject dismay on her face.

Norman put the doll down and reluctantly pushed it back in Flo's direction.

'I was probably getting a bit carried away,' he said to Betty, forcing a chuckle. 'I've got so much time on my hands these days, I don't know where to put myself.'

Betty appeared to consider his words. 'I have no doubt you miss being on the road,' she replied, raising the newspaper between them again.

# 33.

Norman and Florence stayed the night about an hour from Farnham. Without June's budget for a lavish hotel, the best that Norman could justify was an anonymous motel-type place near the M25, its metal roof proving to be a fitting reflection of its interior comforts.

Nervous about meeting Flo the next day, he lay awake most of the night, the distant drone of traffic compounding his growing sense of dread – not at how Flo might react to him, but rather how he might yet again fail her.

Under the circumstances, he was grateful for the opportunity to wear some makeup the next morning; anything to hide his tired, sallow complexion. Although his clothes that day were resolutely Norman, he took some pleasure in the fact that his silk scarf, red nails and lipstick were pure Ethel.

They met in a park not far from Flo's place, the grey concrete misery of her neighbourhood briefly giving way to trees and grass and a small lake where ducks frolicked happily – presumably because they alone were free to move elsewhere whenever they wanted.

Norman found her waiting beside an aged oak tree, its trunk sprayed with graffiti. In those final seconds as he approached, neither of them appeared comfortable making eye contact. They greeted one another more like old work colleagues than family, Norman feeling relieved that he had a gift to hand over – a physical proxy for the intimacy that they were not yet capable of sharing.

'It's a selection of fudge,' he said. 'A little taste of Cornwall for you.'

Flo looked at the picture on the box: a coastal village, its white-washed cottages tumbling down to a harbour. 'It looks lovely.'

'Oh, it really was,' he replied. 'Makes me wish we'd gone years ago.'

'Mum would have loved that,' said Flo.

The mood instantly faltered. 'That's what I keep thinking, too,' said Norman. 'It's not the best feeling in the world.'

They wandered in silence, Flo mostly staring at the ground.

Norman was wondering if he should say something when she beat him to it. 'Did you love Mum? I mean, really?'

'Of course,' he replied. 'She knew about me from the very beginning. We were very happy together.' But he could see in her eyes that the words rang untrue; that he was doing what he'd done for so many years, saying something in the belief that repetition would make it fact. 'Did we not seem happy to you?'

'I don't know,' she replied. 'There were just lots of little things. Like, I never saw you and Mum being romantic. Even when we were kids, it was like you just lived together rather than really loved each other.' It took Norman so long to reply, Flo began to appear concerned. 'We don't need to talk about it if it's difficult.'

'No, I think it's an interesting observation. It deserves a proper response, I just ... I suppose you can't make other people feel loved and wanted if you don't really like yourself. That was prob-ably my biggest failing with Betty, with all of you.' He waited, hopeful that Flo might grant him forgiveness without the need to wade deeper into the swamp between them, but she was looking away again – at her feet, at the sky, anywhere but Norman. 'I can't tell you how sorry I am for keeping things from you. For keeping *myself* from you.'

'You had your reasons,' she said, softly. 'I understand that.'

'But you deserved better. You did back then, and you still do.'

In the silence that followed, he worried that the words still weren't getting through. 'I was sorry to hear you've had such a rough time of it. I wish I'd known.'

'Has Florence told you everything?' she replied, sounding worried.

'Only that I should have been there for you. Which I should have.'

'Oh, I don't know what you could have done,' she said, sighing. 'I felt bad about the divorce, and then bad about my weight, and then bad about feeling bad. It sometimes seems like that's the one thread running through my whole life: feeling bad about myself.'

'I'm sorry to hear that,' he replied, his heart breaking a little that his own daughter could have struggled for so long and he never even knew. 'How are things at the moment?'

'There are still some rough days. It's hard to describe the feeling; a bit like there are clouds blocking the sun.'

'You can always talk to me about it.'

It took her a few moments to reply, as though unsure whether to say what she was thinking. 'To be honest, I used to think of you as one of the clouds.'

Norman winced, so shocked by the words that he pretended to watch the ducks while he struggled for a response. He knew the old Norman would have railed defensively or simply run away, probably even both, but he was standing there in lipstick and nail polish – it was a matter of public record that the old Norman was gone. So instead he just smiled.

'Now you mention it,' he said, 'I think that's pretty much how I used to feel about myself, too. That's why I was always so gruff in those days.' He forced himself to say the words on his lips. 'I was probably a bit of a ... curmudgeon, to be honest.'

Flo said nothing to correct him. 'I suppose I can't judge, can I? It's not like I've been the best parent in the world.'

'But you haven't had the support you needed, I'm sure that

hasn't helped. And if I'd somehow made you feel like you couldn't ask for help, that's all on me.' He caught her eye and smiled again. 'It's mad, isn't it? The things we do to ourselves. The things we do to the people we love. It's taken me a lifetime to realise that.'

She finally smiled back. 'I suppose we live and learn.'

'Let's hope so, eh?' he replied, his face lighting up. 'I'd like to think there's hope for all of us.'

# 34.

Norman was only driven back to Clacton in literal terms. In every other sense, he was carried there on a wave of euphoria, certain that his relationship with Flo was changing in unexpected and magical ways. There was such a light-heartedness to that journey, he even repurposed his colourful silk square as a headscarf, riding the rest of the way with his window down, feeling like Grace Kelly on a grand tour.

'What's your strategy for Sally?' said Florence, as they neared home.

'Oh, that'll be fine,' he replied, saying it so dismissively he didn't notice how doubtful Florence looked. 'After everything I've been through, Sally's the least of my concerns.'

He arrived home feeling impossibly elegant as Florence parked the car in the driveway; marvelling at how much he'd changed since leaving home less than a week before.

He was reaching for the door handle when he saw Sally rushing from her house, hurrying towards them much as a bull might charge a matador.

Suddenly panicked, he pulled the scarf from his head.

'No!' said Florence, already disappointed, but Norman's mind was too busy racing with thoughts of Sally getting closer and closer. Before he even knew what he was doing, he was using the scarf to wipe at his face. Florence sighed loudly and got out of the car, while Norman desperately tried to remove the last of his makeup.

He still had his head down when Sally appeared beside him, peering at him through the car window.

'Are you not getting out?' she said, sounding confused.

Sheepishly, Norman opened his door, his face coming into full view.

Sally stared at him, horrified.

'Are you wearing makeup?' she said.

'This?' he replied, trying to laugh it off. 'It's nothing. It's, er, just a silly game I was playing with Florence.'

From behind him, there was an angry slam of the car boot. Norman watched as Florence took their bags into the house, her irritation clear to see.

Sally turned her attention to his fingernails, no hint of admiration for the colour.

'I've called a meeting for tomorrow morning,' she said, her eyes still fixed firmly on his hands, her face furrowed in a frown. 'It's about the interview. My place at ten.'

'Of course,' he replied, both feeling and sounding like a chastened child. 'I'll see you in the morning.'


Norman could find no comfort in his beef stew that night. What was usually a hug for the soul was now just a plate of hot, lumpy liquid, its ingredients spliced and diced who knows where – some anonymous factory just churning the stuff out, no one caring that it brought an old man pleasure. Since his run-in with Sally, he'd replayed their conversation on an endless loop, each time asking himself why, at the age of eighty-six, he couldn't give an honest answer to a simple question – *Are you wearing makeup? Yes, it's called Candy Girl Fantasy, do you like it?* And yet the worst part was being with Florence in the aftermath: feeling too embarrassed to discuss it with her; and the longer it went unsaid, the more his embarrassment festered into shame, which made it even harder to broach the subject, so that the one thing they weren't discussing soon became the defining aspect of the day, everything else seeming to exist in its shadow.

'So,' he said, with a sigh. 'I cocked things up with Sally, didn't I?'

'Yeah,' replied Florence, finally looking him in the eye.

'I panicked, that's the trouble.'

'You don't need to worry about what other people think. Especially someone like her. I reckon you should go and put your makeup back on.'

Norman laughed. 'You what?'

'The first thing you did when you got indoors was wash your face. I'm not implying anything about your personal hygiene, but honestly, I've never known you to wash your face before.'

'I do it every morning, thank you very much. While you're still asleep, I might add.'

'Then it's interesting that today you did it twice. Like you needed to wash away all traces of Ethel.' Norman marvelled at how casually she said it, as if it was nothing out of the ordinary to perform open heart surgery on his most painful secrets. 'Though it's just a theory. I might be wrong.'

'No, no,' he replied, already putting his fork down. 'I think you might be on to something.'


Given how long it had taken Norman to get ready on previous occasions, Florence assumed that she'd be spending the rest of her dinner – not to mention most of the evening – alone. She was just scraping the last dregs of stew from her plate when she heard footsteps on the stairs. Moments later he entered the room in his blond wig, sparkly cardigan and pencil skirt, his lipstick reapplied with enthusiasm rather than precision.

'Thank you,' he said, as he sat back down. 'That feels much

better.' He started eating again, appearing to find infinitely more pleasure in his food, despite it now being cold.

'Will you go to Sally's meeting tomorrow?' she said.

He looked surprised at the question. 'Of course, I still have my committee responsibilities. Though, granted, I think the atmosphere might be a little tense.' He started chuckling to himself. 'She's never going to live that down, is she? Even if I never touch makeup ever again, she's always going to keep today as a black mark on my record.'

'That does sound like Sally,' replied Florence, smiling. 'The real question is, what are you going to do about it?'

# 35.

In the three weeks that Florence had been staying with Norman, she'd grown accustomed to the symphonic progression of her mornings: waking, bleary-eyed in an underheated room to hear the radio playing downstairs in the kitchen, punctuated by mutterings as Norman struggled with yet another crossword.

As she awoke the next morning, there was nothing – such a striking absence of sound, Florence found herself sitting up, faintly alarmed by it.

Heart pounding, she went out to the landing and called downstairs. 'Granddad?'

Norman's voice replied from the living room. 'I'm in here …'

Confused, she made her way downstairs and entered the room to find Norman dressed like a 1950s Hollywood starlet – a blond bombshell in a cashmere twinset and pearls, with a circle skirt that accentuated his every move – so glamorous it was easy to believe that Cecil B. DeMille might shout through a loudhailer at any second.

'Wow,' she said.

'Is it all right?' he replied, nervously touching his clothes, his hair.

'You look amazing.'

He turned to face her. 'My makeup is very simple, but better that than look like Jezebel.'

'I have no idea who that is.'

'She was a famous harlot. In the Bible, not Clacton.' He turned back to the mirror, still fussing over his costume jewellery. 'It's taken me ages to settle on a look for the meeting. And I was trying to be quiet; I thought you must be tired after all that driving.'

'I'm fine, I'm just ... Are you really sure you're ready to face Sally again?'

Norman took another look at his reflection, this time with a hint of confidence that Florence hadn't seen before. 'I think the more important question is, is Sally ready to face me?'

Despite a chill wind, Norman chose not to wear a coat when they crossed to Sally's house, his outfit on display for all the world to see; his pearl necklace giving him the air of a minor royal on walkabout in the streets of Clacton.

'I probably should have worn something more form fitting,' he said, as his skirt rose and billowed around him. 'I'll be going full Marilyn if I'm not careful.'

Given this slow-moving spectacle in the street, Sally must have been heavily preoccupied doing something for Ernie or Horace, because Norman and Florence made it all the way to her front door without her noticing; even needed to ring the doorbell to announce their arrival. Sally was in the middle of saying something when she opened the door, her words cut dead as she laid eyes on Norman.

She stood there in the open doorway, dumbstruck.

'We should really get inside, eh?' said Norman, stepping through the gap. 'You don't want to let the cold in.'

Sally stirred back into a semblance of life as they took their shoes off, her manner still discombobulated. 'Norman,' she said, 'I don't think you should be here. Not like that.'

Her eyes dropped to his feet; his toenails painted a luscious garnet. She was still staring at them when Ernie shouted from the living room. 'Norm! Get in here, mate!'

And then a new wave of silence as Norman stepped into the room, this one feeling even more profound given that it was Ernie who'd been rendered speechless. He stared at Norman with a look that was hard to read at first, Florence deciding that it was one part shock, two parts confusion, and the slightest dash of admiration.

'Bloody hell,' he said, finally. 'Is this part of your new diet, too?'

'I'm dressed as Ethel today,' replied Norman. 'She's my alter ego.'

By then, Sally had joined them, lingering in the doorway as though unsure whether to stay or flee.

Ernie took another long look at Norman, eventually just shrugging. 'Well, whatever floats your boat, mate. Though I'll be honest with you, I'd need more than a few pints before I made a move on *that* in the pub.'

'Here . . .' said Norman, proffering his sleeve. 'You've got to feel my cardigan. It's so soft, you won't believe it.'

Ernie did as instructed, his face instantly registering a look of wonder. 'Blimey, that's lovely, that is.'

'It's mad, isn't it?' replied Norman. 'When you think of that scratchy knitwear we had when we were young, it makes you wonder if they don't do something different to the animals these days.'

Ernie nodded sagely. 'It would stand to reason, wouldn't it? Everything else is so different, why not knitwear as well?' He turned to Sally, oblivious to her catatonia. 'It's like that Japanese beef they sell in fancy restaurants. When I was a boy, we felt lucky to get a plate of mince and potatoes, now people are paying two hundred quid to eat a cow that's done nothing all its life but listen to music and drink beer. They even get massages!' he added, sounding more envious than outraged. 'It wouldn't surprise me if they get a happy ending, too. The way things are these days, there's probably someone whose sole job it is to jerk off Japanese cattle while they listen to Enya.'

Sally remained in the doorway, her face rigid; Ernie appearing to mistake the expression for rapt attention.

'Mate,' he said, as Norman took a seat. 'I think Sally's too polite to ask, so I'll go ahead and say what's on everyone's lips. You dressing like this, does it mean, you know, you prefer ...'

Trying to be discreet, he made a vulgar gesture of cock rather than saying it.

This was the final straw for Sally. She stormed away, leaving the room so abruptly, Norman appeared rattled.

'I'm just in touch with my feminine side,' he said. 'We all have one, Ernie. Even you.'

Sally returned as brusquely as she'd left, this time with a lemon chiffon cake, carrying it across the room with a stern expression better suited to bomb disposal. She set it down with a bang and began to cut into it, every move an angry stab. She plated the first slice, so overcome with emotion she didn't seem to notice that it was a giant wedge.

Ernie craned his neck, eager to relieve her of it, but instead she just kept cutting more slices, each as random as the one before it, until finally she span around to face Norman. 'I just keep thinking of Betty. That poor woman must be turning in her grave.'

'She did know,' replied Norman.

'That's even worse! To put her through that kind of anguish.'

Despite being the sole target of Sally's invective, Norman appeared surprisingly calm. 'I don't doubt Betty might have preferred some classic Hollywood leading man – she often used to admire Rock Hudson back in the day, which is quite ironic when you think about it – but we both loved each other. It only got complicated once we had children. I tried so hard to keep this part of myself out of sight, I ended up keeping myself out of sight, too.'

This only bewildered Sally even more. 'Of course, you had to keep it from the children! Imagine how this would have confused them.'

'But I did confuse them, that's the thing. By trying to hide who I am, I just made it worse.'

Overwrought, Sally turned back to the cake, randomly cutting yet more slices, every movement a venting of aggression. The cake was starting to look like a complex pie chart when she stopped and turned back to Norman. 'Please tell me you're not going to dress like this for the newspaper.'

'Honestly, I haven't decided yet.'

'What do you mean?' she shrieked. 'They're coming to meet *us*, Norman. To learn about who we are.'

'But this *is* a part of who I am.'

'No, it's not,' she replied, so emotional by that point, even hacking at the cake offered no comfort. 'If you won't do it for us, at least think of your leeks.'

Getting no response from Norman, she turned to Horace, sitting as silent as always in the corner of the room. 'Horace, you can't just sit there, not this time. Not in the presence of this *outrage*.'

Horace began to quiver, as though cogs and cranks had started turning somewhere deep inside. Staring intently at Norman, his lips broke into a crooked smile as he raised a trembling thumbs-up.

Sally groaned loudly and stormed from the room. 'I need to lie down,' she shouted.

Everyone listened to the sound of her footsteps as she stomped upstairs, until finally there was the slam of a bedroom door and then total silence.

Down in the living room, no one seemed to know what to say or do.

It was Ernie who eventually spoke first. 'Do you think we're still allowed to eat the cake?'

# 36.

Although Norman felt for Sally – how could he not after knowing her for so many years? – he also understood that her reaction was her own business; a window on where she was in her life, not where he was in his. Like the survivor of some terrifying near miss, he left her house feeling stronger and more alive than he ever had before. After a brief stop to collect his coat and something from the garden, he suggested to Florence that they drive out to Betty's grave.

'I'd like you to see it,' he said. 'And I know she'd love to see you.'

'Sure, I'd like that,' she replied. 'If you tell me where it is, I'll put the route on my phone.'

'Actually, I was thinking we could drive around town for a bit first. I don't want to call it a victory lap, but, you know ... it's been a special kind of day.'

Florence took the request in her stride, driving them through the centre of town, while Norman sat in the front passenger seat wearing his blond wig and pearls. Having lived his entire life in Clacton, having spent eighty-six years becoming so intimately familiar with the town that he'd almost stopped noticing it, he hadn't expected that riding through it in a wig would make such a difference: his blond bangs reframing every scene, offering a new perspective on places he'd known for a lifetime. Whereas Norman would most often see what he didn't like about the town – the boarded-up shops, the daytime drinkers – as Ethel he chose to see what the place still might become.

'It just needs a little love,' he said, as Florence did yet another loop of the town centre. 'Some love would work wonders for this place.'

Florence smiled. 'I'm not sure things will be so easy to fix with Sally.'

'Oh, she'll come round in time,' he replied. 'She just has to get used to it, that's all. Lord knows it's taken me years; I can hardly expect her to change overnight.' For the umpteenth time, he checked the mirror, certain that he would never tire of seeing that reflection: the public arrival of Ethel Cartwright. 'I've been thinking, maybe next time you come and stay, we could invite your mum and Gerry over for lunch.' He heard Florence chuckle. 'Do you think it's still too soon?'

'It's not that,' she replied. 'I think it's a lovely idea, but it sort of implies that at least one of us knows how to cook.'

'Oh, I wouldn't worry about that. I think you'll find the most important thing on the menu is Ethel.'

After their third lap of town, they headed out into the countryside, driving through open farmland until they arrived at a small church, as aged and weathered as the landscape itself.

'It's pretty out here,' said Florence.

'It is, isn't it?' he replied. 'Betty always loved this place.'

Florence pulled to a stop by the church gate, the only car in sight. Together, she and Norman walked up through the graveyard, nothing to hear but the sound of birdsong. He led her across to the far side of the churchyard, stopping at a modest and unassuming grave.

'Here we are,' he said, giving the marble headstone an affectionate pat. 'It's not much, but I think she would have approved.' He noticed how Florence looked saddened at the sight of it. 'You're with her now. Better late than never, eh?'

He began doting over the grave, picking up some dead leaves, brushing away some dirt.

'How does it feel?' said Florence. 'Being here as Ethel.'

'Oh my ...' he replied, letting out a long sigh. 'Right ... wrong ... lovely ... sad. Everything all at once. I can see I handled things the wrong way, but to be honest I'm still not sure what the right way would have looked like. I suppose I'll never know, will I? The only thing I can say with certainty is that I never regretted marrying Betty, not once. If you took me back, I'd do it all again in a heartbeat.'

'I've never asked how you two met.'

Norman smiled, the memory of it still fresh even after all those decades. 'She was on holiday here with her family. We hit it off at the Blue Lagoon one night. I took her for ice cream a few days later and that was it, really.' He paused. 'I want to say we had a good life, but after the last few weeks, maybe I need to re-think it all. Maybe she wanted to do more with her life. For all I know, she wanted to be a physicist, too. She certainly had an enquiring mind, much more so than me.'

Florence put her arm around him. 'She sounds like a strong woman, you should give her some credit for the decisions she made. Maybe she loved being a wife and mother. Maybe that was exactly the life she wanted.'

'I'll tell you something else she loved ...' He glanced around. 'Oh, I left my bag in the car.'

'No problem,' she replied. 'I can go and get it.'

No sooner had she said the words than she was off, hurrying back across the graveyard, so lithe and full of life.

'Isn't she amazing?' he said, one hand resting on Betty's gravestone. 'Imagine if we'd known all those years ago that all this could come from two strangers meeting at the dance hall. And a scientist, no less. Who would've thought?' He noticed his nail varnish, vibrant against the marble. 'I'm sorry you never got to meet this side of me. I know you didn't want to, but I think we might have found a way to make it work.' He held his nails up to the light, admiring their wine-like hue. 'This colour's called *Berry Feast*. I know you'd approve of that name.'

Basking in a rare ray of sunshine, he closed his eyes, his thoughts drifting through a lifetime of memories: he and Betty driving home from somewhere or other, pootling down the motorway while the world rushed by; pulling over in a lay-by for a cup of milky tea, lukewarm from the thermos.

'You missed a shocking episode of *The Archers* last week,' he said, his eyes still closed. 'It turns out that the new people on the neighbouring farm are actually right-wing terrorists. They're planning to make bombs that look like hay bales.'

He was interrupted by the sound of Florence laughing.

'You tell her about *The Archers?*' she said. Norman opened his eyes to find her standing in front of him, a plastic bag in hand. 'If you're going to believe she can hear you, you may as well believe she listens to the radio, too.'

'But where's the fun in that?' he replied. 'Anyway, I'd like to think she's much too busy larking about in Heaven with Greta Garbo and Cleopatra.' He reached into the bag, taking a handful of blackberries from it and gently putting them on her grave. 'Here you go,' he said to Betty, 'these ones are lovely and sweet . . .' He offered some to Florence as well. 'I can't tell you how much pleasure she used to take in finding blackberries. It's mad, really. We've probably wandered through some lovely landscapes in our time, but all I remember is the way her face used to light up whenever she found some ripe berries. It was one of the many things I loved about her: that her favourite treat in the whole world wasn't something rare and expensive, it was fruit that grows wild in the hedgerows.' He put some more on her grave. 'If we're lucky, we might get a blackberry bush growing here one day. She'd love that.'

229

'I don't want to rain on this moment,' said Florence. 'But that's not how germination works.'

Norman patted the headstone. 'See what I mean, Bets? She's definitely a scientist.'

# Sixty-six years earlier

## 1956

Holiday season was in full swing, though clearly no one had told the weather that. After an Easter more suited to polar bears, the month of June had arrived on a virtual tidal wave of rain. So much rain that even among people in Clacton, who were no strangers to bad weather, the overriding topic of conversation was how wet it had been.

And yet still the holidaymakers poured into town, the trains bringing hundreds more of them every Saturday; rain-sodden hordes tramping through the streets, grimly determined to have their summer holiday regardless.

If nothing else, the endless rain at least gave the Blue Lagoon a turbo-charged quality, everyone doubly determined to make the most of their night out. Unlike Norman, who was happy to stand to one side and watch the room, most people were running on a different voltage: a seething mass of local youths and hopeful visitors, everyone using the dancefloor as a testing ground of sorts, trying to work out who might be up for physicality of a different kind later that evening.

Norman was sipping his beer when he realised that he was being watched: a young woman, no older than he was, clearly more interested in him than the action on the dancefloor. As their eyes met, she hurriedly looked away, her cheeks flushing. Norman was still peering around, wondering if she'd been looking at somebody else, when she stole another glance in his direction, this time breaking into a shy smile.

Before he'd even considered how to respond, he was smiling back, admiring how her black hair fell in soft curls around her shoulders, her green swing dress tightly cinched at the waist. And then he was moving closer, his feet seeming to move independently of his conscious mind until there they were, standing face to face.

'Hello,' he said, feeling unexpectedly bashful. 'I'm Norman.'

The girl blushed again. 'Betty.'

On the dancefloor, a cheer went up as the band began to play some rock and roll. 'I would ask if you wanted to dance,' he said, 'but I've got two left feet, I'm afraid.'

She laughed as she took him by the hand and led him deeper into the crowd. 'It just so happens I have two left feet as well,' she said, shouting over the music. 'I reckon we could be the perfect match.'

On other occasions, that would have been the beginning of an awkward evening, Norman only pretending to enjoy himself, but with Betty it was all a joyous blur, everything around them reduced to a mere backdrop: the rest of that night in the crowded dance hall; the damp, silent streets of Clacton as he walked her back to her digs; the darkened windows of the B&B as he leant in and gave her a decorous goodnight kiss.

'I won't be around tomorrow evening,' he said, the two of them still standing there on the cold pavement, neither of them wanting to move. 'I have to see some friends.'

'In Clacton?' she replied.

Norman felt the words on his lips – *No, up in London* – but somehow it felt wrong to say it; to end the perfect evening by mentioning that other part of his life. 'No,' he said, 'they're in a different town, but I'll only be gone the night. I'd love to take you for an ice cream when I'm back.'

'Well,' she replied, blushing, 'I'd never say no to an ice cream. But don't dilly dally, Norman. I'm only here for another week.'

The train the next day was full of holidaymakers heading home, many of them looking depressed to be returning to their everyday lives. As the train sped inland, Norman found himself watching them with a strange sense of guilt, aware that he was wilfully leaving their holiday paradise behind; yet another way in which it seemed his life was out of step with most people's.

There was plenty of time to think of Betty, too: remembering the warmth of her pressed against his chest while they'd danced the night before, and the unexpected joy of kissing her good-night, the two of them having transitioned so easily from total strangers to potential lovers.

And yet there he was on a train to London, with all that that implied.

It was hard to imagine that Betty, all sweetness and laughter, would be quite so giggly if she knew about Ethel.

Under the circumstances, it was just as well that Rex and Suzie had suggested meeting in Soho, an experience as far removed from his life in Clacton as it was possible to get. Even before Norman reached the bar, the seedy streets had begun to slough away his concerns. Soho was no place for blushing innocence; there were no demure smiles in its shadowy doorways. It seemed especially fitting that the final stage of his journey was to knock on a small side door, unnoticed by most people, and step down into a parallel world where there was no choice but to leave all other thoughts behind.

It was even smokier than usual as he entered the bar, as packed as always, the whole room softened by a grey fug. The people nearest the door turned to look as he entered, doubtless wanting to assess the arrival of fresh meat. It was a process that followed him across the room, each of the patrons sizing him up as he squeezed his way past, trying to avoid eye contact lest he lead anyone on.

Suzie was holding court at the far end of the room, entrancing her audience in an ensemble of black feathers and sequins, a swan of the rarest kind. She was mid-sentence when she saw Norman approaching.

'This is Ethel,' she announced, as she beckoned him closer. 'That's Ethel as in the great Ms Merman,' she added, doing the sign of the cross and genuflecting. She turned to a handsome young soldier on her left, sitting there in his uniform, hanging on her every word. 'Be a darling and get Ethel a drink. And another one for me, too.'

'I don't need a drink,' replied Norman, but Suzie shushed him.

'Ethel, darling, gin is the bedrock of civilised intercourse.' She glanced back at the soldier and gave him a sly wink. 'All sorts of intercourse, for that matter.' She patted the empty stool and waited for Norman to get seated. 'Gentlemen, if my friend Ethel here looks like a straight bricklayer from Essex, that's because she is.'

'I'm a lorry driver,' said Norman.

'Same thing,' replied Suzie with a wink. 'What matters is she's one of the loveliest people I've ever met. Not to mention she looks *stunning* in a damask gown.'

In the moment of awkward silence that followed, Norman was aware that all eyes were on him, doubtless wondering why he was wearing a drape jacket and drainpipe trousers; his feet clad in chunky brogues. 'It's my night off,' he said.

'And thank heavens,' added Suzie. 'I wouldn't want anyone stealing my limelight.'

With all eyes on her, she launched into a colourful recap of her week, managing to make even the most mundane events – picking lint from an armchair, say – sound like something far more interesting than Norman ever had or ever would experience. At some point, the uniformed young man returned with their drinks, as transfixed by Suzie as ever.

'Aren't you a darling?' she said to him, as she handed one drink to Norman and took the other for herself. 'I'm sure I can work out some way to repay the favour.'

The alcohol helped ease the concerns that Norman had carried with him from Clacton, but new ones came in their place. He couldn't help looking towards the door whenever someone new arrived, constantly aware that it could be a police raid. And what then, he wondered? They were cornered down there, there would be no escape. To think he could be strolling on the promenade hand in hand with Betty – or at the very least sheltering from the rain with Betty – but instead there he was, in danger of having his entire life burnt to the ground as a public spectacle. And all for what? For the simple feeling of acceptance, a birth right society had denied him.

Suzie was still in full flight while Norman continued looking around the room, wondering if anyone else shared his fears, but the place was abuzz, so much life and energy crammed into one small space, it reminded him of the tales he'd heard from the Blitz: rather than living in fear as bombs fell from the sky, many people felt a strange kind of freedom, surrendering to a fatalism that only heightened life's remaining pleasures.

Suzie had just started talking about picking some flowers near her bedsit – a tale that somehow managed to involve an angry vicar, a drunken gardener and several shocked passers-by – when Rex approached from elsewhere in the room, puffing away on a cigar, appearing to take endless pleasure in adding to the ambient air pollution.

'Ethel,' he said, his face lighting up. 'Our very own Miss Clacton.'

Norman glanced down at his clothes. 'I'm not really dressed for that today.'

'Which is why I was thinking, we could have a little soirée at my place next Saturday. For family only. We can make a proper night of it.'

'I'm not sure I can,' replied Norman. 'I've just met a girl.'

Rex stared at him through a fog of cigar smoke. 'A *girl*. Now that's a word that doesn't get said in this place very often. Who's the lucky lady?'

'Well, it's still early days ...' he replied, blushing.

This provoked a belly laugh from Rex. 'If she's got you this tongue-tied, she must be very special, indeed. I'm happy for you, I really am.'

'My point is,' said Norman. 'I'll probably be seeing her next weekend. She goes home on Saturday.'

'Then please consider doing both,' he replied. 'I presume she'll be heading home by lunchtime, so you can still come and join us for supper. Which promises to be an absolute triumph, by the way. I've recently found a new fishmonger. Hand on my heart, he has the most heavenly dover sole in the *entire* history of this great nation.' A man at the bar signalled for his attention, the two of them smiling at one another like old friends. 'Ethel, darling, if you'll excuse me ...' He began inching in the man's direction, raising his voice to Norman as he melted back into the crowd. 'Please don't forget next Saturday. Really, I won't take no for an answer. Not to mention, I've just bought some new fox furs. I can assure you, they will suit Ethel Cartwright to a tee.'


Norman's next date with Betty was perfect in every way, even the weather gods seeming to ordain that they should have a lovely time together: he was still waiting for her down by the pier, a bunch of sweet peas in hand, when the skies parted and a beam of sun shone down on the sea, a rare reminder that there was another world above that dense grey canopy of cloud.

It was only as Betty approached that Norman realised this was the first time he'd seen her in daylight. Perhaps with someone else it would have been a rude awakening, but as she got closer he could only think that she was even more beautiful than he remembered.

She came to a stop in front of him, neither of them saying anything for the first few seconds, both too busy blushing.

'Here,' said Norman, handing her the bouquet. 'As soon as I saw them, I thought of you.'

'Thank you,' she replied, holding them close, as though they were something much more precious than mere flowers.

'And it looks like we won't have to eat ice cream in the rain,' he said.

She gave him a shy smile. 'I still would have said yes.'

Without even asking, she took his arm, the two of them starting to stroll along the promenade as if they'd always been a couple. Even the other people out that day seemed to recognise it; smiling at them as though they were emblematic of all that was right and good about the world. And although there were so many things Norman wanted to ask, it felt just as right to say nothing at all; to simply wander along basking in this sensation of being normal and accepted.

It was Betty who eventually broke the silence. 'Did you have a nice time with your friends?'

The sensation of normality began to fracture. 'Yes,' he replied, more hesitant than he'd intended. Betty glanced at him, confused by the tone. 'I spent the whole time thinking of you, to be honest.'

She blushed all over again. 'I was thinking of you, too. I can't even imagine being back in London. Do you ever go up there?'

Norman swallowed the words down. *I'll be there on Saturday. Having supper with homosexual friends in the West End.*

'Now and then,' he said. 'I was thinking, I can walk you to the station on Saturday. That way you won't have to carry your suitcase.'

*And I'll know which train you're on.*

'You're so sweet,' she replied, pulling his arm closer, the warmth of her pressing against him.

Norman responded in kind, leaning into her as they ambled

along, preferring the safety of silence to communicate his true feelings. It was soon after that he heard the music drifting in the air from the ice-cream stand, growing louder with every step: Ethel Merman belting out her belief that there's no business like show business.

'Oh, I love Ethel Merman,' said Norman, the words bubbling up from a place of uninhibited joy.

'Me too,' replied Betty, seeming to take this as yet further proof that they were destined to be together forever.

'You know what they say. Imitation is the sincerest form of flattery.'

'Are you suggesting I should dress like her?' she replied.

'Maybe we both should!'

Betty giggled, this time rising on tiptoes to give him a peck on the cheek. 'Oh, Norman, you do say the funniest things. It makes me like you even more.'

# 37.

As he'd done every day for his entire adult life, Norman woke early the next morning, going down to the kitchen to make himself a mug of tea. It hadn't been that long ago that Betty would have been down there, too, cooing over this or that – the roses in the garden, the shape of the clouds, the neighbour's cat sitting on the fence – and all the while there'd be some mellifluous voice on the radio easing them into another day.

It was strange to think of life's repetitions. It seemed like only yesterday that Betty had passed and he found himself alone in the house, unsure how to go on without her. And now there he was on the cusp of Florence going back to university, frightened all over again about the future and what it might bring.

Like so many other occasions when life felt overwhelming, he pulled on his gloves and went out into the garden, busying himself with digging and weeding and tending to that little world of his own creation; the cold air and the scent of damp soil soothing his heart, reminding him that there is a season for all things.

An hour or two had passed when Florence came out to see him, her hair still damp, a lack of warm clothes making it clear that this was only a fleeting visit.

'I'm obviously losing track of time,' he said. 'If you're up already, it must be late.'

She looked confused. 'It's only just gone nine.'

'Exactly,' he replied. 'Most of the morning's gone. But I've made good use of it.'

Florence stood there looking at the vegetable patch – not admiring it as such, but at least giving it some attention.

'I don't want to know what you've been digging into the soil,' she said.

'I've just been tidying it up a bit. I want everything to look its best for the photographer this afternoon.'

She smiled at him. 'Don't forget to think about how *you're* going to look. You don't want to be upstaged by a leek.'

'Don't you worry about that; I've already been giving it some thought. I'm going to pop over to Colchester this morning.'

'I can drive you,' she replied.

'No, no, this is something I need to do on my own. I'll be fine.'

Florence looked concerned. 'Last time you said that you ended up "falling down some steps".'

Norman put his hand over his heart. 'It'll be a very quick trip. In and out, I promise.'


Florence watched from the living room window as Norman reversed the car out into the street, unable to shake the fear that history was about to repeat itself. He gave her a cheery wave as he drove off, but that only made the situation feel worse – a reminder not only of how much she loved that frail old man, but also the utter impossibility of keeping him out of harm's way.

She was still standing there when she noticed Sally was also in her window, looking out into the street, not surveying the neighbourhood this time, but rather staring out blankly.

The thought was still half-formed in Florence's mind when she found herself going to the hallway, pulling on her shoes, and stepping out into the fresh morning air.

Sally immediately noticed the movement; remained there in her window, watching with growing confusion as Florence made a beeline straight for her house; was still there in the window, looking perplexed, as Florence rang the doorbell.

Moments later, Sally warily opened the door.

'I wanted to make sure you're okay,' said Florence. 'I mean, I know you don't like me, but—'

'What are you talking about?' replied Sally, shocked back to her usual self. 'Of course I like you.'

Florence scoffed. 'You've been nothing but cold with me since I arrived.'

'I can be a little aloof with people I don't know,' she said, her tone proving her point. 'But that doesn't mean I—' She stopped, her face breaking into a smile. 'Did you really come just to ask if I'm all right?'

'Yeah, I mean, yesterday was ... it's a learning curve, isn't it? For all of us. Granddad included, by the way.'

'Well, yes,' replied Sally, her smile fading. 'I'll need some time with it, but I do appreciate your concern.'

Florence stood there, the wind tugging at her black jumper. 'There is one other thing ... I was kind of wondering if you could teach me to bake.'


Having seen, and eaten, some of Sally's prolific output over the last few weeks, Florence assumed that her kitchen would be reminiscent of a Nasa facility, a gadget to hand for everything. It came as some surprise, then, to find that her kitchen wasn't so unlike Norman's. Neater and cosier, of course, and more thematic – florals were a constant leitmotif – but in every other respect the only difference was Sally herself, a lifetime of baking know-how hidden beneath her perm.

'I'm glad you suggested this,' said Sally. 'Baking always helps me relax.' With the same look of peace that Florence had seen on Norman whenever he was working in the garden, Sally took out a handwritten recipe book, its pages dog-eared and food stained. 'I'll be honest, part of me's quite pleased you can't cook. You have so much else going in your favour: youth, looks, your whole life ahead of you. And then to find out you're a physicist, too . . .' She laughed. 'Talk about rubbing salt into the wound!'

'Literally, I can only make cheese on toast,' replied Florence. 'I mean, I can ruin anything, but if you want to actually eat it at the end, it's got to be cheese on toast.'

'Well, today we're going to add cupcakes and quiche Lorraine to your repertoire. I think cupcakes are the right choice for the newspaper people this afternoon, don't you? That's how I imagine media people: very grab-and-go.' She began gathering jars of flour and sugar, mixing bowls and scales, seeming to find endless joy in the process. 'I'm still a little shocked you thought I didn't like you.'

Florence smiled. 'You definitely don't like how I dress.'

'Well, yes, okay,' she replied, laughing. 'That's true. It's all a bit too "devil worshipper" for me.'

'It's just black!'

'But as long as you're not *actually* worshipping Satan, I see no reason why it should get in the way of a good quiche.'

Together, they began weighing out ingredients – a meticulous process of measuring, as scientific as anything Florence had experienced in a lab.

'You'll have to excuse me,' said Sally, as she added a near-invisible quantity of flour so that her digital scales displayed the precise number she wanted. 'I like to be exact.'

'Hey, you're talking to a scientist, remember. I'm right there with you.' She chuckled to herself. 'I know for a fact that Granddad would not have the patience for this.'

There was a shift in atmosphere at the mention of Norman; not a rise in tension, but rather a sense that they'd arrived in orbit around a subject that would need to be discussed sooner or later.

'How's your mother doing these days?' said Sally, her slight frown making it clear that they were really talking about Norman.

'She's okay,' replied Florence. 'She's had depression for a long time, but, you know, I think things are picking up.'

'Does she know about your grandfather?'

'Yes, she's even met him like that. They haven't been on the best of terms for a long, long time. The way I see it, Granddad can't be Ethel without being open and honest and vulnerable; those are all qualities that were missing from their relationship before.'

Sally appeared to acknowledge the comment, her frown fading.

'Betty was very kind to me over the years,' she said. 'Has Norman ever mentioned my late husband?'

'He doesn't talk about the past. That's one of his problems.'

'My husband wasn't the nicest person, let's put it that way. Betty was a rare ray of sunshine for me. She offered the kind of support that only another woman could.'

'And Granddad loved her,' said Florence. 'I'm sure of that.'

'I do know that,' replied Sally, sounding sad. 'I know he's a good man.'

'And he's still that same good man, even when he's in a dress.'

Sally said nothing and Florence knew better than to press the issue; some things simply required time and patience. So they busied themselves with the sifting of flour and the beating of eggs; continuing the slow, steady sequence of steps that would take them from where they were to where they needed to be.

They were dividing the cake batter when Sally spoke again. 'Do you think your grandfather will be dressed as a man or a woman for the interview today?'

Florence shrugged. 'I wish I could tell you, but I honestly don't know. This is a journey for him as much as the rest of us.'

'I just worry,' she said. 'Worry for him, as much as anything. For what people will say, what they might *do*.' She hesitated, appearing more self-conscious. 'But, of course, I'm thinking of myself as well. Imagining it splashed all over town, in the *newspaper* of all things. What are people going to think of us?'

Florence gave some thought to the question, but even more to the woman asking it; to the way that Sally was standing there, looking so frightened of the unknown.

'Do you want to know what I really think?' she said. 'Most people are going to see you as accepting and open-minded; that you live and let live. That's an amazing reputation to have. I think you're worrying that Norman wearing a dress somehow makes a mockery of your values, but it really doesn't. It affirms them.'


Norman only realised the profundity of the moment as he entered the department store, pushing through the main doors into that perfumed air, the scent alone taking him back to his last visit, when he'd been so scared and self-conscious, he hadn't allowed himself to enjoy the experience. Determined not to make the same mistake, he ambled through the cosmetics hall at a leisurely pace, letting his eyes take in the gorgeous selection of lipstick colours, the dizzying variety of eyeshadow; moving through that brightly lit hall of mirrors with a calm, steady confidence he didn't have before.

As he neared the makeup counter, it looked like no one was there, but then the same young woman as last time popped up into view, her arms full.

'Hey ho,' said Norman. 'I didn't see you down there. You're like a jack-in-the-box.'

'I've not heard that one before,' she replied. 'But you're right, you can't keep me down for long.' She put her things to one side, one eye on Norman. 'I remember you now. Did your sister like her makeup?'

'I want to be honest with you, I don't have a sister. The makeup was for me.' In the silence that followed – a millisecond that might as well have been hours – it seemed to Norman that this is how baby birds must feel on their first flight: plunging earthward, forced to choose between death or spreading their wings. 'I was hoping you could give me some tips. I've heard about contouring, but for the life of me I can't work it out.'

She gave him a disarming smile. 'It can be tricky, but I promise you this, it feels like a superpower once you've nailed it. Get yourself comfy and I'll take you through it step by step.'

Norman heaved himself onto a stool and closed his eyes as she pulled a bright lamp overhead and started to cleanse his face, wiping away what he could only imagine were a lifetime of unwanted layers, all the while her voice soft and reassuring. 'I meant to tell you when you were here last time, your cheekbones are gorgeous. I'd kill to have them.'

He laughed. 'I'd happily swap them to be your age.'

'If you knew how much I earn, you might think twice about that. But I basically get free makeup forever, so it's not all bad, is it?'

After making his skin feel cleaner and lighter than it ever had before, she began to apply foundation, each gentle stroke of her fingers seeming like a gesture of acceptance.

'If you've got the time this morning, I reckon we should do a full makeover,' she said. 'Not just the contouring, but your eyes and lips, too, the full Monty.'

'That sounds lovely,' he replied, his eyes still closed, the warm glow of the light making it feel like he wasn't sitting in a shop at all, but rather on a sun-kissed beach in paradise, the luckiest person alive.

# 38.

Norman arrived home to an empty house, Florence's absence seeming to have a prophetic quality; a taste of how things would be once she'd gone back to university. Trusting that she would be back soon enough, he busied himself deciding what to wear for the photo shoot, poring over the options in his wardrobe like a nervous debutante.

He'd settled on a floral blouse, a spring renaissance of flower buds and blooms, when Florence opened the front door.

He called to her from the landing. 'I'm up here.'

After climbing the stairs with her usual lithe ease, she came into his room.

'Wow,' she said. 'Forget the local newspaper, you're ready for the cover of *Vogue*. Your makeup is amazing.'

'You may as well enjoy it while it lasts,' he replied. 'It will never be this good again.'

He pulled on his blond wig – the perfect counterpoint to the blouse – and clipped on a pair of bulky diamond earrings, the kind that would require an oil fortune in real life.

Florence smiled at the sight of them. 'Going for a bit of bling?'

'It's not like any of it's *real*.' He touched an earring fondly. 'It's just a little bit of sparkle, isn't it? Lord knows, the world needs more sparkle.'

'By the way,' she said. 'I know what we can serve Mum and Gerry when you invite them over: quiche Lorraine and cupcakes.'

'Ooh, that sounds lovely,' he replied.

'That's probably just as well, because it's what you're getting at Sally's this afternoon.'

It took Norman a moment to understand the implication of what she'd just said, his eyebrows rising as the penny dropped. 'And how is Sally today?'

'Nervous.'

'Well, that makes two of us . . .'

They were interrupted by a loud scraping noise from downstairs in the hallway. Going out to the landing, they watched as the postman put more than the usual effort into squeezing a package through the letterbox, eventually just thumping it a few times until it fell to the doormat with a solid, satisfying thud.

'Do you want me to bring it up?' said Florence.

'No, we may as well go down,' he replied. 'I'm gasping for a cup of tea.'

She went ahead of him, picking the package off the floor and waiting with it as he slowly descended the stairs.

'I have no idea what it could be,' he said, taking it from her. 'I'm not expecting anything.' He weighed it in his hands. 'It's neither heavy nor light, if you know what I mean.'

'You could just open it,' she replied.

'But the anticipation is half the pleasure.' He looked at it more closely, his face falling. 'Oh, dear.'

'What's wrong?'

'It's from June's nursing home. What if something's happened to her? What if she left instructions for them to send it if she died? I mean, look at the handwriting, that's not June's.' He held it up so she could take a closer look: every 'i' of the lolloping script crowned with a heart-shaped dot. Alarmed, he handed her the package. 'You'll have to open it. I can't, just in case.'

In nervous silence, Florence carried it through to the kitchen table, the two of them taking a seat before she started tearing into it, layers of brown paper and cardboard finally giving way to an old book and a single sheet of paper.

'There's a note,' she said. 'Of sorts, anyway.'

She passed it to him; such a dense cobweb of pen strokes, at first glance it was hard to recognise what language it was, let alone what it might say.

Recoiling, Norman handed it back. 'No, no, that's definitely a task for a scientist. I'd never figure it out.'

Instead, he picked up the book, recognising it straight away. 'It's one of Suzie's. A book of poems.'

Florence stared harder at the letter, slowly making sense of the words, all written free of punctuation. '"Dear Norman or should I say Ethel no I'm not dead I finally found what I wanted to give you I know Suzie would want you to have it I have so many already they're lovely reminders and now you have that as well sorry if you can't read my writing I can't read it either God I hate writing letters I will ask one of the nurses to write the address on the envelope otherwise this will probably get lost forever love June."'

But Norman was barely listening, too transfixed by the book. He smiled to himself as he touched its pages.

'Suzie was always trying to memorise some poem or other. Badly, I might add. She used to just fill in the gaps with whatever came to mind at the time.' He gently flicked through it, many of the pages containing pressed flowers, gossamer thin. 'I knew it would be full of these. She couldn't help herself when it came to flowers.'

'That one's pretty,' said Florence, reaching for a violet, its petals fragile with age.

'It's probably seventy years old, maybe more.'

'That's a crazy thought.' She held it up to the light: its beauty frozen in time, preserved over the years when so much else had been lost.

'I might even have been with her when she picked some of these,' said Norman. 'She was always stopping to pluck a flower from somewhere or other.'

Florence returned the violet to the arms of Tennyson. 'I like that idea, that each flower represents a moment in time.'

'And probably an irate gardener, but it's a little late to worry about that now, eh?'

He continued flicking from page to page, every flower a reminder that we must each decide what's important to us and then treasure those things for as long as they're within reach.

He looked up at Florence. 'If there's time after the interview, we should go for an ice cream down by the beach. We can talk some more about that lunch with your mum and Gerry.'

'Sally said it's going to rain later.'

Norman gestured dismissively. 'That was probably just a figure of speech.'

'No,' replied Florence, laughing. 'I'm pretty sure it was based on an actual scientific forecast.'

'Still, we may as well hope for the best, eh?'

He looked out into the garden. It was true, there were some dark clouds gathering, but the same could be said of life itself. Sometimes the sun shines, sometimes it doesn't. All that matters is what you do with the day.

# Acknowledgements

I'm grateful for the support of everyone at Little, Brown, especially James Gurbutt, Phoebe Carney, Alice Watkin, Olivia Hutchings, Katy Brigden and Niamh Anderson. My heartfelt thanks also go to Juliet Mushens at Mushens Entertainment.